Shadows danced beneath the moon

Her heart halted as something appeared to shift. It was only the wind. She forced herself to turn her back on the window and face the door, waiting for Jeff.

The glimmer of a small, shiny object on the floor caught her eye. It was a cuff link, a button, or something like that. She could hear Jeff coming with the drinks.

"A little toddy for a cold night," Jeff said as he walked toward her carrying two glasses. The object caught the light again, and she bent to pick it up just as the glass wall behind her shattered with an explosion. The blasted glass flew in all directions, and Ronnie tumbled to the floor. She lay motionless as shards of glass rained down on her, biting her skin in a thousand places....

ABOUT THE AUTHOR

Caroline Burnes is a former journalist who is teaching and writing fiction in the Mississippi area.

A Deadly Breed

Caroline Burnes

Harlequin Books

TORONTO • NEW YORK • LONDON
AMSTERDAM • PARIS • SYDNEY • HAMBURG
STOCKHOLM • ATHENS • TOKYO • MILAN

For Marsha Nuccio

Harlequin Intrigue edition published March 1988

ISBN 0-373-22086-3

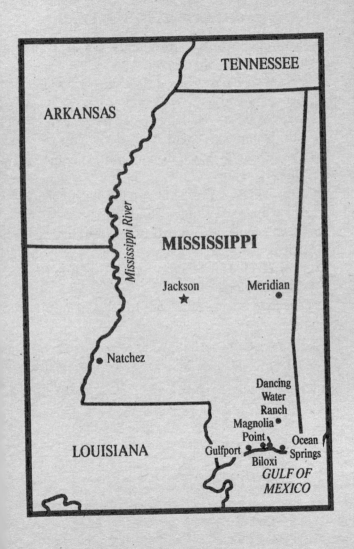

ARKANSAS

TENNESSEE

MISSISSIPPI

Mississippi River

Jackson ★

Meridian •

Natchez •

Dancing
Water
Ranch

Magnolia •
Point

Gulfport •

Ocean
Springs

Biloxi

LOUISIANA

*GULF OF
MEXICO*

CAST OF CHARACTERS

Veronica "Ronnie" Sheffield—On the trail of a story she ran into danger.

Jeff Stuart—Was he on the take, or was he being framed?

Neil Brenton—Had Jeff's old friend and mentor now become his enemy?

Sally Duvall—She'd do anything to come up with the truth.

Jay Carlisle—The man who always made the scene but stayed in the shadows.

Stella—Was she protecting Jeff and hiding the real facts?

Ann Tate—Her peaceful ranch becomes the scene of violence.

The bald man—What was his real identity?

Prologue

"That's her," the tall, slender man whispered, pointing to a flash of silver that moved swiftly through the dark green foliage.

"Good. Make sure she gets inside. Distract Dennison's men if you have to."

"You want that reporter in there?" the first man asked, incredulous. "If she sees something, she'll spoil it all. What about the shooting? We didn't bargain for members of the press as witnesses," he said.

"Ed's an excellent shot. No one will ever know it's a hoax, and what better publicity is there than a member of the press as an eyewitness?" The light from several lanterns caught and reflected the starched whiteness of the second man's tuxedo. Carefully he lit a cigarette, his hands more expressive than his voice.

"I don't like it. This whole idea is too dangerous. If Senator Stuart . . . But you're the boss."

For a moment the shorter man inhaled his cigarette, the orange glow illuminating a face that showed concern and a trace of doubt. If tonight's happenings were traced back to him, he could lose everything.

"Just let Miss Sheffield in. It will be very interesting t watch her reaction tonight, and to read her account in to morrow's newspaper."

The tall man nodded once, very quickly. "We'd better g and pull Dennison's men off her tail or she'll never make inside."

"Do that. And tell Eddie not to worry. Hopefully ou target will get the message and back off."

He was left alone in the shadows of a small patio near th main ballroom to finish his cigarette as the taller man with drew. Grinding the butt beneath his heel, he looked up at th huge, two-story stone house. Over his head there was a ba cony, and above that a widow's walk. He inhaled sharpl straightening his sleek bow tie as he headed for the bal room, where Veronica Sheffield would soon be an unir vited but very desirable guest.

Chapter One

The metallic silver dress swooshed about her legs as she took the stairs two at a time. Heedless of the delicate material, Veronica Sheffield concentrated only on speed. She was three steps from the top when a sudden tug almost pulled the tight-fitting, strapless bodice down to her waist.

"Damn!" she whispered emphatically.

Grabbing the stair railing, she shook her skirt only to find that her high heel was snagged in the hem. As she clutched the gown to her full breasts with one hand, she sat on the stairs and removed her shoes. Clasping both silver slippers in nervous fingers, she dashed up the last steps.

At the top of the stairs a small, dimly lighted landing gave sheltered view of the deserted, upstairs hallway. Veronica forced herself to stop and gather her frayed composure. Suppressing her nervousness, she whispered, "Thank goodness. No one's here yet."

A darkened bedroom directly across the hall promised a temporary haven. Rushing in, Ronnie softly closed the door and slid the latch before she leaned back and expelled her breath. Her heart was pounding crazily, but there was a smile of elation on her face.

Getting inside Grover Dennison's party was only the first step, she reminded herself as her breathing regulated. Her

reasons for crashing this party tonight were two of the mos
prominent politicians in the state of Mississippi: the attorn
general, and one very handsome, much talked-about stat
senator who was pushing a highly controversial horse rac
ing bill into state law.

The ball was the absolutely perfect place to begin her fact
finding expedition, she thought as she secured a long stranc
of silky black hair in her chignon. Under cover, as "part
guest," she'd get a chance to peek beneath the mask mos
politicians wore in front of members of the press.

Her newspaper, *The Louisville Star* had received a tip tha
large sums of money were being channeled into Jackson
Mississippi, to stop the racing legislation. The source sai
the Mississippi racing bill was upsetting some very power
ful people who had interests in other tracks, people wh
didn't want their names known. Big money was allegedl
headed toward Jackson to buy off politicians who coul
stop the track. When Ronnie's editor heard that the attorne
general or a state senator might be the targeted recipients o
illegal funds, Ronnie found herself back in Jackson. Un
cover the story of who was paying and who was taking wa
her assignment. Her growing reputation as a political re
porter was based on past achievements in ferreting out an
writing about corruption.

She'd been reluctant at first to return to the South, but he
boss, Kurt Chambliss, had insisted. He knew her well, an
thought her last assignment in Chicago had been harder o
her than she would ever admit. The grin faded from her fac
as she remembered some of the difficult stories she'd had t
write. One thing about corruption was that it often ruine
innocent people who got trapped in the cross fire.

Standing up, she twisted to make sure the dress hur
properly in the back. "It's a job," she reminded herse

uietly. "I'm not supposed to judge or defend, just report
acts."

With a quick jerk she readjusted her bodice, tugging up
he glimmering material to more fully cover her breasts. *If
'm going to get arrested tonight, I hope it's not because of
his dress* she thought dryly. One last tug on the glittery
abric smoothed the snug waist around her slender frame
ntil the material flowed perfectly from top to toe. She
iggled her stockinged feet into her shoes and put her ear to
he door to listen for sounds of a party in full swing.

Patience wasn't one of her virtues, she reflected, feeling
er nerves tighten. She picked up her silver-spangled hand-
ag and opened it. Inside lay a single tube of lipstick, two
eys and a large chocolate bar. She quickly broke off a
quare of chocolate and hungrily pushed it into her mouth.
ince she'd given up smoking, chocolate had become her
ibstitute whenever she felt nervous. It might not help her
omplexion, but it did keep her from jumping out of her
kin.

Just as the last sweet taste disappeared, the orchestra
wung into an easy tempo fox-trot. She applied a thin glim-
er of lipstick and opened the door a tiny crack, her hands
noothing down the silver fabric of her dress one last time.

Three elegantly gowned women walked down the hall-
ay, intent on returning to the party after a trip to the rest
om. Ronnie stepped casually behind them and descended
he stairs, listening to their casual chatter.

"He is an extraordinary man," a petite, well-groomed
dy said. "Such charm."

"I pity the woman who loses her heart to those blue
yes," another added. "He is something of a rake, you
now."

The third laughed. "My husband says he's one of the
iost powerful men in the state, even the whole South."

"He is powerfully appealing," the smaller woman adde
with a good-natured laugh. "George says the women's vot
alone would give him a U.S. Senate seat if he wanted t
run."

"He has my vote."

"The problem is that no one is really certain what Jeffe
son wants. George says he acts as if politics were a game t
pass time."

"Hmm! If Jefferson wanted to pass the time, there ar
plenty of young ladies who would entertain him with othe
things than legal technicalities and irate ministers fussin
about the morals of gambling!" Laughter tinkled abou
them as they took the last step.

Veronica bit back her sarcastic opinion of women wh
judged politicians by a handsome face. *Keep a low profile
Ronnie, or they'll be asking who invited you to this ga*
event! Her thoughts were interrupted by the enchantin
melody the orchestra was playing as the women she'd bee
following drifted off in separate directions, leaving Ronni
to gaze into a roomful of total strangers. She wondered i
the Jefferson just mentioned might be the state senator.

"Would you care to dance?" The offer came from be
hind her and she jumped guiltily.

"Certainly," she said, turning to an elegantly groome
middle-aged man. She immediately recognized Neil Brent
on, attorney general of the state. "I'd be delighted." Th
silver dress had snagged one of her prey. She stifled her im
pulse to laugh, giving Neil Brenton a wide smile instead.

Leading her to the floor, he held her lightly. "You're
fresh face at this party," he said, his brown eyes assessin
her.

"Yes, this is my first time." Veronica smiled up at hin
Fate was certainly being kind to her tonight. Neil Brento
was the most powerful politician in the state, and Jefferso

Stuart's mentor. She hoped she'd be able to get his opinions firsthand on Senator Stuart's bill. His gaze was cool, and she could easily imagine his effectiveness in politics or before a jury.

"You know this dance is a tradition in Mississippi. It's a night where decisions and careers are made and broken." His lips smiled, but his eyes remained alert, watching. "I suppose your husband told you that already."

She laughed, her voice low and soft. "Are you trying to find out if I'm married, or if I know the traditions of the state?"

"Both," he said quickly, catching her around the waist as the dance concluded. His touch was a fraction too insistent.

"A woman has to have an air of mystery to keep her charm," Veronica said, forcing a mischievous smile. "I refuse to answer any questions tonight. I'm just here to enjoy the dancing." As the music ended, she stepped lightly out of his arms, giving him another smile. When she was a safe distance away, she exhaled on a sigh of relief.

The man had power, and knew how to use it. At a later date, he might cooperate with her research; many politicians did. But she wasn't ready to reveal her reasons for moving to Jackson, particularly not to Neil Brenton. It would be best to observe him with discretion. If he checked out clean, there would be plenty of time for formal introductions.

At the punch bowl she picked up a delicate crystal cup, barely tasting the drink before putting it down on the table. She watched the dancers intently, taking note of the faces she recognized from her files and searching for others of importance to her assignment.

The Dennisons had taken great pains to host the traditional party with elegance and style. She watched the white-

haired Dennison and his much younger redheaded wife
chatting in a corner with the chairman of the state's Dem
ocratic party. She couldn't help but wonder if the party wa
a gesture of Old South hospitality, or a bid for persona
gain. For a moment she felt ashamed. "Always on the
lookout for ulterior motives," she chided herself silently, her
full black lashes sweeping down on her cheeks as she briefly
closed her eyes.

A passing waiter graciously handed her a brimming glass
The wine was delicious, but she felt she had to address the
warning rumbles of her stomach and find something other
than chocolate.

Exotic colors and dishes tempted from the buffet table
and Ronnie sought the fresh seafood. She put several deli
cate shrimp on her plate, and then raw oysters with sauce
and crackers. Avoiding the crowded dance floor, she drifted
back toward the staircase where she could observe and yet
remain as unobtrusive as possible.

"There is a small dining area on the second floor," a
waiter said. "May I carry your plate?"

"No thanks," Ronnie said, smiling widely. Innocently
the waiter had given her the perfect excuse to investigate the
rest of the house. If anyone asked, she could say she was
looking for a dining area. "Thanks a lot."

She was halfway up the stairs when she remembered her
shoes and the dress and slowed to a dignified walk. The up
stairs dining room was filled with older ladies, and Ronnie
moved on quickly, memorizing the layout. When she passed
the bedroom where she had hidden earlier, she impulsively
decided to step inside.

In the privacy of the darkened room, she could let down
her guard a little. Though Veronica Sheffield, reporter, was
used to the pressures of her job, tonight she felt overly keyed
up. The brilliant stars hanging outside beckoned her to the

window, where she discovered a small balcony she hadn't noticed earlier. Graceful stone arches exotically framed the crisp night, making it look like the perfect place to take a breather and eat. Carefully balancing her wineglass on the rail and leaning on her elbows, she held her plate in one hand as she speared an oyster. It was as delicious as she remembered from her summer visits to the Gulf coast as a child. She dipped a second one into the tart horseradish-laced sauce. A slight movement in the grounds below caught her attention. Focusing her eyes on the darkness below, Ronnie scanned the dimly lighted garden that stretched away from the house into blackness. There was nothing there, just flickering shadows. She immersed the oyster in the tangy sauce and then lifted it toward her mouth. From the shrubs twenty yards away, a large dark figure moved into deeper shadow, a flash of light glimmering for one brief moment. Ronnie felt herself freeze. There was no doubt, a man had just pulled back out of the lights, a big man in black clothing wearing something that gleamed. Before she could move, the oyster slipped from the toothpick and fell into the darkness below.

"What in the hell?" a very deep, very masculine voice from directly beneath her asked in irritated disgust.

"Oh, no!" Ronnie gasped as she leaned over the edge of the balcony to discover a small patio below. A tall man with broad, powerful shoulders was fishing around in his collar. To her horror, he extracted a blob of oyster, still dripping in cocktail sauce. Before she could draw back, his angry eyes found her in the semidarkness.

"Is this your idea of a joke?" he demanded, keeping his voice controlled and low. His sharp anger seared her burning ears.

"It was an accident," she said lamely. "I meant to eat it." Her eyes darted to the edge of light. There was no sign of the

other man, not even the gentle movement of a breeze. She
looked down again at the man directly beneath her as he
held the offending oyster between his thumb and forefin-
ger, dropping it on the ground with a splat. Ronnie could tell
by his stance that he was indeed very angry.

"If you'll come upstairs, I'll see what I can do about the
damage to your clothes," she said. "I'll certainly pay for
it."

"If I get any closer, you'll probably set my clothes on
fire," he remarked acidly, giving her a black, unpleasant
look as his fingers returned to his collar. "I doubt if anything can be done."

"At least let me apologize and give you my name. I can
pay for the cleaning bill."

"That won't be necessary if you'll give me a hand removing this, uh, sauce from my neck. I'll be right up."

Ronnie drew back, brushing a cold hand across her
burning face. Of all things to happen! The night was quickly
taking on an air of burlesque. First she had almost torn off
her dress and then, just when she spotted a possibly clan-
destine meeting, she'd assaulted someone with an oyster.
I'm certainly doing a fine job of maintaining a low profile,
she thought sarcastically.

Waiting nervously at the doorway, Ronnie was joined in
a few seconds by the unlucky party-goer. His lean body
seemed to fill the corridor, and her eyes widened in shock
and further embarrassment.

"I don't look that bad, do I?" he asked, stepping toward
her with an easy, self-confident movement.

"No," she managed to reply, still reeling from this new
source of humiliation. "There's a bath in here, and I think
I may be able to get the worst out before it sets." Her heart
was dancing a wild double beat. The man she'd smacked
with a wet hors d'oeuvre was Jefferson Stuart! But no

where in the painstaking biographies meticulously collected by the newspaper's research staff had there been any indication that he was such a handsome, charismatic man. The intensity and intelligence radiating from his blue eyes seemed to pass right through her.

Ronnie walked in and turned on the cold tap in the bathroom, quickly finding a cloth. She returned to the bedroom where he stood completely at ease, watching her with a mixture of curiosity and pleasure.

"Let me see what I can do," she said nervously, applying the cloth to his neck. He was tall, a ruggedly built man with a wide chest and lean hips. She stood on tiptoe to reach the stain. When she tottered unsteadily his hands captured her ribs, holding her.

"How's it working?" he asked, his voice amused.

With his hands around her, Ronnie found it hard to speak. She stepped back, an edge in her voice. "You're either going to have to sit down or take your shirt off." She was too conscious of him, too aware of his broad chest.

"Are you always so direct on the first date?" he asked, teasing her with a smile while he flipped open his black silk bow tie.

The color rode up her cheeks, making her skin burn. "Only when it's necessary. I'm not in the habit of trying to wash people who stand over six feet tall."

The black silk dangled loosely around his neck as he slipped off his coat and began to undo the buttons of his shirt. His fingers were quick and sure, and the white material parted to reveal a well-defined chest, darkly tanned and matted with hair.

Veronica's pulse quickened, and she walked to the balcony door as he finished removing his shirt. She concentrated on the material she'd memorized from Jeff Stuart's biography. He was something of a low-profile playboy,

never married, schooled in Europe at Oxford, law degre
from Harvard. An interesting family history. His grandfa
ther and namesake had been a riverboat gambler who'd wo
their Mississippi family estate on an outrageous bet that ir
volved the color of a thoroughbred foal at birth. Jefferso
Stuart had horses in his blood, and after experiencing hi
charisma firsthand, it came as no surprise that he wa
pushing the most controversial bill in current history straigh
to voter acceptance. She understood how he might be a ta
get for a bribe.

"Now what?" Jeff waited for her, shirt in hand, as hi
bronzed chest caught and reflected the light from the bath
room in a series of contrasting highlights and shadows.

The answer died in her throat. Her mouth was suddenl
dry, and she touched her tongue to her lips. "Cold water,"
she said, her voice a whisper.

"I beg your pardon?"

"Cold water for the stain," she said abruptly. "Soak th
collar in cold water." Before he could answer she took i
from his hand and went back into the bathroom. She ease
the stain under the tap, hoping the water would make it di
appear. After a few moments of scrubbing, the result wasn'
perfect, but it was acceptable.

"It's the best I can do," she said, blotting the collar on
towel. "I'll have a new shirt delivered to your house tomor
row."

"That won't be necessary. Besides, you don't even kno
my name." He watched her closely. "And I don't know th
name of the woman who pelted me with an oyster."

"I'm sorry. Veronica Sheffield. My friends call me Ron
nie."

"Jefferson Stuart," he said, taking her hand in his larg
one. "Soon to be known to my friends as The Target."

"I am very sorry."

"I'm only kidding you a little," he interrupted. "To show
you that I'm truly not mad, I'd like to ask you for the next
dance. Just as soon as I put on my shirt." He slipped into his
clothes as unself-consciously as he had disrobed.

"Is it cold?"

"The sauce was worse. After the shirt dries, this whole
thing will be just a funny memory." His strong fingers
closed around her elbow, and he nodded toward the door.
"The orchestra calls and I recognize a waltz."

On the dance floor his arm circled her waist and pulled
her against his hard frame. She didn't have to imagine the
rippling muscles beneath his clothes; she'd already seen
more than enough.

"What brings you to Jackson, Miss Sheffield?" he asked.
His breath touched her ear, sending a shiver of delight
across her too-warm skin.

"New opportunities, new job, maybe a sense of adventure." She relaxed in his arms, forcing herself to meet his
questions with a daring smile. She'd had plenty of practice
in putting off personal questions, and Jefferson Stuart was
one man she didn't want to know too much about her.

"That's fairly vague," he said, his blue eyes narrowing to
a calculating glint.

"Not intentionally," she hedged, keeping her smile.

Suddenly he spun her out to the length of his arm, then
pulled her back with an expert gesture that brought his hips
firmly against her.

"Why are you in Jackson?" he asked again, his tone
leaving no room for casual bandying.

Too aware of his body pressed to hers, Ronnie felt the
first flare of her temper. He was trying to corner her, and she
knew instinctively that he wasn't a man who could be
fobbed off with a laugh and an easy answer. Again she
feared that her party-crashing plan had been too impulsive.

If she lied and he discovered her, he'd have her thrown ou in public humiliation. She wouldn't learn anything, an worse, she'd be labeled an incompetent. Her eyes widene as she met the cool curiosity on his face.

"I'm a reporter," she said. "I crashed this party." Th risk had to be taken. Something about him made her wan to be straight and on the record.

"You aren't an invited guest?" He hesitated a moment but before she could answer he brought his leg against he and forced her over his thigh, tilting her easily until her hai almost touched the floor.

The rush of blood and the sense of lost balance was diz zying. Her hands clung around his neck for support as sh heard his delighted laughter. She tried to stand, but he wa in perfect control of her body. When he finally swung he back to her feet and into a series of breathtaking spins tha sent the flimsy skirt of her dress swirling in a glittering ar around her long, shapely legs, his smile was wider. "You'r good-looking for a party-crashing reporter. What shall I d with you?"

"Talk to me," she replied breathlessly.

He cradled her tightly in his arms, and his blue eyes rake her face. Ronnie felt her heart thumping against him as sh tried to read the thoughts swirling in his sea-blue eyes.

"You're the one who needs to talk. What are you look ing for?" he challenged.

"I needed a story. I thought I might find one here. It wa worth the risk." Her words were choppy and breathless. Sh couldn't tell if it was from the dancing or his powerfu closeness.

"And have you found a story?" he asked as they circle the room.

"Maybe." There was defiance and spirit in her reply.

"You think I should let you stay?" he asked, holding her back a short distance while he carefully watched her face. "This is a terrible reflection on security here." There was laughter in his voice.

"I didn't think you would tattle on me," she said hotly.

"I'm not exactly certain what course to take." A slow, sensual smile touched his lips and smoldered in his eyes. "You're really too attractive to evict. But you do need a lesson in manners."

"And you think you're the man to give it to me?" she asked, her anger making her speak before she thought.

"Step outside on the patio, and we'll see." As his fingers firmly grasped her arm her first inclination was to balk, so she braced her back to stop him. He turned, giving her a roguish, expectant look—then the ballroom was plunged into near blackness.

Chapter Two

Ronnie had no time to think. Jeff's grip on her arm tightened as he dragged her across the dance floor. On the wa
behind her, sconces of burning candles created a feeble, eeri
illumination. In the confusion, people crashed into one an
other. They had gone barely four steps when the nea
blackness was shattered by an orange balloon of flame fror
the doorway and the paralyzing sound of a gunshot. Tw
more shots came in rapid succession, orange blossoms syn
onymous with death splitting the night. All around her, th
guests began to scream and thrash about. Before she coul
take a breath, Jefferson Stuart's weight toppled her onto th
ballroom floor, his broad chest covering her completely.

"Stay down," he warned, his voice calm and authorita
tive.

When she struggled to rise, he quickly applied his hand t
her neck and pressed her to the floor.

"Keep down!" he ordered.

She could feel him above her, his body tense and wait
ing. Several women were screaming, short regular bursts o
hysteria. In the darkness, confusion ruled. She felt th
careful pressure of Jeff's fingers on her back. The touch o
his hand was oddly soothing.

"Stay right here and don't get up," he said. His weight owly shifted off her and then he was gone into the panemonium of the room.

Ronnie's reporter instincts quickly kicked into gear. She ad to get the facts. There was no way to tell who had fired le shots, no clue as to whom they'd been directed at. Lying gainst the cold parquet dance floor, Ronnie suddenly reembered the large, black-clad stranger in the garden. He'd een watching someone. Could he have been waiting for the oment to step inside, to kill? The thought made her heart onstrict. Was he still in the house, hidden and waiting? ifting herself to her hands and knees, she began moving ward the edge of the room. In the darkness he could be nywhere, his finger on the trigger. She edged slowly across le floor, aiming for where she thought the patio door was. t least there were lights outside, foolish little lanterns, but etter than nothing.

"Everyone stay calm. There's nothing to worry about. Ir. Dennison will have the lights back on in a moment."

Jeff's voice echoed through the ballroom, calm and ressuring. Ronnie felt the tension in the room begin to ease, nd her memory of his touch reawakened. Were the shots leant for this man? she wondered, shuddering at the modrn madness of such anonymous death.

"Is anyone hurt?" Jeff asked.

Several fresh outbreaks of tears answered, but no one eemed injured. Ronnie finally stood, pulling her dress back ito order as electricity flooded back through the wires and lled the room with light.

The entire ballroom was littered with people hugging the oor. Near her, two women leaned against their escorts in eak relief, and every face was drawn into a tense mask of ar or anger.

Across the room, Ronnie caught Jeff's intent gaze on he
His look was unreadable.

"Stay calm. If you need medical attention, just let M
Dennison know," Jeff said. He pointed to his right whe
Grover Dennison and his wife stood, a united front again
the terror of the night.

Ronnie circled the room, kneeling to assist people still to
frightened to stand, yet searching, remembering all the d
tails. Security guards moved authoritatively through tl
lower floors, and the sight of them was reassuring. Thou
the Dennison property was outside the city limits, Ronn
expected the wail of sirens at any moment. After all, tl
state's biggest powers were endangered.

Jeff was still assisting the Dennisons, talking calmly wi
frightened guests. He seemed to have forgotten all abo
her. Clutching the skirt of her dress in her arms, she ran u
the stairs. She had only a few minutes to look for eviden
before the police arrived. The official version of the gu
shots might not actually reflect the truth, she knew. She'
dealt with political situations far too long. If the gunma
was a paid hit man, Ronnie knew she'd have to figure o
who the intended target was on her own and quickly, b
fore the evidence was impounded and the site sealed off.

A security guard, his posture tense and wary, disap
peared into the second-floor dining area. Ronnie took thre
long steps across the hall and slipped into the bedroo
where she had originally started the evening. So much ha
happened; the scenario she had imagined—dancin
watching and minor sleuthing of a social situation—ha
turned into a nightmare of violence. How odd! Thoug
three shots had been fired, there were no injuries. She ha
to get her purse and take another look at the shadows ou
side. Had someone been waiting there? All of the gues
were already whispering that Jeff had to be the target. Sl

remembered his earlier joke about the oyster and shuddered. His touch was so warm, so vital. Was it possible that whoever opposed his horse racing bill had decided to kill instead of trying to bribe him? Once again she pressed her ear to the door and listened to make sure no one was headed her way.

When the police came, they'd question every guest. The procedure would be long, tedious and also completely blow her cover. She sighed, and thought once again of the half chocolate bar nestled in her purse. A cigarette would be better, but the chocolate was handy, somewhere in the bedroom. One little piece, and then she'd start her search.

In the glow of a small lamp near the bed, she walked to the balcony for one more look at the patio. As she pushed open the door, her lungs squeezed into a painful knot. Two large, muddy footprints were at the balcony railing.

Her heart gave a triple beat as she realized that someone had stood in the exact spot she'd stood. Someone who'd come up here from the garden. Someone with large feet. A big man.

Forcing the air from her lungs, Ronnie took a short, shallow breath. Goose bumps danced down her back, and she turned slowly, ready to face whoever stood behind her. But the patio was empty, the bedroom undisturbed.

For a moment she simply stood, sorting through possible alternatives. She was at a party of strangers. Anyone could be involved in the shooting, and she was a possible eyewitness with potentially dangerous information. Whom could she turn to? Whom could she trust? Carefully she stepped over the muddy prints and closed the balcony door. Jefferson Stuart was the only name that came to her mind. He had been with her the whole time. While they were dancing, anyone could have slipped into the room, leaving behind muddy proof of his existence. She had to trust him.

When she went back to the ballroom, Jeff was still help-ing the Dennisons. Her sudden entrance didn't raise a flicker of interest in the still panicky room. Catching Jeff's eye, she nodded at his warm smile and meaningful wink. Against all of her natural instincts, she moved to the fringes of the crowd, helping herself to a glass of champagne and trying to act as calmly as possible. Her eyes never left Jeff's busy figure, and he periodically glanced over to give her a smile of encouragement.

When the room settled into an uneasy calm, Jeff strode eagerly to Ronnie's side. "Any bruises?" he asked. His hands rested on her shoulders and gently traveled down her arms. Then he felt her back. His fingers moved with exper-tise and gentle concern.

"No, I'm fine," she said. "What is this all about?"

"That's a question a lot of people would like answered," he said. His sea-blue eyes swept the room, making sure that everyone was unharmed. "Let's step out on the patio where we can talk," he said, guiding her toward the door.

"Senator Stuart," she said, trying to hang back.

"Call me Jeff," he said over his shoulder, but he didn't slow his pace or release her arm.

"Jeff, dammit!" she snapped, bringing him to a sudden halt. "Would you please wait long enough for me to tell you something I feel is important?"

He paused, his hand pushing the door open slightly. A cold burst of January air curled into the room, chilling Ronnie and making her shudder.

"I saw a man out here earlier tonight," she said, step-ping closer to him. The cold, and Jeff's sudden nearness made her bite out her words quickly. "He was hiding in the bushes at the edge of the patio. I saw him from the bal-cony." She had to tell him the facts in order, in some sensi-ble fashion.

"Are you certain? What did he look like?" Jeff's reaction was terse. He seemed to find her information annoying more than helpful. She watched the caution creep into his eyes, caution and worry.

"I didn't get a good look at him. He was dressed all in black, more of a shadow than anything else. A big shadow." Ronnie felt like a schoolgirl. Something about the way Jeff watched her made her feel as if she'd done something wrong.

"Was it a man or a big shadow?"

"Listen, I'm just trying to be helpful," she replied hotly. "I saw a strange man lurking in the bushes. I thought he might have been involved in the, well, the gunshots. I thought since you're the reputed target, you might want to find out who's shooting at you. I know I would. Maybe the police will find it relevant information." She was back on track, ready to begin to hunt for answers.

"Why didn't you tell someone about the man before?" Jeff asked.

"It didn't seem relevant before. I figured it was a waiter. A guest. In fact, it could have been someone you were talking with. He was out there just a few seconds before I dropped the oyster...."

The realization of what her words could mean made her stop. Jeff followed her train of thought, she could see it in his eyes, in the frosted anger that made them change from deep blue to turbulent navy.

"Where did you see him?" Jeff asked.

"Just at the edge of the light," Ronnie said, "just past the lanterns."

The door swung open under his light push, and he stepped back to allow her to pass. The night was bitterly cold, but she had no choice. She walked onto the patio and started toward the dark shrubs. Casting a look up at the balcony, she realized Jeff could have been hiding beneath the balcony, in the niche below. He could have seen the strange man, the big man who had hidden in the darkest shadow and left muddy prints. Her shoulders shivered sporadically, and she had a wild craving for a piece of chocolate. When she'd spotted the footprints, all thoughts of candy had been forgotten.

"Exactly where was he?" Jeff asked from the end of the patio, his lean form stooping to examine the area.

"To your left," Ronnie said. "Maybe there are some prints that..." She started to tell him about the muddy footprints in the bedroom, but something made her stop.

Jeff searched the bushes, and she moved to his side. She was cold and worried, but the excitement and fear sent powerful surge of adrenaline through her.

"What's this?" Jeff asked. His powerful shoulders were bent and his hands riffled through the dark leaves of a camellia bush. With an exclamation, he pulled a glittering evening bag from the interior of the shrub.

"Our first clue," he said, turning to Ronnie with a smile of elation. "Are you sure the person you saw was a man? It could have been a woman, couldn't it?"

Ronnie felt her reply stick halfway in her throat. The silver bag glittered in the erratic light of the lanterns. Silently she reached a hand out to take it, but Jeff pulled it away.

"Our first clue to the elusive stranger, and perhaps to the person who fired those shots. The crime lab ought to be able to trace whoever it belongs to. We might have the criminal behind bars in a matter of hours."

"Don't bother," she said, the words tasting rusty and old in her throat. "That's my bag."

She looked directly into Jeff's eyes as she spoke. She saw his surprise, then doubt and suspicion, the very same thoughts she'd had about him only moments before.

"Who are you?" he asked, his voice colder than the wind
that stung her bare shoulders and back.

"I told you. I'm a reporter. I'm with the *Louisville Star.*"
She talked fast, jerkily. "Call my boss and check it out. Call
him now," she insisted.

"You're with a Kentucky paper and you're working here
in Jackson, Mississippi?" he asked, not bothering to hide
the fact that he found her story incredible.

"It's the truth," she said. "I'm here on special assignment."

"Horse racing!" he said, putting it together. "That's a
big interest in your part of the country, isn't it?"

"Yes," she said.

"This whole night was a setup, wasn't it? The oyster, the
dance..."

"Listen, Jeff, I intended to meet you, that's a fact. But
not this way." She had to make him believe her. She was a
good reporter, willing to take a risk, but she didn't manip-
ulate people the way he was implying. The image of him,
standing in the bedroom with his shirt in his hand, came
back to her. She couldn't let him believe that she'd deliberately created such a compromising scene.

"I've always respected the press and realized what a hard
job they had to do. But now I'm beginning to see why my
associates have such distaste for the type of people who do
anything to create big, ugly headlines. I'm surprised you
didn't have a camera crew set up!" His voice was angry.

"That's not fair!" she said, taking one step closer to him,
tilting her square jaw up to his chest. "I'm not that kind of
reporter, no matter what you think. I didn't design this evening. I came to watch the interaction of politicians, to find
out who supported your bill and who didn't. I had no
idea..."

The patio doors swung open, pushed from within by determined hand.

"Jeff, I warned you this might happen! Now I hope you' listen to reason and kill this damned bill before it kills you!' Neil Brenton crossed to where Ronnie stood concealed b Jeff's burly frame.

Stepping around Jeff, Ronnie saw the surprise on Bren on's face as he saw her. He'd obviously thought he wa alone with the senator.

"We've been looking for you everywhere, Jeff. When yo have a moment—" he looked inquisitively at Ronnie "—I' like to see you."

"Miss Sheffield needed some air after the scare tonight But she was just going back inside. The night is too chill fo her without a wrap." His entire demeanor changed, and h touched her shoulder possessively, his eyes mocking her a ger. "I know you won't be at all interested in this politica talk, my dear. Go on inside and have a good time." With casual gesture, he handed her the silver bag. "Be carefu dear, this was expensive," he said.

Ronnie almost choked. Jeff was covering for her, glos ing over his darkest suspicions. She'd fully expected him t turn her over to the police. But he didn't want Brenton t know about the bag, or about her. And he didn't want h to hear this conversation! Questions multiplied in her brai but she was helpless to do anything except smile and wal inside. She didn't dare risk asking even a single questio He'd put her in a completely unacceptable position, b holden to him. Turning on her heel, her anger-filled ey caught his for one brief, daggerlike stare.

"I'll be waiting for you inside," she said as sweetly as sl could.

"I'll be in soon," he promised, a glimmer of dark h mor in his voice.

She took one step—and once more felt an awful tug on er dress. Her bodice slipped several inches, her hem rapped itself around her leg and threatened to throw her the ground.

"Damn!" she said, grasping her bodice with both hands ad pulling it over her blushing skin. Her high heel was once gain caught in the delicate material. She stumbled off, not othering either to untangle her shoe or retort to Jeff's easy ughter ringing behind her.

The ballroom was too hot after the chill night. Ronnie mped in with a straight back and spots of high color on her heeks. Jeff seemed to have a peculiar sense of humor, but e wasn't ready to laugh. At least not yet. She found an conspicuous position near a wall and concentrated on orting through the questions in her brain. So Neil Brenton ought the gunshots were aimed at Jefferson Stuart because of his horse racing bill!

The orchestra was playing softly, but no one had any interest in dancing. City, county and state law officers had rived, sans the sirens. They were already questioning the uests. That procedure was something she wanted to avoid, or as long as possible. What could she possibly tell them? hat was Jeff going to tell them?

As she gradually worked her way back to the patio door, e decided she must talk with Jeff before the police talked her. She could wind up in jail if Jeff told them she was an ninvited guest. That fact would make her a suspect, and tempted shooting of a political figure was a very serious ffense. Jeff had the ammunition to direct that charge quarely at her, if he chose to do so.

Taking a deep breath, Ronnie pushed the door open and epped into the night. To her surprise, only Neil Brenton ood on the patio. Smoke curled elegantly from a cigarette

he held in his right hand, and his dark brown eyes watch
her in an unwavering stare.

"Where's Jeff?" she asked.

"You should have told me you were his date."

"I believe I did tell you that a woman likes an air of my
tery," she managed to say. "Where did Jeff go?"

"He had some serious business to attend to, my dear. B
that will give us a wonderful opportunity to talk. Jeff an
have always been very close, and I'm pleased to see that he
now dating a beautiful intelligent woman, and an excelle
dancer."

His words of flattery were strangely cold, and Ronnie fe
as if a trap were gently closing about her.

"I do love to dance," she said, trying for a light soci
note. "Right now, though, I'd really like to talk with Je
It's a personal matter," she said.

"I thought I detected a note of tension in paradise wh
I came out here," Brenton replied smoothly. "I hope
didn't interrupt a tender scene of reconciliation with n
concerned uncle routine."

"Of course not," she said, almost snapping at his imp
cation.

"Jeff is a difficult man," Brenton said, walking over
her and placing a gentle hand on her shoulder. "He h
great ambitions, great desires. And sometimes he isn't to
careful of other people's feelings, even his own safety. Li
tonight. Any man with half a brain would be out her
making sure that you're unharmed. After all, that terrib
gunfire was something of a shock, even to the brave
heart."

"I'm perfectly fine," Ronnie said, wanting to walk aw
from his hand but forcing herself to remain still. "Je
doesn't need to baby-sit me."

"As much as I love Jeff, I have to accept the fact that he's a man who demands the spotlight." The attorney general laughed. "I guess perhaps I'm to blame for teaching him that trait."

"He told me that you were close," Ronnie said, suddenly deciding to gamble. All of her background information indicated that Jeff had been taken under Brenton's wing as a fledgling lawyer. Brenton had schooled and prepared him for state office. Some even said governor and then U.S. senator. Now was a perfect opportunity to find out what Jeff's true aspirations were. The horse racing bill could be a ploy in a more complicated web of political moves.

"Yes, we have been very close," Brenton said. His eyes dropped and there was a twist of sadness to his mouth. "Jeff is a remarkable man, one of the most able I've ever met." He paused, turning just slightly, as if he wanted to avoid further discussion.

"But," Ronnie prompted him.

"I shouldn't be talking with you this way, my dear. Jeff must find his own destiny. If I don't always approve of his tactics, then so be it. I'm a politician of the old school. Jeff is younger. He must contend with different pressures, different issues and the constant scrutiny of the press. And the danger."

Ronnie kept her face expressionless. "What tactics are you talking about?"

"These younger politicians have learned that the public thrives on intrigue, suspense and emotion. Take this incident tonight. No one was injured. There is no apparent reason for such a vicious attack. But properly managed, it could center public sympathy on some lucky politician."

Brenton's words were carefully chosen, but Ronnie saw behind them the foundation he was laying. Was it possible that Jeff had engineered the whole thing to create an illusion that his life was in danger? The notion was despicable Even under the best circumstances, someone could have been hurt.

Neil Brenton's eyes were sharply focused on her face gauging her reaction.

"Jeff's ambitions are his concern," she said. "My concern now is the fact that I'm freezing to death. Would you mind if we went back inside. I can't imagine where Jeff go off to." She babbled on, fighting for time to compose her self.

"Please don't think that I'm trying to cast doubt on Jeff I view him like a son," Neil said. His hand turned her to ward the door. "I just can't believe that he's abandoned such a lovely young woman so soon after a scare."

"I hardly think abandoned is the right word," she said making her voice light and happy. "As I told you before I'm very capable of taking care of myself."

They entered the ballroom, and Ronnie turned to than him for his concern. Her eyes caught Jeff's gaze just be hind Neil's shoulder. The anger that shot across the roor was almost more potent than the gunman's bullets, and only Ronnie's firm resolve kept her from taking a step back.

"Something wrong?" Brenton asked.

"Not at all," Ronnie said. "Nothing at all. Thanks fo your concern." She walked away from him.

Jeff and the police officer arrived at her side simulta neously.

"If you don't mind, I'd like to ask a few questions," th officer said. He was young and very animated.

"This is Veronica Sheffield, my date," Jeff interjected "She was with me at the time of the shooting and didn't se anything. The whole ordeal has shaken her terribly, and you don't mind, I'd like to get her home."

"Certainly, Senator," the officer said. "We're just relieved you weren't injured. Those bullets could have been meant for you."

"If they were, the man was a terrible shot," Jeff said quickly. "Now please, I think enough has been said about this for tonight. If you need me for anything, I'll be at home."

His hand circled her arm and gently propelled her toward the front door.

"Now go home," he said. "I'm not certain exactly what involvement you have in this, but I'm going to find out."

"I could say the same for you," she answered hotly.

The police officer's words were too close an echo of Neil Brenton's predictions. She glared at Jeff with suspicion.

"Where do you live?" he asked.

"I don't think that's any of your business."

"I'm making it my business, my little reporter. We have some unfinished matters to attend to. Tell me where you live, or I'll simply let the cops take down all the information very neatly, and a lot more."

"2121 St. Ann," she said. There was no point in fighting him now. Besides, there were questions she wanted to ask him as well, after she saw the newspaper headlines of the morning editions.

"I'll be in touch," he said, his voice edged with warning.

"I'll be waiting."

Chapter Three

Jeff's jaw clenched in weary apprehension as he pressed harder on the accelerator. The endless, speculative questions from the press brought home to him that tonight's happenings would truly change his life. He crossed the railroad tracks and checked his watch. At two in the morning, the entire Jackson downtown was asleep. Pulling to the curb near a corner restaurant with a glaring neon sign, he allowed himself one thought of the beautiful party-crasher who'd almost gotten herself seriously hurt. Was she safely asleep at her St. Ann Street residence, that incredible dress a slinky pile at the foot of her bed? He sighed and got out of his truck, an old Chevy that he preferred driving to a car.

There was only one customer in the whole place, a man who waited, shoulders slumped, in the very back booth. Jeff watched him through the café window. When he looked up, Jeff nodded a greeting. The man lifted his coffee cup in a salute, and Jeff swung around to enter the dingy structure.

"You're late."

"You know why," Jeff answered. "I thought your people could take care of things. They missed one gunslinger and..."

The stranger's face hardened and he rested both hands on the table. The waitress came and placed a cup of coffee in front of Jeff. After a long look, she withdrew without asking for an order.

"The Sheffield woman, she's a reporter," the man said, studying his large hands on the table. "She could expose everything. Do you think it's wise, larking around with her on the dance floor?"

"She thinks she saw someone in the garden," Jeff shot back angrily.

"Can she identify the man?"

"No," Jeff answered. He paused. "We might have gotten lucky. I don't think she saw anything, although I did find her purse in the garden."

"That's great!" The other man chuckled. "Just like I planned. So now I guess she's riding out the night in police custody for questioning?"

Jeff shook his head, disbelief and anger combined in his eyes. "You planted that purse?"

"Sure. She broke into the party for a story, so I thought I'd really give her one." He laughed cagily. "You don't know the times snoopy reporters have gotten under my feet. It's great to get one back."

"You're a fool, Carlisle," Jeff whispered. "If she gets onto what's behind this, she could ruin months of work."

"You don't think I know?" Carlisle snapped, rubbing his hands together. "She could blow the whole thing. So it's up to you to keep her under wraps."

"How the hell did she get in?" Jeff asked. Weariness had replaced the anger in his voice.

"That's a question for the books. Dennison had six security guards there. They never saw her. Maybe she had some outside help?" he asked.

"The Dennisons didn't know her, I checked that out," Jeff said. "Maybe Neil." He looked at the other man.

"Mr. AG, now that's a possibility," Carlisle said with a sneer. "He's getting bolder by the minute." He laughed as he pulled a small clipping device from his pocket and started to snip at his cuticles. "He's crafty, all right."

"Being smart isn't a crime," Jeff said tightly.

"No, but it's useful if you're bent that way, Senator. You should know, since you're such good friends." He laughed again, folding the clipper back into his pocket.

"One day, Carlisle, I'm going to make you eat those words."

"Can the tough act, Senator," Carlisle said, leaning back in his seat. "We got business. What was the media reaction to the shooting?"

"If they play this for a murder attempt, it could work in our favor," Jeff said reluctantly.

"Good. If we're careful, tonight's mistake won't affect our plans," Carlisle said leaning forward. "It's a shame Ms. Sheffield has involved herself in this, but we can't let one person interfere with our plans. Her job involves risks. She knows that. You know that."

"I know that if you'd been doing your job, you would have stopped her from getting into the party," Jeff said, his anger erupting suddenly as he, too, leaned forward across the table. "Where were you?"

"Trying to cover your butt," the other man snapped back.

"If this continues, Carlisle, I'm going to withdraw from our deal," Jeff said. "One more slipup like this and I'm out!"

"The damage is minimal. At least for now," he insisted. "You just take care of Sheffield. I don't care what you have to do, just keep her busy and off our tail. Think about the money, partner."

"Fine, but no more mistakes," Jeff said rising. "I mean ." He strode from the table, putting a dollar beside the ash register before he pushed through the swinging door.

The other man rose slowly, his eyes following Jeff's movements to the truck. He stood for several moments, then reached for the clippers as the old pickup disappeared down he empty street.

"SHUT UP!" Ronnie grumbled at the telephone as her hand waved about the bedside table trying to find it. "What idiot would call in the middle of the night?"

She found the receiver and pulled it quickly to her lips.

"Hello and this had better be good," she said.

"What the hell is going on down there?" Kurt Chamliss's voice barked down the telephone line. "There's an attempted murder and I don't get even the first paragraph of copy from you!"

"Kurt," Ronnie said, sitting up in bed and pushing long strands of black hair from her face. "What time is it?"

"Seven here, so it's six there," he snapped. "Too early for national story?" he asked sarcastically. "Or have you been too busy to notice that Senator Jefferson Stuart was nearly murdered last night?"

"It was hard for me to see, since he was on top of me the whole time," Ronnie answered.

Her reply succeeded in attaining Kurt's silence.

"What did you say?"

"I thought that would catch your interest," Ronnie said, humor replacing her early morning grogginess. "I was at the dance last night, Kurt. I crashed the party and I was dancing with Jeff, uh Senator Stuart, when the shots were fired. He threw me to the floor. That's what I meant."

"Are you hurt?" The question was terse and shot like bullet down the telephone line, but Ronnie knew her boss gruffness was often a cover for his concern.

"No. No one was hurt. The shots came close, but no on was hurt."

"We just got a wire story. It says three shots were fired i the middle of a party. The story says Jeff was the target."

"Maybe," Ronnie said, once again remembering he conversation with Neil Brenton.

"What's going on down there?"

She reminded herself that Kurt was adept at picking u verbal clues, and she wasn't certain how much she shoul tell him. "I'm not really certain." She hesitated. "There wa something strange about the whole incident last night."

"Too strange for a brief story?" he asked, his tone gen ler.

"I didn't want to blow my cover yet," she said, swingin her feet out of bed and picking up the telephone. The lon extension cord allowed her to travel down the hall, into th kitchen and to the counter where she turned on the coffee pot. "I knew the wire service would carry the basic detail I wanted to try and uncover something else, something di ferent, before I told everyone down here that I'm a re porter."

"Are you onto an angle?"

"That might be putting it too strongly. Just let me sa that things are more complicated down here than I firs thought."

"Not the simple little state capitol you left five years ag to make it big in the big time?" Kurt teased.

"Exactly," she said. Jeff's and Neil Brenton's words wer colliding in her head. She drummed her fingers on th countertop and impatiently waited for the coffee. "When

greed to take this assignment, I thought it would be a va-
ation, a reprieve among old friends.''

''Are you sure you weren't hurt?''

''Not a scratch, Kurt. Can you get me the background on
Neil Brenton and Jeff Stuart's falling-out over the horse
acing bill? Something's not quite right.'' At last she poured
 cup and took the first sip. The rich taste of the coffee made
he morning a little more bearable.

''Yeah, sure, and don't worry about the story. I was a litle upset when the wire came across with something and our
est reporter was down in Jackson sending nothing in. I
hould have known to trust your judgment.''

She smiled to herself. That was the biggest compliment
Kurt could pay a reporter. He wasn't exactly known for his
ind words and encouraging attitude. In fact, many of the
eporters called him The Slave Driver behind his back, but
he'd grown and improved so drastically under his wing that
he had no complaints.

''I'm really not convinced there was a real murder at-
empt, but I can't prove it.''

''Just trust your instincts, Veronica. I've never met an-
ther reporter with a better nose than you. Trust what you
eel, and send me a story. Soon. That's an order.''

''Right, boss,'' she said, hanging up the phone.

The sun was just peeping over the edge of the kitchen
urtain, and she stifled a yawn. With the hot cup of coffee
 her hand, she went into the living room.

''I can't face this yet,'' she said to herself, standing over
ozens of unpacked boxes. ''I get four hours' sleep, and
en I'm expected to open up everything I own just to find
ome clean underwear. It's too much.''

She stood looking at the crates, and then walked toward
er bedroom. The silver gown was lying on the hall floor,
here she'd abandoned it the night before in her hurry to get

into bed. She picked up the shimmering material and hel
it to her face. There was a lingering scent of spice, th
vaguest memory of Jefferson Stuart's cologne. Her finger
tightened on the material. The implications of what Brent
on had said about Jeff were very ugly. And they could als
be very true. That was the job she'd taken on when she cam
to Mississippi, to find out whether they were or not. Sh
took the dress to the closet and hung it on the sole coa
hanger. The rest of her clothes were in suitcases, boxes an
packing crates. She shut the door and leaned against it
There was just too much to do, and she was due to mee
Sally Duvall at nine-thirty.

As she tackled the job of finding her clothes, her min
went through the years she'd known Sally. In her fifties
Sally Duvall was one of the best reporters in the business
Her family responsibilities had kept her in Mississippi, ou
of the national competition, but she'd been instrumental i
encouraging Ronnie to pursue her own dreams of workin
for a nationally respected paper. Sally had faith in her whe
no one else did.

After a shower she pulled on a pair of gray slacks and
turquoise sweater, gathering her shoulder-length hair at he
neck with a ribbon. Steadfastly ignoring the chaos of he
house, she opened the front door and stepped into the cris
morning air. The cold made her pull in her breath, and whe
she exhaled, a frosty cloud circled her face, making he
think of long-ago school mornings when she'd loved th
excitement of winter. She'd been lucky to rent the ol
brownstone in one of the historic sections of town, only
hop, skip and jump from the state capitol where she'd b
spending most of her days and nights.

The morning newspaper was lying near a line of camelli
bushes, and she was smiling as she walked over to retriev
it. When she was a little girl, she and her brothers had ofte

had wars with the soft camellia blooms, hurling them at one another so that they struck and burst into showers of beautiful petals.

She reached for the paper, eager to find out how her competition had handled the story of the gunshots. As her fingers grasped the plastic wrapper, she saw the footprints. Large and deep, they were directly in her line of sight near the living-room window. The ground was soft from the melting frost, and she knew the prints were fresh. She could still see the treads, a pattern common to many brands of running shoes.

Instinctively, she tucked the paper under her arm and stepped into the bushes. The prints led back to her half-opened bedroom window, and over to the point where the telephone lines ran into the house. The prints were deeper here, as if the man had stood for some time.

A curl of fear traveled from her stomach down her back. In the cold air, her breath churned out in a series of short, harsh clouds. She leaned one hand against the cold bricks of the house to steady herself until the worst of the fear passed. In Louisville there were people she could call, law officers, reporters, a few trustworthy politicians. But in Jackson she was on unfamiliar ground. She had no idea whom she could trust. Jefferson Stuart came to mind, and the memory of his broad shoulders and confident handling of the night before gave her a moment's respite from her fear. But as she walked around the house to the sidewalk, she knew that was only an illusion, a game she played with herself like a little girl in a fairy tale. Life was more complex. There was every possibility that the man who had stood outside her window and watched her was someone Jeff knew. Someone Jeff had sent. She realized she must first find out what he really wanted before she could trust him.

The moment of peace fled like birds before a storm. He face was pulled into a frown as she stepped into her car and carefully backed toward the street.

St. Ann was a quiet street of mostly elderly Jacksonian who had been born and raised in the houses they still occu pied. Ronnie loved the neighborhood, the gently rolling hill and the solemn, private homes.

The street was always empty, but she checked carefull before backing out. There were a few parked cars, bu nothing else. She pulled out the map Sally had sent to di rect her to The Deadline, a hangout for reporters, and sh was on her way.

The renovated old café wasn't difficult to find, and sh pushed open the saloon-style door with an eagerness tha made the hinges squeak. Sally's flaming red hair was eas to spot at a center table. At Ronnie's approach, Sally lifte her Bloody Mary and gave a silent greeting.

"How's life been treating you, kid?" Sally asked, signal ing the waiter for immediate service. "You look great. A littl̇e pale, but other than that, great."

"I've missed you," Ronnie said warmly, at last shakin; the sense of doom that had accompanied her on the drive.

"Kentucky is a long way away, but it isn't too far for a) occasional visit home," Sally said.

"Nor for you to come up," Ronnie countered with a smil as color finally returned to her face. The waiter placed an other Bloody Mary before her, and Sally ordered tw brunches.

Ronnie still held the morning newspaper, and she place it on the table. "I want to check out the competition," sh said.

"You're a little late, kiddo," Sally replied. She pulled paper from her briefcase and tossed it to Ronnie. Th headline was bold and black; "State Senator Target c hooting." Though she'd been a witness to the event, Ronnie couldn't stop the involuntary jolt the words gave her.

"I'm glad Jeff is still alive. I'd hate for you to have missed the opportunity of meeting such a handsome, healthy male specimen. His only drawback is his profession," Sally said with a grin.

Ronnie quickly scanned the story. Either the writer had been given a series of false facts, or he'd deliberately jumped to the wrong conclusions.

"This isn't right," she said, pushing the paper back to Sally.

"Well, I know you're a star, but isn't that sort of harsh judgment for one of the *Daily Sentinel*'s reporters? How do you know it isn't right?"

"I was there last night, at the party," Ronnie said softly. "I was dancing with Jeff when the shots were fired."

There was only a second of silence as Sally's lips spread into an admiring smile. "I'll be damned! I tried to call you last night to see if you wanted to come over and have dinner with Frank and me. When you didn't answer, a little voice in the back of my head started singing out. I knew you were up to something. How did you get in?"

"I walked in the front door," Ronnie said. "I just didn't have an invitation."

"You crashed?" Excitement made Sally's green eyes glitter. "And you were there for the shooting?"

"Yeah. Three shots, nobody hurt. I don't see how they can tell who the shots were intended for. The whole place was crowded...."

"Wait a minute," Sally said, uncrossing her legs and leaning forward. "You don't think Jeff Stuart was the target?"

"I didn't say that," Ronnie answered quickly. Neil Brenton's words had been so allusive, filled with innuendo

rather than fact. She told herself that another priority would
be to determine what Neil really believed—that Jeff was the
target of antiracing elements or that he was the worst sort of
grandstander.

"What exactly are you saying?" Sally didn't miss a single movement or inflection. She earned a living as a free-
lance reporter because she was good.

Ronnie took a sip of the spicy drink and carefully broke
open a croissant the waiter had left in a basket. "There's the
possibility that the whole thing was a setup."

"To what purpose?" Sally asked.

"Maybe to gain public sympathy, just an added boost for
his horse racing bill." Ronnie crumbled the delicate roll with
her fingers as she talked. For some reason, she didn't want
to look Sally in the eye.

"That's interesting," Sally said, pushing the butter toward her friend. "Eat your food, don't play with it. I never
would have given the incident that coloration, but then
maybe I've known Jeff too long."

"What was your first thought?" Ronnie looked up at
last, catching the full impact of Sally's searching green eyes.

"That someone wanted to make trouble for Jeff, one way
or another."

"I saw Jeff Stuart on the patio last night, before the
shooting. I, uh, hit him with an oyster," Ronnie said, unable to suppress her grin. Then she abruptly grew serious.
"Right before I dropped the oyster, I think I saw a man, a
big man who disappeared into the shadows around the garden. I couldn't tell much about him, but there was something odd. Anyway, it could have been the gunman."

Her final words were soft, punctuated by the familiar
restaurant noises of dishes and silverware, laughter and
conversation. The two women looked at each other.

"Was Jeff talking to the man?"

"I don't know. I walked out on this balcony to eat. I saw the man in the garden, and then I dropped the oyster."

"This is a little hard for me to grasp, Ronnie. Are you sure?"

"Very sure." She paused. "That's not all. Jeff found my purse in the garden shrubs after the shooting. We were looking for the place where the man was hiding."

"How did your purse get into the garden?" Sally asked. Worry was slowly etching a firm line across her forehead.

"The man must have thrown it down from the balcony. I found muddy footprints. So whoever he was, he must have gone upstairs to look for something." Maybe he was looking for her! Ronnie felt her heart racing. The footprints were too vivid in her mind. "I think someone was trying to incriminate me."

"This is beginning to sound ominous," Sally said, trying for a smile, and failing to hide her concern. "Anything else?"

"There is one thing more. This morning, I found similar large footprints around my house."

"Oh," Sally said, sitting back in her chair and reaching for her drink. Her eyes never left her friend. "Did you call the police?"

Ronnie shook her head. "I wasn't certain who to call. I thought I'd talk it over with you."

"I can see where you'd be reluctant, especially after they knew your purse was out in the shrubs at the Dennisons after the shooting. Boy, you sure kick up a storm when you come to town."

"The police don't know about the purse. Jeff covered for me. He even acted like my date so I wouldn't have to answer any questions." As Ronnie spoke, her voice dropped. "He didn't seem to want me to talk with the police. Any idea why?"

"No, but now I understand why you walked in here so pale. When you get ready to go home, I'll follow you. I'll also call a friend of mine at the phone company and have your lines checked out. We don't want any taps, any problems." Reaching a hand across the table, Sally rubbed her friend's arm. "Hell's bells, Veronica, you don't just cover the news, you make it. That's one way to keep ahead of the competition." She smiled, this time actually suppressing her worry.

"I know it's just a series of strange events all falling together at one time," Ronnie said, but her voice held no conviction. "Next week, we'll be laughing about the crazy scare I had my first two days in town."

"Excuse me, Mrs. Duvall, there's a call for you. The phone is at the bar."

"Thanks, Mike," Sally said as she rose from the table. "If that's Bertha at the answering service, I'm going to skin her hide. I told her not to bother me this morning, that I had an important meeting with my collaborator. Sometimes I think she delights in doing just exactly the opposite of what I tell her," she grumbled as she walked across the room.

Ronnie watched her petite friend sweep past tables and people as if they didn't exist. Sally had been born with a pen in her hand and a question on her lips. Her husband, Frank, always teased her by saying that their children had learned to say "Who, what, when, where, why and how" before "Mama" or "Daddy." The thought eased the tension that was building between her shoulders, and she buttered a piece of pastry and popped it into her mouth. Was Jefferson Stuart a victim or a perpetrator? The question refused to leave. She couldn't shake the memory of his touch, the way his hands had traveled over her so carefully when he thought she'd been hurt. She sighed, shifting her focus to find her friend.

Sally was coming back across the room, and Ronnie gave her a cheery smile. Something about her walk made her look closer. Sally's green eyes were wide open and her mouth was drawn into a straight line.

"Grab your purse," Sally said firmly. "We're leaving here, right now."

"What is it?" Ronnie asked, picking up her billfold and newspaper. "We didn't really get a chance to touch our eggs."

"We'll go somewhere else." There was no arguing with Sally's tone.

"What's going on?" Ronnie asked, her husky voice rising slightly.

"Get going. I'll explain in the car. My car. We can send someone for yours later."

"I'm perfectly fine to drive, if you'll tell me where to meet you."

"Ronnie, that phone call was about you." She grabbed Ronnie's arm and held it tightly. "A man said for me to tell you to get on the next plane back to Kentucky. He said not to finish our breakfast, or our Bloody Marys. He said if you valued your hide, you'd be gone within the hour."

Sally's green eyes burned with a cool glint of fire. She kept Ronnie's arm in her hand and gently directed her toward the exit.

"Put it on my tab, Mike," she called over her shoulder.

"What was his voice like?" Ronnie asked. The threat was like a dim echo in her head. Ever since the party she'd had my warnings going off. Now she had proof that it wasn't just her imagination. "What else did he say?"

Sally whirled around, startling her friend. "He said the bullets last night weren't meant for Jeff. They were meant for you!"

Chapter Four

"Go straight outside and get in my car. Burgundy Lincoln right at the door," Sally ordered, nervously biting her bottom lip.

Ronnie allowed herself to be pushed, but something was very wrong about the message Sally had delivered. Very wrong. Why would someone want to shoot at her? None of it made sense. She didn't know anything. Not yet, anyway.

"That's it," Sally said soothingly. She opened the door. "Now get in."

Ronnie obeyed, turning to look down the street. There wasn't much traffic. The Deadline was too far downtown yet not really close enough to any bank or business. Only members of the press would champion such an unlikely place for its character.

In the clear January sunshine, Jackson looked very much as it had during her childhood and teenage years before she went away to college. Before she became a reporter. Her eyes swept up the street and found nothing. Ordinary parked cars. Like cars on every street in the world. Like the car parked in front of her house this morning. The realization was almost too subtle. She wasn't shocked to discover the black sedan. She even smiled, noting the clichéd "mysterious dark car."

Sally was on the driver's side, sliding behind the wheel.

"This is no time for grinning like a simple-minded idiot," she commented. "What is it?"

"I'm not certain, but see that black Buick up there. This morning when I left the house, there was one just like it parked on my street."

Sally glanced casually in the direction indicated. "Don't go bonkers on me, Ronnie," she said slowly. "There may be a thousand black Buicks like that in this city."

"I know," Ronnie said, "that's why bad guys use them, because they're so anonymous."

"I'm going to take you to the Capitol because I don't know where else to take you," Sally said, grinding the Lincoln's balky starter into action. "Once we're there, we'll call Kurt and decide what to do. I can book you a flight out of here by two."

"Forget that plan of action right now," Ronnie said. The motion of the car seemed to release her from inertia, and she felt her energy return. "I'm not going anywhere."

"Don't be a fool," Sally said. "The guy on the phone was serious."

"What did he sound like? Deep, Southern, rough, what?"

"He sounded like he was disguising his voice. Does that come as a surprise?"

Ronnie pressed against the window trying to see in the side mirror if the Buick was following them. "Did he sound like a big man?"

Sally pondered the question. "I'm not certain what a big man should sound like, but for some reason, I want to say so. Average, maybe. I'd say educated, though I don't know why. It could have been the authority in his voice. He expected me to believe him because *he* said it." Sally's gaze

darted to the rearview mirror as she talked. "There's no one
on our tail. We're not far from the Capitol."

Ronnie forced her shoulders to relax while reaching in her
bag for the ever-present candy bar. "I'm not calling Kurt,
and I'm not going back to Kentucky. And that's final," she
declared. "I came here to do a job, and I'm going to do it.
Remember when I said those shots couldn't have been meant
for Jeff, because there were so many people dancing. Well,
the same applies to me. Whoever fired the gun would have
had to kill twenty people to get to me. And they didn't try."

"That doesn't mean they won't again," Sally said slowly.
"Remember, there's been someone standing outside your
house, watching and listening to everything you do."

Fear curled slowly inside her, and she felt for a moment
like a child waiting for the dentist's drill. "I know. But it
doesn't mean they will. I think it's all just an attempt to run
me out of town. The only thing I don't know right now is
why, but that's something I intend to find out."

"Here we are," Sally said, turning left onto Capitol
Drive. "I don't like this, but I know you too well to push.
You're like a mule bogged down in the mud. Unless you
want to, you won't budge."

"The legislative session doesn't start today. Will anyone
else be here?" Ronnie asked, hoping that a change of subject would relieve her friend's anxiety.

"Maybe, maybe not. The security guards will be here,
though. They're not cops, but they're highly trained."

"I'm not worried about safety," Ronnie said, reaching
across the seat and giving Sally's arm a squeeze. "I was
wondering if I'd meet more politicians, other members of
the press. You know, new girl on the block syndrome."

"That's a possibility." Sally swung the car into a parking
space reserved for the press. There were several cars a

ady on the lot. "I'd say some other members of the fourth state are certainly here. I wonder what gives."

"Maybe every single member of the press is being hotly ursued, and they all decided to hide at the Capitol," Ronie said, joining her friend at the front of the car.

"Your humor leaves a lot to be desired," Sally said dryly. Want to check out the situation?"

"I'm with you, partner," Ronnie said. "I came all the ay to Mississippi for a chance to work with you again. ead on."

Sally only shook her head. "You're putting on a brave ct, but I want you to know I think you should go back to entucky. I'm a little older, and a little wiser. This situaon could be dangerous, really dangerous. It's not the time kid around or act like you're invincible. I don't want to e you hurt."

"And I don't want to be hurt," Ronnie replied, grasping ally's shoulder and turning her around so that they faced ach other. "I'll be careful. I promise. If it really looks angerous, I'll leave."

After a second, Sally smiled. "Okay. Now let's go."

They strode down the leaf-covered walk toward the inting steps of the imposing old state building. Sally called greeting to the guards, briefly introduced Ronnie and urried on. They had just stepped into the rotunda when a age ran to Sally's side.

"I've been trying to reach you for over an hour, Mrs. uvall," he said breathlessly. "Mr. Brenton's called a press nference for right now. He said it was urgent and he asked e to call all the press. He especially wanted me to get in uch with you. I tried and tried, but we couldn't locate ou."

"It's fine, Timothy. Where's Brenton now?"

"Second floor, outside his office." He took a long brea
while giving Ronnie a look of pure curiosity.

"This is Veronica Sheffield, a friend of mine who is al
a reporter," Sally said smoothly. "Timothy is Neil's aide f
this session." She turned back to the young man. "Be
nice to Miss Sheffield as you would to me. We're worki
together for a while."

"You bet," Timothy said. "I'd better go. Mr. Brent
sent me for some copies of proposals at the clerk's office

He dashed down the hall, his highly polished shoes cla
tering on the tile floors. Ronnie watched him hasten throug
the high arches and graceful columns that created the r
tunda. The Capitol was still as impressive as she remer
bered it from her high school trip to watch the legislature
session. It had been one of the experiences that forged h
desire to become a reporter, to keep the public truthful
informed.

"He's a good kid, if you ever need anything," Sally sai
"We'd better find that conference. I wonder what Neil ha
up his sleeve today."

"Does he usually have something up his sleeve?" Ronn
asked quickly. Sally's comment made her wonder agai
about Neil Brenton and the concern he'd expressed for Je
Stuart. Two men who were known to be as close as fath
and son, a controversial bill, the possibility of big mone
and now, violence. She chewed the inside of her lip as sh
walked.

"Neil's been a politician long enough to know the valu
of always having a trick up a sleeve, but I didn't mean th
in a derogatory fashion," Sally said pointing toward a fligl
of spiraling stairs. "Neil's done a lot of good for this stat
He pushed for education reform, civil rights, insurance r
form, banking reform, not very popular political stance
but he made them. He's taken some hard knocks, b

omehow he's managed to hang on and survive. This is his
ixth term as attorney general. A record.''

They reached the top of the stairs, and the hubbub of
ews people at work ended Ronnie's opportunity to further
robe Sally about Neil Brenton, most particularly about his
elationship with Jeff Stuart.

"Hey, Sal," A tall, slender reporter with silver hair
reeted Sally. ''Too bad you came. We thought we'd have a
hance to cover this without you around to steal it from us.''

"Keep practicing, Douglas, keep practicing," Sally said,
aughing. She made quick introductions to the twenty-odd
eporters as they stood outside Neil Brenton's door, wait-
ag for him to come out. Television crews checked lights, ran
able and tested microphones. When Neil stepped into the
ull glare of the television lights, a hush fell on the group.

"I called this press conference to say that this office has
egun an investigation of the shooting at the Grover Den-
ison home last night," Neil began.

His face was haggard, as if he'd gone without sleep,
onnie noted.

"We have organized our best law officers in this effort to
pprehend whoever fired those three, potentially deadly
ots," Neil said. He was calm and possessed as he spoke,
ith just an edge of anger.

"Police Chief Clive Davis is coordinating his investiga-
on through my office. Though the shots appear to have
een random, I want to emphasize that the state's most im-
ortant elected officials were present. This is *more* than a
andom shooting.'''

He paused a moment, and Ronnie saw his expression
often. He seemed to gather himself, cleared his throat and
poke again. Ronnie's background information was lengthy
nd clear on the paternal relationship between Neil Bren-
n and Jeff. The older man had not only encouraged the

younger, but he'd made political opportunities, pushed t
have Jeff accepted by the Democratic party even though h
was younger and more liberal than the old lions of the or
ganization liked. It wasn't hard to see the attorney general'
emotion. He was visibly shaken.

"Jeff Stuart is a dear friend of mine. I cannot compre
hend why anyone would take this action against him. Whe
there are political disagreements, the only acceptable wa
the people of America resolve them is with a ballot, not
bullet. This office condemns such acts of violence, and
pledge to you that we will do everything in our power to ap
prehend the criminal who invaded a private citizen's prop
erty to perpetrate this reprehensible act. Thank you.
Stepping away from the microphones, he looked around th
gathering and caught Ronnie's eye. Surprise stole over h
face as he signaled recognition.

Several reporters moved forward with notepads and m
crophones and began asking about the investigation. Sall
scrawled a few additional notes on the steno pad she'
pulled from her purse. "I think I want to ask Mr. Brento
a few questions," Ronnie said softly.

"Are you going to tell him about the phone call th
morning, and about the footprints outside your house?
Sally's voice was hopeful.

Ronnie pondered the question, then shook her hea
"No, not right now."

"You need to tell someone, Ronnie. This is serious."

"Give me a little while to think this thing through.
doesn't make sense that anyone would have it in for me.
just got into town." Before Sally could protest furthe
Ronnie moved through the reporters to Brenton's side.

"Excuse me, Mr. Attorney General," she said, "I have
few questions when you get a moment."

"Miss—? You never told me your name, preferring to remain the lady of mystery for the night. Now I know why." He smiled, but once again, only with his lips. Ronnie forced herself to step up and extend her hand.

"Veronica Sheffield, with *The Louisville Star.*"

"And I thought you were merely another of Jeff's lovely ladies. But I knew there was more to you than simply a graceful dancer and a lovely face."

This man had spent too many years kissing babies and wooing voters, she thought grimly. He was a professional politician, able to match anyone in Washington with the know-how of manipulation and rhetoric. She didn't like the type, but it didn't mean she wouldn't like the man once she knew him better.

"Thank you, Mr. Brenton," she said, matching him look for look. "Do you have any clues as to who is responsible for the shooting last night?"

"I can't discuss the details of the case, you understand we wouldn't want to jeopardize our investigation. But I can say that the police have uncovered several very significant leads. The crime lab is running an analysis on the bullets, but we're low on clues. Unfortunately when the light fuses were pulled, most of the people at the party panicked."

"No one can give a description of the gunman, then?" Ronnie asked pointedly.

"You don't waste time, do you?" he asked, smiling to let her know he appreciated her directness. "I thought perhaps you might have some ideas about the motive behind the gunshot. Reporters are always full of ideas." He watched her closely as he spoke.

"I'm afraid my job leaves little room for speculation. I prefer simple questions, and honest answers," she said.

"Step into my office for a moment," he offered. "Since you were there, I would like to ask you a few questions. I believe you were with Jeff just before and after the shooting."

"That's right," Ronnie said, following him to the impressive oak door he pushed effortlessly.

"Excuse me." He turned back to the members of the press. "Don't hesitate to call my office with any questions. When I receive further details, I'll be sure and notify you all." He ushered Ronnie past his secretary and into his private office, then closed the door.

"Did *you* see anything unusual, anything at all?" He stood like a prosecutor, one hand on his desk for the appearance of balance. His question came at her fast, trying to throw her off guard.

The question was to be expected, but still, Ronnie felt the nerves flutter through her stomach. She'd put herself in an awkward position.

"I didn't get a look at the gunman, if that's what you're asking."

"Jeff told the police officers on the scene that you were his date." The first note of hardness crept into Neil Brenton's voice. His eyes were calculating, and the image of a hawk came to Ronnie's mind. A hawk flying high in the air with a prey sighted on the ground.

"I was very tired and shaken by the whole incident. Jeff knew I'd seen nothing, and he was trying to spare me the long ordeal of standing around waiting to answer routine questions." Next he would be asking her how she'd got invited to the party. That whole can of worms would be spilling out everywhere.

"Jeff's a very compassionate man," Brenton said. He walked behind his desk and for the first time Ronnie noticed his office. There was a portrait of Governor Bilbo on the wall behind the desk, obviously a state heirloom. The carpet was a deep blue and matched the comfortable ooking sofa. The broad oak desk gleamed with polish. The attorney general sat down in a brown leather chair. His walls were lined with law books, but no personal mementos, she observed. He signaled Ronnie into a blue suede wing chair n front of the desk.

"How long have you known Jeff?" he asked suddenly.

"Not very long," Ronnie responded. "I understand, hough, that you two have been friends since Jeff was a litle boy."

"That's true," Neil Brenton said, leaning back and smiling. Once again, Ronnie was struck by the hawklike quality n his eyes, as if he'd see even the slightest movement, the witching of a toe inside her shoe.

"You introduced Jeff to politics, didn't you?" she asked.

"If you can say that a mother duck introduces her ducklings to swimming, then you can say that I introduced Jeff o politics." He laughed. "I've never met anyone more natural. When Jeff went for his law degree, I knew he'd never be content to have a small practice on the coast. He's always had ambitions, bigger ambitions than the state of Mississippi can offer him." A muscle twitched in his jaw.

Ronnie felt her pulse quicken. She was on to something, ome important facts. "As big as the U.S. Senate?"

"And what's wrong with that?" Brenton asked, suddenly leaning forward. "Mississippi would be lucky to have a man like Jeff represent her in Washington." The mask was back in place.

"I didn't mean to imply that anything was wrong with wanting to be a U.S. senator," Ronnie said easily. "I'm new here, and I have a lot of catching up to do. I don't know the hings that other reporters take for granted."

"Jeff's a good man, Miss Sheffield, a fine man for this tate." He watched her again. "Can I tell you something?"

His question caught her off guard, the confidential tone rattling her. "Of course. But I must know, is it on or off the record?"

He laughed, a sudden burst of sound. "Always the good reporter." He laughed again. "I suppose this is off the record. It's just some of that background you've missed. This horse racing issue could prove to be very bad for Jeff's career. He sees it as a way to bring business and jobs into the state, to generate taxes for the schools. Now that's all well and fine, on paper. But the fact of the matter is that gambling won't bring in anything but trouble. I've told Jeff this, and now I'm telling you. We need industry, but legitimate industry like computer technology, factories to hire our unemployed. Horse racing is a dirty business. Gambling brings a bad element with it, and if you have any influence with Jeff, you should persuade him to look for other means to promote the state, and his future."

"The tracks in Kentucky generate tremendous amounts of revenue for the state," Ronnie said. "At home I have figures, statistics...."

Brenton waved a hand at her, shutting her off. "I think you have to remember, young lady, this is Mississippi, and we don't want track riffraff down here." His voice was hard and unflinching. "I wouldn't be encouraging Jeff in this endeavor. It's political suicide. Jeff has been misled. He seems to be choosing the wrong friends lately, and I'm worried about him. I'd do anything to make him understand how wrongheaded this endeavor is." He turned away from her and stared at the portrait of Bilbo. "Now if you'll excuse me, I have to be down at City Hall."

He rose suddenly and left the room. Ronnie stood, smoothed her slacks and gathered her composure before she walked back out past the secretary and into the empty hallway.

The attorney general's figure disappeared down the spiraling steps. As Ronnie watched him depart, she felt someone behind her. The hair along her neck rose, and she forced herself to remain perfectly still. She didn't believe someone was trying to kill her. Not really. But there had been those footprints and that threatening phone call at the bar. How had the man known what she and Sally were drinking?

"None the worse for wear, I see," Jeff Stuart said as he came to her side. "But dressed very casually for work." His eyes moved from her soft cotton sweater to her grey slacks and flat, comfortable shoes.

"I didn't actually expect to work today," she said, unable to suppress her exhaled breath. When she looked into his deep eyes, she couldn't hide a smile. "You scared me half to death, coming up behind me like that. You're quiet as a cat, and in a nicer mood than last night," she added dryly. There was none of the anger she'd witnessed firsthand. Perhaps the tension of the shooting had made him too aggressive. Today he was all charm.

"I was watching the conference from up there." He pointed to the third floor, which was used for access to the galleries of both chambers and to house the press. "You've blown your cover now. Neil is sure to have a file on you by closing time tonight."

"A file?" she asked.

"Yep. Every traffic ticket, misdemeanor and dirty thought you've ever had."

"That's no problem, Senator. I had a good upbringing. I've never had a dirty thought."

Jeff's chuckle was warm and contagious, and Ronnie felt the release of laughter.

"How does it feel to be the target of an attempted shooting?" she asked. The question was half joke, but she also wanted to gauge his reaction. "I heard you were a danger-

ous man, but I never realized that a single dance could cos
me my life."

"Do we have to talk about that today?" he aske
smoothly. "Every reporter in town has had a field day, an
to be honest, I'd much rather think about you and that sex
dress." His eyes were sparkling with high spirits.

Ronnie dropped her gaze before she was completel
drawn in by his merry eyes. "I'm sorry, but it *is* my job t
ask questions. Do you believe the shooting was a result o
the horse racing bill, some rabid opponent trying to knoc
off the champion of horse racing?'"

"No," Jeff said patiently.

"What do you believe?" she asked.

Her determined jaw was tilted up to his, and the sincerit
in her eyes made him want to answer her. Unfortunately, th
black lashes that fringed her serious gray eyes and her fu
lips made him want to do more than talk.

"Actually, I think it was some crazy who stumbled in o
the party, had a gun and decided to create a little excit
ment. You were there. Those shots were wild."

Watching him, Ronnie almost forgot that he could hav
set up the entire thing. She could see the definition of h
chest beneath the crisp white shirt he wore. if she lifted on
finger and touched the starched material, she would feel th
cushion of his chest hair.

"I have my opponents," Jeff said. "But no one is tha
insane."

"Neil Brenton thinks horse racing is a mistake for th
state," Ronnie said, jerking her mind back to the busines
at hand.

"Neil and I have discussed this issue until we're both blu
in the face," Jeff told her easily. "He's wrong. He doesn
believe we can set up a clean track, and I do. Neil's pi
headedness has gotten completely out of hand, and he

pushing the limits of his office to try and stop me." Jeff forced a smile and swallowed his sudden anger. "The thing you should remember is that Mississippi is the poorest state in the nation. The tax revenue generated by a track could go for teacher pay raises, school improvements, medical benefits, a million other things that are desperately needed here. And racing is one of the most beautiful sights you've ever seen."

"I know very little about it," Ronnie said.

"You've never seen a race?" Jeff asked, disbelief ringing in his deep, rich voice. "You live in Kentucky and you've never seen a race?"

"Only on television."

"That doesn't count."

"Jeff, I was raised in the country. My friends had horses, but not me," she said, laughing at his expression of chagrin. "I was always reading, writing, studying."

"This has to change," Jeff said, his eyes brightening. "I have an idea. I can arrange for you to talk with a horse breeder, someone who can give you the business facts about the horse industry in Mississippi, what it could mean to this state. That way you can see in action how they're bred, born, raised and trained."

"You know a breeder?"

"It's a wonderful farm. The owner has experience, and knows cold, hard facts about breeding racehorses in a state that forces you to export your finest foals at giveaway prices."

"Jeff, I'm not in this business to make people like me," she warned him. "I do have some hard questions about finances, employment, the money and risks."

"That's exactly the kind of thing horse breeders would like to get published," Jeff assured her. "There's no question too hard, because the track will be good for Mississippi. We have the climate, the soil. . . ." He stopped. "And if you've never seen a fit horse run, you've missed one of the most beautiful sights in the world."

"It's a deal then. When can I meet this breeder?"

"This weekend. I'll be in touch with the arrangements."

"You can reach me at—"

"555-1604," he interjected. "I'm good with numbers."

"I'd better go find Sally," Ronnie said, suddenly feeling awkward. She was pleased that Jeff knew her number. Pleased and skittish. His boyish excitement was highly contagious, and for a moment she'd almost forgotten that she was working on a story, not socializing.

"She's in the pressroom calling in a story," Jeff said. "I told her I'd wait for you and send you up."

"Thanks," Ronnie said. "I'll expect to hear from you."

"You will," Jeff answered, smiling as he started to the stairs. At the banister, he turned and gave a quick wave. Ronnie waved back, feeling sixteen and coltish. She circled the rotunda and found the back stairs that led to the press room. Sally was still filing her story when she entered.

"How'd it go?" the redhead asked.

"I'll tell you over some lunch. If you remember, we never got to eat," Ronnie replied, realizing that she was ravenous.

"Okay," Sally said, grabbing her purse. "I have a genius of an idea. Remember the desk you were looking for last month when you called? Let's go downtown to some of the junk shops and check it out. There's a great little café I know with the best home cooking you've ever tasted. Plenty of food and not much money."

"What can I say?" Ronnie laughed. "You're the driver."

"If I had my way, I'd feed you and put you on a plane," Sally said, suddenly too serious. "I have this gut feeling that phone call was only the beginning of some big trouble."

Chapter Five

"Let's stop by The Deadline and get my car," Ronnie said. "It's easier to park than your bus."

"You just like driving that hot rod. Infantile urges," Sally observed sourly, but she turned the big Lincoln in the right direction nonetheless.

"Before we were interrupted this morning, I wanted to ask you something," Sally went on. Her eyes were on the road, and she didn't look over at Ronnie. "If you want to say it's none of my business, fine. I understand."

"This sounds terrible, Sal. What is it?"

"Why didn't you marry Craig Bellafonte?"

"Oh," Ronnie said. Craig seemed like a million years ago. She had trained herself not to think about him, not to wallow in the pain that even the mention of his name had once brought.

"Bad question to ask?" Sally said. "I'm sorry."

"No, it's a legitimate question. You deserve an answer. After all, I practically invited you to the wedding, and then never explained why there wasn't one."

"I don't need an explanation, kiddo. I just really wanted to be sure that you were okay. For months you were so excited, as if you'd finally found the right man to complete your life. Marriage isn't the be-all and end-all of the world, but as you know, I'm a strong supporter of it."

Ronnie forced her hands to lie still in her lap. Craig Bellafonte. What could she tell her friend? "Craig wasn't the man I thought he was. I guess it's that simple. I fell in love with a make-believe person, a mirage."

"How so?" Sally probed.

"You know he worked for the competition, and he was and is a very capable reporter. It's just that a few weeks before the wedding, I found that he was reporting only the facts that suited him."

"Holy cow," Sally said, letting her breath whistle out between her teeth. "You tied up with a man who wasn't ethical?"

Ronnie smiled at her friend's disbelief. "He was a very convincing liar, Sally. He fooled me and a lot of other people. When I found out the truth, I felt like such a fool I didn't want to tell anyone. I just wanted to forget the whole thing ever happened."

"That was a good idea," Sally said. "I'm sorry to drag up the past."

"I was going to tell you later, anyway. Now it's over. And that was all two years ago. I'm pretty much over the hurt. I'm just a little more cautious."

Sally maneuvered the Lincoln into a parking space, and they got out and walked to Ronnie's silver 280Z.

"Now that's a hot car, sweetie. But where do you put your legs when you get in?"

"Sally, you're only fifty, but sometimes you like to sound like Grandma Moses. Get in and let me show you what a car can really do." Ronnie laughed. "We're on the trail of antiques."

She slammed her door and revved the engine. Sally was laughing as she quickly fastened her seat belt. "Go down to

Conti, cross the tracks, turn left, go three blocks and turn right and then go right again on Alley Street.''

"Sure," Ronnie said. "Is this a memory test?"

"Just drive," Sally said. "You wanted to, now go."

Twenty minutes later they were still hunting for the shop. "If we don't find that antique store in the next fifteen minutes, I'm going to go on strike and insist on food!" Sally exclaimed, exasperated.

"Not a bad idea, but this isn't exactly a neighborhood for dining." Neglected stores lined the potholed road. They were in the old business district of the town, a place filled with secondhand stores and bargain shops.

"There's a pretty good café only a few blocks away," Sally assured her. "Remember, I mentioned it earlier. Good home cooking, and an interesting clientele."

Ronnie turned the car down another block, her eyes seeking the small antique store she'd read about. She had a million boxes to unpack, and she needed some furniture to unpack her things into. Jackson had a reputation for being an antique collectors' haven.

"What type of clientele dine at this establishment you're so interested in eating at?" she asked, her eyes probing the dark brick buildings.

"Oh, werewolves, dragons, a few hookers, just your ordinary psychos and murderers." Sally suppressed a smile.

"That doesn't sound too bad," Ronnie said, her attention still focused on the storefronts. "How's the food?"

"Well, the last three people I know highly recommended the daily luncheon special, but that was before the funerals."

Ronnie slowly turned her head, giving Sally a long look. "What funerals?"

"I didn't think you were paying a bit of attention to what I said. And you weren't."

"I'm sorry, I just have a one-track mind. Let's get some lunch and see if that doesn't clear up my dull brain cells." She nosed the car slowly down the street, creeping cautiously around parked delivery trucks and what appeared to be abandoned vehicles. "I'd give up, but if I don't get furniture this week, I won't have time to do it later."

"I know." Sally sighed. "This is going to be one grueling session. At least you've gotten most of the technicalities down."

"At least," Ronnie said. "I haven't had any sleep for the last three nights. If I haven't been crashing parties, I've been reading history, laws, probability studies. Ick!"

"Maybe you should have spent more time dancing with Jeff." There was a teasing note in Sally's voice.

Instead of taking the bait, Ronnie paused, her brow furrowing above her oversize sunglasses. "I've given a lot of thought to Jeff Stuart. I know I need to work with him, but I want to keep as much distance as possible between us...." Her voice faded.

"And he's damned attractive," Sally finished for her. "He's an integral part of our assignment. I don't know if you can avoid him."

"Not totally. In fact, he's supposed to arrange for me to interview a Mississippi horse breeder this weekend. I can work with him; it's just that I don't want to be in a position of relying on him." She cleared her throat, hoping to cover the nervousness. Jeff had invaded her life in a hundred small ways. She found herself thinking about him in the middle of work, remembering the teasing corners of his smile, the touch of his hand on her back. The situation was worse than distracting, it was completely crazy.

"Where's the ranch?"

"Oh, he didn't say. Somewhere in the state."

"That would be an excellent story. No one else has even begun to think along those lines. Jeff's a shrewd politician."

Ronnie slowed to a halt in front of a tiny diner built in a shotgun design. "Is this the place?"

"The Minny Mouser, that's it," Sally said, patting her stomach. "The best corn bread in the city."

Ronnie parked the car, and they entered through the swinging glass door. As they found a back booth and settled in, Ronnie's gaze swept the interior, taking in the old furnishings and the cleanliness of the counters and grill. The place wasn't bad at all. The smell of home-cooked meals was decidedly tantalizing. As she smiled at Sally, in the corner of her eye she caught a glimpse of a broad, muscular back disappearing down an alley across the street. Something familiar about the walk and the set of the shoulders made her stare.

"Take a look, I think I've just seen Jeff Stuart," she said softly to Sally, her eyes never leaving the rapidly diminishing back.

Sally craned her neck, letting a low whistle escape her lips. "You've got the eyes of an eagle. I think you're right."

"I wonder what he's doing here?" Ronnie asked. She tried to keep her voice casual, but there was an underlying wistfulness.

"Probably the same thing we're doing. Looking for bargains. He's an antique collector, and I hear he renovated his family home and added some extraordinary pieces."

"I don't know," Ronnie said. "He acts like he's hiding."

"Want to follow him?" Sally's eyebrows rose over green, catlike eyes. "We haven't had a good game of hide-and-go-seek in years."

"I don't know." Ronnie hesitated. Her first instinct was to satisfy her curiosity, to find out what task had brought Jeff to the low-rent side of town. But something stopped her.

"Are you getting to be a softy?" Sally asked, amazement apparent in her voice.

"Not on your life," Ronnie said. She eased from the booth. "If we're going, we'd better go now or he'll be gone."

They hurried out of the café, darting across the street and down the darkened alley.

"I feel like Nancy Drew," Ronnie commented sarcastically.

"Maybe so, but Lois Lane would approve," Sally replied with a wicked grin. "Isn't this the way they do it in the movies?"

"Sure, and it's a great way to embarrass yourself."

They came to a corner, and Ronnie peeped around, hoping that she wouldn't find herself face-to-face with Jeff. She could imagine the anger his blue eyes would direct at her. Flames couldn't begin to match the heat.

Among the large boxes and garbage cans, there wasn't a sign of a living soul. The alley had come to a T that was empty on both ends. Jeff had vanished.

"Where'd he go?" Sally asked, walking down the alley to the left. There was no sign of any business entrance, only a few barred doors that apparently led to warehouses.

"This is odd," Ronnie said softly. "Maybe it wasn't Jeff after all."

"Well, it could have been someone else," Sally conceded. She turned her curious eyes on Ronnie. "If it was Jeff, I wonder what he was doing. And more importantly, where he went."

They turned back, retracing their steps to the café and resuming their seats.

"So you had to chase down your appetite?" the waitress said, dropping two plastic-coated menus before them. "Try the special, it's the best thing today."

Without even consulting the menu, Sally ordered two specials with iced tea. "I've got to get back to the Capitol," she said. "If we hurry, we can try a few more streets to see if we can locate that antique shop. This isn't our day for finding what we want."

Ronnie didn't answer. Her eyes were focused outside the window of the restaurant and down the shadowy depths of the alley. She was almost certain the man was Jeff. Her body had recognized the broad stretch of his shoulders, the casual grace of his walk. She knew intuitively that he was nearby. There was the slightest disruption of her heartbeat, a speed that had nothing to do with her run down the alley. What was Jeff doing? she wondered, remembering his cautious yet purposeful stride. Why did the thought of seeing him unnerve her so?

"Earth to Ronnie, come in Ronnie." Sally pointed her fork at the steaming plate on the table before her. "Your food has been here almost two full minutes. If we're going to find your furniture today, you'd better get busy."

Ronnie picked up the fork and automatically ate. The fresh vegetables and corn bread were delicious, but she couldn't appreciate the food. Her mind was filled with a thousand questions and a variety of emotions she found hard to untangle.

THE HEAVY WOODEN DOOR slid shut behind Jeff as he stepped into the dark, open room. A few feet away a match struck harshly on the roughened exterior of a matchbook.

The small orange flame illuminated Jay Carlisle's beefy face.

"The meeting's set for next Tuesday," he said. The slender tip of his cigar glowed orange, and the match sank into darkness.

"Are the dramatics so necessary?" Jeff asked, nodding at the darkened warehouse around them.

"Yes. The meeting is set for here. We're not really expecting too much. This is a negotiation, a time for them to feel you out. If they suspect you aren't on the level, then you'll be in a lot of trouble."

Jeff watched the cigar glow in the darkness. He could barely distinguish Carlisle's features. "When are you going to tell me the specifics of the deal?"

"When I'm ready."

Anger swept over Jeff, and he fought down the urge to collar the man who stood only a few feet away.

"Listen, Carlisle, I'm not interested in losing my life because you won't share your secrets with me."

"Oh, don't worry, Senator, when the time is right, you'll know everything you need to know. But if you know too much now, you may be uncomfortable."

"What exactly is that supposed to mean?" Jeff's voice echoed harshly off the metal walls of the warehouse, creating an eerie, hollow sound.

"I wouldn't want your good friend the attorney general to get wind of this."

"If you think I'd ever..."

"Hold on, Senator, I'm not accusing you of anything. Yet. But I've seen a lot of strange things come down, and I've learned to be real cautious. You can't blame a man for taking precautions." The orange stub dropped to the ground and was immediately crushed out.

"I'd like to take a few precautions of my own," Jeff said.

"Good. Then be here exactly at midnight, Tuesday. Park ver on Conti Street and walk. I'll have you in sight the hole time. Listen to the offer, and see if it's something you uld reasonably live with. Once you're in here, you're on ur own."

"Will I meet Johnny Deluchi?"

"Mr. D? I doubt it. He'll send a secondary for this meet-g."

"I'll hear from you before Tuesday?"

"Yes. In the usual manner."

"A phone call from Christine. Isn't that a little too much ke a bad television script?"

"Who cares? It works." The man started to step slowly ackward. "What about the reporter? Have you taken care that problem?"

The mention of Ronnie made Jeff's anger flare again. She d complicated his life, drastically. "She'll be gone this eekend," he said. "It's all arranged."

"It had better be," Carlisle said. "She's a nervy broad. I now her type, and she won't take no for an answer. You ould have let the cops find her purse at the shooting. That ould have kept her busy and out of the way."

"Nice talking with you, Carlisle."

"Yeah, Senator, enjoy the weekend. I'd make it memo- ble, if you know what I mean." He laughed in the dark-ss.

Jeff strode briskly to the heavy door and pushed it ughly to one side. A beam of midday light flooded the om, revealing an almost empty interior. In the far back rner cardboard boxes touched the ceiling. He took his ne examining the room, memorizing the contours and the ptiness. Then he slid the door back into place and walked rough the sunshine toward the street.

Half a block from his truck he saw the silver sports ca
The thought of Ronnie made him quicken his steps, h
long, powerful legs devouring the sidewalk as he hurrie
When he came to the plate glass window, he peered insi
and spotted Veronica's dark hair and Sally's flaming r
curls. With a grin he tapped on the glass, drawing their a
tention.

Jeff's face in the window sent a sudden lurch throu
Ronnie's chest. She felt her stomach unaccountably dro
and she demurely dabbed a napkin to her mouth to cov
her discomfiture. Jeff waved a greeting, and she signal
him to join them.

"What's the matter, don't you like the Capitol snack b
sandwiches?" he asked. His lean body slid across the boo
beside Ronnie, his hip touching hers only for a moment.

"We're looking for an antique shop," Sally said. "Wh
are you doing here?" Her eyes briefly touched Ronnie's,
small but definite signal of alertness.

"Looking for a reporter," he said with a laugh. "I ha
the most wonderful scoop, and no one is at the Capitol f
me to reveal it to."

"What kind of scoop?" Ronnie kept an innocent loo
focused on his face, even though she felt a strange ener
tingling through her body.

"Oh, something tantalizing and very significant." Mi
chief, like wind-whipped waves on the sea, danced in l
eyes. He laughed when Sally shook her head in obvio
disgust.

"I'm too old for such foolishness, Jeff," she said. "A
Ronnie's too smart."

"Okay," he responded agreeably, beckoning to the wa
ress, "I don't have a story, but I would like to join you f
lunch."

"Make it quick, we're hot on the trail of antiques," Sally said, "and one of us has to be back at the Capitol by two sharp. Our governor is calling a press conference."

"I should be there, too," Jeff said, "but I think I'm going to skip it." After the warehouse meeting, he was in no mood to spend time in any type of conference or session. He wanted to be outside in the sunshine, taking in the sights and sounds that gave him such pleasure. Danger or no danger, he wanted to be with Ronnie.

"Hey!" Sally exclaimed, a note of inspiration strengthening her voice, "I could go back and cover the press conference, and Ronnie could stay here with you." She took a last bite of corn bread and looked at her friend. "Jeff has a truck."

"I don't know," Ronnie said hesitantly. An afternoon with Jeff was a tempting thought, but this was just the type of situation she had hoped to avoid. Jeff did something to her; he touched nerves that were long dormant.

"That sounds like a great idea," Jeff urged. "I know this area like the back of my hand."

"Even the alleys?" Ronnie said, a little too quickly. She bit her lip and silently cursed herself for blurting out the question instead of casually easing into it. Jeff made her so nervous, she couldn't even act like a halfway competent reporter.

"Alleys are sometimes the best shortcuts," Jeff said easily, but the lines near his mouth tightened. "If we shop, I promise to show you a few."

"Great." Sally picked up the tab and Ronnie's keys. "I'll take your car, and lunch is on me. See you sometime before five." She was gone, her high heels clicking on the linoleum.

The waitress set another steaming plate of food on th
table, nudging the dishes out of Jeff's way. "What type o
antiques are you looking for?" he asked.

Ronnie went over her needs, noting that expense wa
definitely a factor. "I've seen some wonderful pieces, bu
not in my price range," she said, trying to keep the conver
sation smooth and impersonal. "Were you really huntin
bargains today?" she asked, watching him closely.

"I'm always looking for bargains," he replied. "By th
way, you're a hard lady to track down." He bit into the h
corn bread with a sigh of contentment. "I've made the a
rangements for this weekend."

"You mean the interview with the breeder?" Ronni
couldn't hide the excitement in her voice, but she also no
ticed how he'd expertly dodged her question. "Thanks, Jef
Where is the place?"

"Near the coast," he said. "This food is great. Could
tempt you with a little coffee and dessert while I finish?"

"Just the coffee," she said, appreciating the deft mar
ner in which he signaled the waitress and manipulated th
conversation. "You do have a way with women," Ronni
said, giving voice to her thoughts before she could stop he
self, and making herself blush.

Jeff laughed, taking in her embarrassment. "Loose lip
sink ships," he said.

"It's the truth," Ronnie defended herself. "Everywher
I see you, women dash to do your bidding."

"Alas, only the most intriguing ones are immune to m
charms." There was a mocking note in his voice, then l
openly laughed at her. "I don't have much success with yo
Ronnie."

"I'm a reporter, Jeff," she said, feeling trapped and ur
comfortable. "I can't get involved with a person I wri
about."

"Well, you don't have to write everything," Jeff said, feigning indignation. "But then again..."

"You are totally incorrigible," she said, at last unable to hold back her own laughter. "Tell me a little more about this interview you've arranged."

Seeing anticipation in her eyes, Jeff barely stopped himself from reaching out and touching the smooth skin of her face. Instead, he picked up his fork and moved the food around on his plate. "This is a unique situation, Ronnie. You're just going to have to follow my advice, and do what I say."

The tone of mystery around his words acted like an elixir. Ronnie leaned forward in the booth, her gray eyes trained on him with total absorption.

"What's unique about the situation?"

"Well, this breeder isn't really ready to go public, but I did a bit of persuading...."

"Jeff, I'm going to have to ask a lot of tough questions. If this person is a friend of yours, maybe the interview isn't a good idea. I don't want to put you in the middle."

The honesty in her words made him look up. The crystal depths of her eyes were endless. There lay worlds to explore.

"Ann is capable of defending herself, and her business," he said. "I have no worries on that count. But to get the interview, I want you to do a few simple things."

"Like what?" Ronnie asked, slipping her notebook out of her purse.

"Friday afternoon, as soon as possible, drive down to Biloxi. Go to 2334 Beach Road, it's right along Highway 90, you can't miss it."

"Is the horse farm on the beach?" Ronnie asked.

"No, but this is a convenient place to begin. I'll make ar rangements for you to stay there for the weekend." H looked down at his plate.

Unable to read his face, Ronnie turned back to her note book. The possibility of her first big story made her clenc the pen tightly. "I can stay at a hotel," she said. "I don want to be a bother to any of your friends."

"Believe me, it won't be a bother. Just go there, an everything else will work out fine."

"Okay," she agreed, flipping the pad shut and tucking into her purse. "So, the plans for the weekend are set."

"Let's get that furniture you need, and if you don't fin what you want, you can always examine the shops along th coast. There are some exceptional bargains if a perso knows just where to shop."

"And I suppose I have the best tour guide on the whol Gulf coast?" Ronnie's happy smile lit up her face.

"You're pretty smart for a reporter," Jeff said, hopin that fact wouldn't end up costing them both their lives.

Chapter Six

"The whole time we've been shopping, you've bent my ear 'bout horses," Ronnie said as she folded the sales slip for a desk and chest of drawers into her coat pocket. "I feel like 've entered a whole new world." Jeff had talked about orses, but he'd managed to evade all of her important questions.

"The thoroughbred is the most magnificent creature live, bone and flesh transformed into something magical. f you've never seen one run, whether it's in an open pasture or on the track, you've never lived." A small laugh ollowed, and Ronnie felt the brush of his fingers on her arm s he helped her into his truck and then hopped into the river's side. "I didn't mean to get so carried away," he pologized.

"You really love it, don't you?" Ronnie said, responding to his passion and excitement.

"In a word, yes. I don't want to get started again on another lengthy speech. I just can't believe you've never seen race."

"I can't believe it either," she replied. Sitting beside Jeff s they drove down the busy streets of Jackson, what she eally couldn't believe were the events of the past two days. 'he shooting, the footprints, the threat, the terrible sense of fear that she'd felt watching the man hiding in the Denn son garden. She glanced at his clean profile, the tiny wri kles of humor near his eyes and mouth. They'd spent tł last two hours shopping and laughing together as if the were racing headlong into romantic involvement. The ide made Ronnie drop her gaze to her lap. It was wonderfu and also impossible, yet the hours with Jeff had pushe aside her duties, and her fears.

"I've enjoyed this afternoon," Jeff's voice was casual. " hope we can do this again sometime." He chanced a look ∂ her, seeing the strength of her jaw and the way her ha curled slightly beneath the turquoise ribbon. Why did sł have to be so trusting? Why a reporter? He had a momeı of misgiving about his future. "I'm glad you crashed tł party," he said, shaking off his doubts.

"Will you ever forget the way we met?" she asked, tucł ing in her chin in embarrassment. "That oyster..."

"At this moment, our meeting holds too much fascina tion for me." Wanting to erase the shame on her face, h picked up her hand.

Ronnie's delicate fingers drifted into his larger hand. Sł could feel the calluses on his palm, the slightly roughene skin that tantalized, a reminder of his athletic grace an power. His fingers closed around hers carefully, as if he hel a very delicate bird.

He idled the truck at a stop sign and lifted her hand to hi lips. His warm breath touched her skin first, sending shiver of delight through her body. His lips caressed tł back of her hand, moving to the wrist and then to the palm Her skin was soft as silk, and the odor of her perfume wa elusive. He felt her tremble slightly as he applied a littl more pressure.

Her hand was a willing prisoner, and he lingered over tł sensuous elegance of her tapered fingers. When he finall raised his head, he was fully aroused. Her eyes glowed softly, and he could see the faint mist of her breath when she exhaled deeply. With one easy pull, he could have her in his arms, feel her supple body pressed against his so that she would have no doubt what she did to him. But something in the way she sat so perfectly still made him hesitate. He went on holding her hand, the soft warmth enclosed in his harder flesh. She didn't withdraw, but she didn't meet him halfway, either, simply looking down at her lap. Remembering how dangerous this girl could be to his future, he pressed the accelerator and drove single-mindedly toward the Capitol.

Ronnie's heartbeat began to regulate itself as the downtown district passed by the truck window. Jeff's effect on her was both undeniable and surprising. She knew his reputation as a ladies' man. It was in the files, and even Neil Brenton and Sally had made reference to it. That didn't matter, though. She'd never had her hand kissed in such a fashion, and she liked it.

Jeff turned into the Capitol driveway. Instead of going to the Senate parking lot, he pulled in at the front steps. "I have some business to take care of," he said quickly. If she didn't get out of the truck, he was going to have to touch her again.

"Thanks, Jeff. I can't wait for my furniture to be delivered. And now I know a little about racing, from a personal point of view."

"My pleasure, Ronnie. And I'll see you this weekend when I take you to see the breeder."

"I have the address, and the directions," she assured him, climbing out of the truck with a bounce. "Thanks." She waved him off and ran up the steps, moving fast to try and escape her thoughts. She wanted him to kiss her, wanted to feel his lips taking hers, and that was no way for a reporter to react to a news source. She forced herself to think of the

serious complications Jeff Stuart could make in her career.
The idea that he was involved in something crooked seemed
crazy, but it was something she had to remember. As she
hurried inside to find Sally, though, she couldn't suppress
the delight she felt at the thought of the weekend.

THE WHITE FENCE was easy to spot in the dazzling winter
sun. Ronnie put the car in neutral and stopped at the oyster
shell driveway. The peaceful stretches of white, sandy beach
that made up the Biloxi coastline lay to her left, and the cold
winter winds had cleared the beach of sunbathers and all but
a few hardy boaters. She found the stretches of empty sand
breathtaking.

"So, this is the right address," she mumbled to herself,
checking the numbers on the mailbox by the road. She felt
a surge of anxiety but pressed her foot determinedly on the
gas pedal. Jeff had been so mysterious about the entire trip.
He'd told her nothing except that he'd taken care of all
lodging arrangements and that the interview with the horse
breeder, Ann Tate, was set for Saturday morning.

The car coasted quietly down the driveway, and Ronnie
slowed to absorb the gracious beauty of the giant oak trees
that formed a canopy overhead. In the background she
could hear the soft whisper of the Mississippi Sound.

In the distance, the faint outlines of a white Creole-style
home could be detected through a maze of manicured
shrubs and trees. Ronnie was delighted to find she recognized the bare-limbed dogwoods, azaleas, hydrangeas, ca-
mellias, bridal wreath and wisteria. When the flowers
bloomed in the early spring, the yard would be a fairyland.

"I wonder who owns this place," she said to herself,
wishing desperately for a cigarette. The urge hadn't struck
in several days, and the intensity of the longing for nicotine
caught her off guard. "Damn," she added, and dug around

in her purse for some chocolate. The beauty of the estate was making her nervous. She wasn't certain what she'd stepped into, or who would greet her at the door.

"Well, here goes," she said as she eased down on the gas and slowly pulled to the front of the house. A broad, welcoming porch covered three sides, and swings and rocking chairs were an open invitation to comfort. Wide gray steps led to the front door, which had an intricate pattern of leaded glass set in the design of a peacock.

Ronnie got out of the car appearing more confident than she felt and walked quickly to the door. Just as she was about to knock, the door was opened wide by a striking woman almost six feet tall. Her bronzed skin glowed in the sunlight and green eyes probed Ronnie.

"You must be the lady reporter. Please come in," she said in a soft voice that seemed to float.

"I'm Veronica Sheffield," she managed to reply, not knowing whether to get her bags or simply leave them in the car until Jeff appeared to formalize the introductions.

Seeming to read her mind, the tall woman smiled. "My name is Stella. Don't worry about your bags; Earl will bring them in and put your car in the garage. You won't be needing it this weekend."

Ronnie followed her into a beautifully decorated living room. In a large fireplace, wood waited only for a match. At Stella's direction, she took a seat.

"Please, make yourself at home." Stella's Creole voice hinted of exotic places. "Mr. Jeff will be here very soon. He went into town to pick up supplies for my kitchen. Here he comes this morning, wanting this and that prepared, and no warning, so I tell him that if he wants such special things, then he must run about town and find me the ingredients. That is fair, yes?"

"Absolutely," Ronnie agreed, totally confused. Why was Jeff asking Stella to prepare anything?

"But he is such a dear," Stella relented with a broad smile. Her striking eyes grew gentle. "And he rushed out of here with such eagerness. I cannot stay mad at him." She shook her head knowingly. "I am too old to deny him."

Ronnie sank slowly back onto the sofa. She looked from Stella round the room. "I appreciate your inviting me into your home," she said with some hesitation. "Jeff didn't exactly give me the details about my visit."

A look of disbelief was quickly replaced by a knowing grin. "So, he is up to tricking you, is he?"

"Tricking me?" Ronnie asked, the first serious doubts beginning to take shape. "What do you mean?"

"Mr. Jeff did not tell you that this is his home. He means to surprise you with the knowledge. I believe he thinks you wouldn't come and stay with him if you knew the truth."

"This is Jeff's home?" Even as she spoke, the truth was evident to her. The room was well-appointed, but strictly masculine.

"Yes, Magnolia Point has been in the Stuart family for three generations now. Jeff is very proud of his heritage." Stella spoke simply, but with a certain degree of pride.

Ronnie rose slowly to her feet. "I really can't stay here," she said softly. "It's impossible."

"Why can't you stay?" Alarm gathered in Stella's voice. "Mr. Jeff is making many plans for you. All day he has…"

"I'm sorry," Ronnie interrupted her, feeling the color wash across her face. "But you must understand. I can't stay here with the Senator. It wouldn't look right at all." She fumbled, unwilling to put her objections into words.

"Not look right?" Stella's face was incredulous. "Ever since I was a girl and my mother worked for Mr. Jeff's mother, this house has been a place for many people to visit and enjoy. There is a tradition here, a longtime way of life where people talk and share the moments of their lives. This is wrong?''

Seeing the concern on Stella's face, Ronnie paused. She'd take up the issue with Jeff when he returned. At the thought of his trickery, she felt a small burst of anger. He'd really pulled one over this time. She could just imagine the laugh he was having now. No wonder he'd been so secretive about the weekend. She clenched one fist at her side and sat down again.

"So you will stay?" Stella asked, her relief evident. "I don't know what I would tell Mr. Jeff if you were to leave. He would never understand. I will make you a warm drink, some Irish coffee, and you can relax until he returns."

"When do you expect him?" she asked, trying to keep the fury out of her voice.

"Very shortly," Stella said diplomatically. "You must relax. Earl has taken your bags into the guest room, and Elain has arranged your things. If you'd like to freshen up, go up the stairs and to the left."

"I just think I might do that," Ronnie said, knowing that if she were forced to sit still she might well explode.

In the guest room she found her nightgown on the pillows and her slippers already placed neatly on the floor next to the bed. Her cosmetics were unpacked and arranged on the vanity. Sunlight filtered through lace-covered curtains, and from the windows she had a bird's-eye view of the magnificent grounds.

"Jeff Stuart, this time you have gone too far," she whispered under her breath. She felt another jolt of anger, this time at herself. She'd driven half the length of the state just to find herself the butt of a practical joke! Without ever asking even the first intelligent question about her visit to the coast, she'd let Jeff lead her by the nose. The thought was almost too much to bear. "I'd like to bury you in a truckload of oysters!" she whispered vehemently.

"Only if you promise to clean me off again."

She whirled from the window, almost crashing into his strong chest.

"I want to have a word with you," she said, her breath coming rapidly and her gray eyes blazing.

"Has anyone ever invented a better word than spitfire to describe you?" he asked mockingly. When she failed to answer, he nodded. "I guess not; so spitfire it'll have to be."

"How could you do this?" she exclaimed. "I have a million things to do in Jackson, and you want to play games!"

"Spin the bottle was always my personal favorite." His eyes were positively wicked. Laughter danced in them with hurricane force as he lounged in the doorway. "The blast of your temper is hot enough to warm the house. Maybe I should tell Stella to turn off the heat."

"This isn't funny, Jeff," she said, stopping herself just in time from stamping her foot.

Anger had whipped pink stains into her cheeks, and her eyes were luminous with fury. Jeff kept his casual pose against the door, but his body tightened as he took in the angry movement of her breasts, the tension that emphasized her delicate strength. There had always been beautiful women in his life. The coast boasted some of the most attractive ladies in the world. But none had ever captured his imagination like the feisty reporter who stood before him ready to extract out some physical retribution. He'd tricked her into coming to Biloxi, it was true. It was either that or let Carlisle "take care of her." Though he tried to convince himself he'd gotten her to Magnolia Point only to keep tabs on her, in his heart he'd have to admit to other, more personal motives. And if his motives weren't exactly honorable, he'd done what he promised. An interview with Ann Tate was scheduled for the next day.

"I knew if I didn't trick you, you wouldn't come," he said softly. The mischief was gone from his eyes, replaced by something else.

"Jeff, you've put me in a very bad situation. I can't possibly stay here, in your home," she said, forcing herself to speak rationally. "I'm a reporter and you're a politician. How would it look if the public found out that I was your houseguest? I'll be writing stories about you, for God's sake." The last phrase slipped out before she could stop it.

He took a step toward her, his lithe body moving with remarkable speed. "Let's go back downstairs and talk about this over a drink. Stella said she was making some Irish coffee. When she said you were a little distraught, I came right upstairs."

"Let me pack my things," Ronnie said, making a sweeping gesture to indicate her belongings. "Whoever works for you, I hope you pay them well. I've never seen such service."

Jeff laughed, a low warm chuckle that was almost like a touch.

"You notice everything," he said. "Leave your stuff; I'll help you get it back together after a drink."

The thought of hot coffee laced with liquor was tempting. Ronnie lowered her angry gaze and stepped toward the doorway. Jeff's arm came around her shoulders, giving her a gentle squeeze.

"I know it isn't appropriate, but welcome to Magnolia Point. I wanted you to see my home. No compromise of your reputation was intended."

The simple sincerity of his words, coupled with his touch, sent an unexpected thrill through her body. Her hip brushed against his, igniting a sensation that spread to her stomach and down her thighs. The jolt was so unexpected that she faltered. His strong arm tightened around her, supporting her for a brief second.

"Has all of that anger made you dizzy?" he teased.

"No," she said, wanting to move away from him but unable to break the bond between their bodies.

"Shall I carry you down the stairs like an unwilling bride?"

"I believe the bride gets carried *up* the stairs, to the bedroom," she said dryly.

"One day—" he turned her quickly to face him, his breath touching her face "—you're going to find yourself in a position without a quick retort."

Whatever words might have assisted her fled. She was captured by his eyes, by the strength of his hands at her back. Her heart beat with rising passion, and she felt his heart thudding against her palms, which she held pressed to his chest. She saw the generous contours of his mouth, and wanted to taste his lips. He tightened his grip slightly, pulling her closer until her body was pressed comfortably against him.

"What, no sharp reply?" he asked gently.

"No," she whispered, unable to manage more than one word.

He knew she would pull free at any moment, yet the feel of her body was too delicious to resist. He bent his head and let his lips gently sweep across hers. He felt her softness accept his caress with restrained passion. Gently, he withdrew.

"There's more to you than the search for a story," he said. Her heartbeat was her only reply.

"The coffee is getting cold." Stella's voice drifted up to them on the landing. Ronnie stepped back, leaving her hands on his chest for balance. Her eyes clung to his, tak ing a final look into a depth that pulled her under in a whirlwind of dizziness.

"I think I need that coffee," she said.

"And you shall have it," Jeff answered, "and anything else you desire at Magnolia Point."

He guided her to the stairs, his hand a constant support. They returned to the living room, where Stella had prepared coffee and an assortment of sweets. Ronnie's hand shook visibly as she took a cup and lifted the steaming liquid to lips that still tingled from his kiss. She kept her eyes lowered, waiting for her passion to recede. Whether she stayed in Biloxi or not, she had to get a grip on her emotions.

"When we finish the coffee, I'd like to show you the grounds," Jeff said casually. His large frame was sprawled on the sofa, a cup of coffee held easily in one hand. "After all, a walk around the property couldn't hurt, since you've come all this way."

"Driving in, I couldn't believe the beauty," she replied. "I didn't realize how much I've missed the South."

"You've lost some of your drawl," he teased her. "Where were you working before coming here?"

"Chicago, Louisville, different places. When you work for a newspaper, you travel a good bit. I guess you've always lived here?" She wanted to talk, to know more about him.

"Except when I was away at school, or traveling," he said. "But no matter where I was, Magnolia Point has always been my home."

"More coffee?" Stella entered quietly, a silver coffeepot in her hand.

Jeff nodded, affectionately squeezing her arm as she passed. "Stella is responsible for me, so if you have any complaints, you should take them up with her."

"Ah, that is not so, Mr. Jeff," she said, beaming. "I try very hard to make you a good boy, but always you elude my efforts. You have a mind of your own. Be careful, Miss Veronica," she warned, turning the warmth of her smile on Ronnie.

"Yes," Ronnie said, "I'm learning very quickly how careful I have to be around the Senator."

Jeff laughed and picked up a dainty cookie. He put it to his mouth and bit down gently. The message he sent was completely clear. Ronnie dropped her eyes again, trying to subdue the tide of emotion that magically answered to his command. For the first time in her life, she had come up against a force stronger than her own will. Tiny chills of excitement and trepidation danced over her body.

"Mr. Jeff can be a devil," Stella said, watching the exchange of tensions between the two. "If he misbehaves, you must tell me, Miss Ronnie. I will try my best to make him be good."

"I'll keep that in mind," Ronnie said with more calm than she felt. Who was going to keep her in line? she wondered.

"Drink up," Jeff said quickly. "The afternoon is getting away from us. You know twilight strikes early during the winter months."

She savored the whiskey-laced warmth of the coffee. "It's a shame that the fall of night doesn't necessarily mean a time to rest," she said, thinking of the long nights of work the session would bring.

"The nights in Mississippi are made for much more than resting," Jeff agreed delightedly. "In my mother's time, no young lady would ever have admitted it so openly, though."

"Mr. Jeff!" Stella said. "Behave yourself. You have made your guest uncomfortable." There was a note of warning in her voice. "There is no wonder she is afraid t stay in your home. You act like some cat, strutting the fences in the moonlight."

"See," Jeff said, laughing, "you're perfectly safe here with Stella to watch over you. She is a paragon of virtue, and she has already taken you under her wing."

"Thank goodness for Stella," Ronnie said softly, giving the older woman a smile.

Jeff jumped to his feet and grabbed Ronnie's hand. "Enough polite bantering. Grab a coat and let's walk. I've had enough sitting around for the rest of the day. Stella's going to make us a great dinner, then I'm taking you down the strip for a night of Biloxi dancing."

Before she could protest, Ronnie was pulled to her feet and hustled toward the door. Jeff handed her a down coat from the closet and helped her into it. With his own coat in his hand, he hurried her out the door and onto the porch.

The afternoon had sped by, and the sun was taking on the golden tones of the dying day. Jeff's arm slipped around her as he helped her down the steps. A brick path led around the house, and they walked toward the setting sun.

"Stella's husband, Earl, maintains the grounds," Jeff said, looking over the immaculate yard. "He has a talent with plants. Everything he touches seems to flourish."

"I don't think I've ever seen a lovelier place, even in the dead of winter," Ronnie said truthfully. The plantings were thick, full of delightful nooks and hiding places that would be perfect for children. "I'll bet you loved growing up here."

"When I was younger, I used to hide here," he said, his hand sweeping across the dense azaleas. "Stella would come out looking for me, and I would do my best to avoid being caught. She has a great radar, you know, and I could never evade her for long." He chuckled at the memory, turning toward her and pushing a wind-tossed strand of hair from her face. "Are you cold?"

The brush of his fingers sent a rush of heat through her. "Not a bit," she answered, walking on. "I like winter, the way the trees look without leaves." She looked around her. "There's every type of plant here, except magnolias."

"Oh, they're here," Jeff assured her. "In fact, that's where we're going."

The land began to rise slowly. He reached out and captured her hand, gently bringing her back to his side. "Now you have to close your eyes." When she hesitated, he touched her hair, smoothing the dark tresses. "No tricks, I promise."

"You've already tricked me more than once," she reminded him.

"That was for your own good. I knew you wouldn't come unless I did, and I wanted you to be here with me."

The huskiness in his voice ignited her blood. She closed her eyes. "Lead on," she said, forcing her voice to remain steady.

His grip tightened, and she felt herself being drawn up the small incline. The bricks gave way to a carpet of level grass, but he steadied her carefully. With her eyes closed, she could smell the spice in his after-shave mixed with the faintest scent of a salt breeze. The wind cooled the heat on her cheeks.

"Okay, now open your eyes," he directed.

A magnificent winter sunset branded the sky red, orange and a vivid pink. The vibrant colors deepened to shades of purple and mauve. In the foreground an enormous stand of shadow-blackened trees provided a perfect contrast.

His arm tightened around her, pulling her close as he gave her time to take in the dramatic view. From the top of the noll she could see the Mississippi Sound reflecting the colors of the radiant sky.

"The magnolias are much friendlier in the full light of ay," Jeff said, "particularly in late May when the white lossoms fill the yard with sweetness." Her full lips were lightly parted, an invitation that he could no longer resist.

he swung her body against his, he brought his mouth ver hers. She yielded to his superior strength, and his hands oved under the coat to feel the fragile structure of her back nd ribs. With face turned up, she received his kiss, and noved to further encourage him. He felt her trembling, a ightly wound spool of passion so carefully restrained. lowly he pulled back, lingering a moment to brush his lips own the side of her face and to whisper against the soft kin of her throat.

A thousand reasons for running away flew through her mind, yet she did not move. One part of her mind accepted ne possibility that he might be a dangerous man, but that art was inactive, and only her heart ruled. Her body leaned to him of its own accord, and her arms circled his neck. he calm, dangerous waters of the Gulf swirled in his eyes, nd she knew the current was too strong. Yet she was help-ss against her body's needs. She lifted her chin, wanting nother kiss.

Jeff felt his restraint snap, and he captured her mouth, his ongue probing deeply into the secret recesses. At first she mply accepted, yielding slowly to his passion. Then he felt er first, tentative response, the blossoming of her own, ghtly checked passion. He softened the kiss, giving her me to seek his advances. She moved against him, stretch-g her slender frame along his rock-hard body. He gradu-ly increased the pressure of his hands, letting his fingers plore her back with tender power. When he heard a soft gh escape her, he pulled her tightly to him and held her in

a grip of iron. She inflamed his blood, sending it boilin
through him until he wanted nothing but her taste, her ski
under his mouth. He left her parted lips, and moved dow
to her fragile ear. Gently he nuzzled, eliciting anothe
deeper sigh.

Ronnie was powerless to stop. Pressed to his hard length
she accepted the intensity of her need for him. Her lip
turned up to seek his kisses, and her body sought the feel c
him, the totally masculine strength that magnetically fuse
them together. When his lips moved to her ear, she wa
rocking on a storm-tossed sea, clinging to the only thing tha
could save her. Jeff. His name slipped from her, softer tha
a sigh, but he heard. Slowly she felt him draw back, felt hi
scalding eyes gauging the meaning of her whisper.

She opened her eyes, finding that darkness was fallin
around them as they stood on the knoll, locked in each oth
er's arms. In the gray light, she caught the wild desire tha
burned in his eyes. She was transfixed by the images h
conjured with only a look. She saw him, bare-chested
holding out his shirt to her. Beneath her fingers, she coul
feel the ridges of hard muscle. Her fingers pressed into h
chest, kneading and rubbing as her eyes expressed her su
render. With a soft moan, he crushed her to him. When h
lips descended on hers, she asked for no quarter, and he gav
none.

At last he released her, and she straightened slowly, fine
ing her own balance. The passion had been so intense th
it was difficult to think, to try to act normally. His han
still supported her, and she slowly stepped back. What ha
she been thinking of? With one kiss, she'd been more in
mate with Jeff Stuart than anyone else in her life. He gav
and took, such passion.

"Jeff, I, uh . . ." She paused. "This shouldn't have ha
pened. We both know that," she managed to say. There wa

ust enough light to make out his features. Her heart was
eating fast, too fast, and she knew she was scared. Afraid
f what he made her feel.

"One part of me knows that's true," Jeff said softly, let-
ing his fingers pull through her silky hair, "but another part
ells me that it could be the rightest thing I've done in a long
ime."

"Let's go back to the house," she said. Another mo-
ient, another declaration like that, and she'd be back in his
rms.

She walked fast, a little ahead of Jeff, letting the house
ghts lead her. About ten yards from the side door, Jeff
topped her. "Wait here a moment," he said. "I'll be right
ack."

She moved against the house, leaning into it as a block
gainst the chill wind that blew from the sound. She hadn't
oticed the cold with Jeff, but now it was knife sharp, bit-
:r. She huddled against the wall for a full minute, clench-
ig her jaw to keep her teeth from chattering. Where had
eff gone?

Footsteps crunched softly on the shell driveway, and she
oked up expectantly. The rhythm of the steps was strange,
rratic. Listening intently, she smiled to herself. She was
rowing accustomed to his tricks by now, and a game of
ide-and-go-seek wouldn't be out of character. A large
zalea was only two feet away, and she slipped behind it. If
:ff was trying to scare her, he'd have hell to pay, she
romised herself as she ducked into the leaves.

The man emerged from the darkness, hugging the trees
ong the drive. He was only a shadow among the flicker-
g fingers of light that extended from where Ronnie hid. He
as big and extremely agile. Her heartbeat rose in her
roat, a painful thud that seemed louder than the crunch
' the man's feet on the gravel. As he slid into the light, she

saw it for the second time, the gleam of light reflected. H
was bald! She pressed farther back against the wall and hel
her breath. The man in the garden at the party had bee
bald! That was what had originally caught her eye, that gli
of light on skin. And now he was here, at Magnolia Poin

Chapter Seven

Fear pushed Ronnie deeper into the shrubs, and though she felt paralyzed, her mind was spinning wildly. What was the bald man doing at Jeff's home? Had he followed her? Or Jeff? To finish the job he'd started in Jackson? Her thoughts jumped madly. Was Jeff the victim or a collaborator?

Peering through the leaves, she could barely locate the man as he moved around the fringes of the lighted yard. She shifted, trying to get a clear look at his face, but the lighting was too poor. She had a strong desire to try to follow him, to turn the tables, but the memory of Sally's frightened face came back to her. For reasons she didn't really understand, someone could be trying to hurt her. Was it because she was with Jeff? Was he in danger, or was he behind the danger? Was it all just a ploy to gain sympathy, as Neil had suggested? Was Jeff using her because he knew she was a reporter? Craig Bellafonte had found her talents as a reporter very useful. That thought brought a surge of anger, and she clenched her jaw. Carefully she parted some branches, but the bald man had slipped among the shadows. Though she strained to find him, she saw nothing. And where was Jeff? He'd disappeared without a word, leaving her to wait alone in the cold night. She eased up, her back

against the wall. There was no sign of anyone in the yard.
Fumbling a little in the cold, her fingers found the doorknob and she twisted and pushed. In a few seconds she was
inside the house in the most amazing room she'd ever seen.
One entire wall was glass, giving a view of the yard sloping
down toward the sound, and the roof was glass, too, covered with the elegant branches of the oak trees that surrounded the house. She tucked herself into a small sofa,
watching. Her heart was still erratic, but she felt her calm
returning. Was the bald man a friend or foe of Jeff's? That
was the question she had to answer. And soon, before her
heart led her farther down the road to another heartbreak.

CLUTCHING AN ORCHID with gentleness, Jeff left the green-
house, his thoughts on Ronnie and her effect on him. She
was a source of trouble, yet he was attracted to her. There
was no sign of her near the house, and he looked around
several moments before his alarm began to build. She'd been
standing right there. He suddenly visualized a terrible scene.
Ronnie struggling as two men dragged her away. Deluch
wouldn't be above such a tactic to ensure the death of the
horse racing bill. He rushed forward, dropping the flower
onto the shell driveway as he began to call her name.

He burst in the front door, slamming it hard behind him.
"Ronnie!" he called. "Ronnie!"

Jeff's voice was frantic, and for a moment, she didn't
know whether to answer him or not. Fear tingled down her
spine, and she hesitated. It had to be a coincidence that the
bald man was at Jeff's home. It had to be.

"Veronica!" Jeff called.

He was closer, just outside the door. She could tell by the
sound of his voice that he was angry!

A door slammed and she saw his figure flash by the win-
dowed wall that faced the waters of the sound. He stopped

cupped his hands and yelled her name again. Standing with legs apart, he looked directly into the wind.

"Veronica!" Her name drifted indistinctly to her through the glass. "Veronica!"

She burrowed deeper into the sofa and admitted that she was afraid. Her legs were numb with fear, and she wondered if she'd ever walk again, if she'd live through the night to walk a city street, or through a sunlit park.

Jeff hurried down the path to the magnolia grove, and she breathed a sigh of relief. She'd been warned once that the shots were intended for her. She hadn't believed it at the time. But now...it was not implausible. If Jeff knew the big man, was it he who had called the restaurant and tried to warn her? Or was he the bait that had lured her down to Biloxi for the final strike? He'd tricked her into coming to his home. She couldn't deny that. Whatever reasons he had, he'd been slightly dishonest.

Her heart raced again, and she felt the weakness of extreme fear touch her bones. She had to get out of that house. There'd be time to answer the questions later. Right now, she had to get off the estate and get someplace where she felt safe and could think.

She forced her body up, feeling anesthetized, unable to move one foot in front of the other. Each little motion required such concentration, and she knew the depth of her fear. Her car keys were upstairs in her purse. The idea of abandoning the car and walking out to the highway, of facing what could be hiding in the long, winding driveway, was too frightening. She had to get her keys and pray the car would give her some measure of safety.

Jeff was down the path near the water. She was alone in the house, or should be. Stella had gone to her small cottage where she lived with her husband, Earl. No one else was supposed to be in the house. Unless... She pushed her thoughts away from everything except the need to get up the stairs and to her keys. The house was so big, three stories with dozens of rooms, hundreds of hiding places. In the daylight, she'd thought it was such a lovely place.

She slipped across the living room, moving from one piece of furniture to the next, like a burglar she thought. The foyer was clear, and the stairs curved gracefully to the second floor. On those stairs, Jeff had kissed her for the very first time. And if she didn't get out, his lips might be the last she ever kissed. That thought jolted through her and impelled her forward. At the stairs, she ran as fast as she could to the top and skidded into her bedroom. She had only a few items, and she wanted to leave no evidence that she'd ever set foot in Magnolia Point. She threw her clothes and cosmetics into her bag, grabbed her purse and tiptoed to the bedroom door. The upstairs hall was quiet. Too quiet. She took a deep breath and charged down the stairs to the front door and out into the night. She didn't bother to shut the door. She didn't bother with anything except making her feet fly as fast as they could.

The garage was on the east side of the house, and she drove her legs in that direction. There was the sound of crunching gravel behind her and she wanted to scream with fear, but she forced her legs to move even faster, until she gained the garage.

The car door was unlocked and she threw in her bag and flung herself behind the wheel. She put the key in the ignition and hit the accelerator as she turned on the motor. The engine roared into life, then sputtered out. She tried again, her heartbeat sounding like a hard-rock drummer in the night. The car responded, but weaker. There was no real spark of life.

She'd heard footsteps behind her. Her time had run out. She was trapped in the car, and it wouldn't crank. She fe someone watching her, and her hand fell to the automatic lock system. Her fingers quickly pushed the button, and the locks snapped. She forced herself to look up, to face the heavy, dark-clad bald man who pursued and watched her, possibly wanted to kill her. He was in the garage. She felt him looking through the window, waiting for her to look up and see him. This was it. This was the final moment, when she'd see the gun at point-blank range.

She lifted her eyes to the passenger window. Jeff Stuart's angry face was perfectly framed in the glass.

"Going somewhere?" he asked.

The very fact that she was unhurt only fueled his temper. She'd scared him half out of his wits, and now she was playing childish games of hide-and-go-seek around the yard. Surely she'd heard him call, he'd been all over the estate.

Ronnie froze with her hands on the wheel while Jeff stood over the car door, obviously waiting for her to get out. Her mind spun with a thousand fears. The tightness of his jaw and the flames of anger in his eyes were frightening. She tried to look away from him, but couldn't. Did he know the big man? She tried to read the answer in his face, to see her fate, but Jeff was inscrutable.

"Get out of the car," he ordered.

With one last desperate effort, Ronnie reached down and twisted the key. The motor turned over, but nothing happened.

Furious, Jeff reached for the door and jerked at the handle. The locks held, but the car rocked slightly with the force of his anger.

"I don't know what kind of game you're playing, but it isn't very funny," Jeff said through clenched teeth. "Get out or I'll get you out."

There was no alternative. Slowly, Ronnie reached out and unlocked the door. Jeff pulled it open and roughly grabbed her arm.

"What are you doing?" he asked. Seeing her eyes, wide with fear, it suddenly dawned on him that she couldn't understand his own fear, or his behavior.

"What are you doing out here?" he asked again, his voice softer. "Didn't you hear me calling?"

With the slackening of his anger, Ronnie finally felt herself grow calm. "I was trying to start my car and leave," she said with as much composure as she could muster. She'd made a decision, she'd never tell him about the man. If he was an acquaintance of Jeff's, then he already knew. And if he wasn't... It was too complicated to think about. All she had to do was keep calm, survive.

"Trying to leave?" Jeff asked. "You picked rather a strange way to make a departure," he added dryly.

"While I was waiting for you, I remembered I had a story to file. I got my things and decided to go back to Jackson. I thought I'd call later, from a phone along the way. I didn't know where you'd gone. I . . ."

"I think I frightened you," he said, smiling easily. "I'm sorry, but when I couldn't find you, I got worried."

"Worried? About what?" Her heartbeat increased again, and she had the funny sensation that her body would break in half.

"I don't know," he said, smiling at his own foolishness. "You were gone, and I knew I didn't want anything to happen to you."

"What could possibly happen to me at Magnolia Point?" Ronnie pressed.

"Some other Biloxi man could have seen you and decided he wanted you for his very own," Jeff said, teasing her. "It's happened before, in the past. What's wrong with your car?" he went on, deftly turning the conversation.

"It wouldn't start," she said, settling back in the seat. Her hands were shaking as she reached for the key, but her foot went instinctively to the gas pedal. There was no reaction from the car. She tried again, feeling Jeff's eyes on her. The motor didn't respond at all.

"There's something wrong," she said weakly.

"Release the hood."

She obeyed, and Jeff walked around and lifted it. He went over to a worktable and found a flashlight. When he returned, he examined the motor for several minutes.

"I know something about cars," he said, "and I don't see anything wrong right on the surface."

Ronnie slipped out and took a look. In the glare of the light, the motor looked clean and perfect, as far as she could tell. His nearness made her want to touch him, but her doubts held her back. Now she wasn't certain of anything.

"Try it again," Jeff said.

Though they tried several times, the sports car refused to give any sign of life. Ronnie wearily rubbed her fist across her forehead. "Cars don't just die. It worked perfectly when I arrived."

"It could be something as simple as a dead battery," Jeff said. "Sometimes the cold knocks them out."

"Yeah, well that leaves me without a car."

"Let's go back inside. You look really exhausted. Although it will have to wait until tomorrow, Earl can take a look at it, and the possibilities are good he'll be able to put her back in tip-top shape."

He took her arm and directed her back toward the house, keeping the flashlight trained on the ground to guide their steps.

"Here we are," Jeff said at the front door. "You can use the phone to call your boss," he suggested. "It's odd that you were going to leave without even talking with Ann."

His eyes were alert and watching, and Ronnie glanced away because she knew she could never lie to his face. "I was going to drive home, file the story and come back in the morning."

He stopped, looking down at her. Her features were veiled by darkness, but he knew the contours of her face. "I see," was all he said as he helped her up the steps. She was shaky on her feet, from a mixture of exhaustion and slowly subsiding fear. She was in no condition to be driving down dark interstate roads where there were miles and miles of empty woodlands.

At the stairs, he gently led her up to the bedroom she'd been assigned and turned her to look at him. His gaze was clear and concerned. "Why don't you lie down a moment and rest? I'm going to call Stella over to make you something hot to drink."

The sheets were already turned back, and Ronnie sat on the edge of the bed.

"I'm really fine," Ronnie insisted. She straightened her shoulders slightly and lifted her chin. "The car aggravated me. I'm feeling better now." The fear was receding. Looking around the room now, she noted the antique furniture, the beautiful crystal lamps on either side of the bed. Jeff stood only four feet away, strong and concerned.

She stood up. "I'm sorry," she said, feeling her energy begin to return. "I've acted like a baby, I'm afraid. I don't know what got into me."

"I think Stella should take a look at you," Jeff insisted. With her chin up and the fight back in her eyes, she was beginning to look better, but she was still too pale, too drawn

"I wouldn't think of letting you disturb her. I'm sure she has better things to do than take care of someone who runs around at night getting upset." She forced a smile. "See, I'm fine."

"Stella or the doctor," Jeff said without a hint of humor. "Take your pick."

"I don't need medical attention."

"Good, then I'll get Stella."

He walked to the bedside phone and dialed four numbers. After a brief conversation, he looked back at her. "She'll be here in five minutes."

"Jeff, this is really unnecessary," she protested.

"It's too late for complaints," Jeff said. "Now, you rest. There's something I need to check out." He left the bedroom, and Ronnie slipped off her shoes and climbed beneath the covers. She was terribly chilled.

Stella's tread on the stairs was light and graceful. She rapped softly on the door and came into the room.

"You look pale as a ghost," she said, shaking her head. "What were you doing running through the dark like some half-wild creature?"

"I was..." Ronnie swallowed. She wanted to talk to Stella, to tell her about the strange man, but she couldn't. Stella was Jeff's loyal employee, who was more family than hired help. Scaring her wouldn't solve the problem.

"You were what?" Stella prompted. She rested her hand on Ronnie's forehead. "You're too hot."

"I just got overexcited," Ronnie said, drawing her elbows under her and partially sitting up.

Stella pierced her with a look. "Too many strange things happen here lately, too many," she said. Her green gaze was level, unflinching. "People prowling, footprints in the flower beds. You know something about this?"

"Some of it," Ronnie said, her voice a thin whisper.

"Folks taking shots at Mr. Jeff at parties, phone calls late at night with mean voices. Is this something you know about?"

"There was a man outside," Ronnie said, holding the look the other woman gave her. "I think it was the man saw hiding in the garden at the Dennison house the night the shots were fired."

Stella didn't react at all. She held herself rigid. Then large tear rolled out of the corner of one eye and down her cheek. "Mr. Jeff is in some kind of trouble. I can tell it You're a reporter, Miss Sheffield, you can help him. You've got to help him."

Sitting up completely, Ronnie grasped Stella's shoulder with one hand. "Hush now, Stella," she said softly. "Mr Jeff wouldn't want you to cry."

"Mean men call here, rough and ugly. I don't know what's happening. When you came today, I thought the house would be happy again, good company with laughter and dinners." She brushed her face with the back of her hand. "The badness is still here. If I try to talk with Mr Jeff, he tells me not to worry. But I can't help it. There's something wrong in this house, and I'm afraid for Mr Jeff."

The words were like little daggers of fright. "Is someone really trying to hurt Jeff?" she asked.

"He says no, but he acts different," the other woman answered. "Can you help him? If you could find the truth about the money, then the bad men would go away and leave us alone."

"The money?" Ronnie asked.

"That has to be the trouble," Stella said. "Money is always the source of the trouble. Always."

Ronnie drew a deep breath and asked the question she dreaded. "Stella, have you seen Mr. Jeff with a big, bald man?"

Stella's eyes widened like green mirrors, but she said nothing.

"Have you...?" Ronnie stopped speaking as Jeff entered the room.

"How is she, Stella?" he asked. The lines around his eyes were deeper and the sensuous fullness of his lips was narrowed to a thin line.

"She's not hurt, Mr. Jeff," Stella said calmly, as if she'd never had a moment of turbulence. "A good night's rest and she'll be fit as a fiddle. I was just going to the kitchen to make some tea for both of you." She stood and walked to him, placing the flat of her hand on his cheek. "You, too, are flushed. Even as a child you always wanted to rush into the night and play. I told you then, and I'm telling you now, the night air brings sickness."

"But I have you to make me well," Jeff said, forcing a light note into his voice. "A good cup of tea does sound wonderful, though. How about it, Ronnie?"

"Perfect," she said. Wild horses couldn't drag her out of the house until she had another opportunity to talk with Stella. The woman knew more than she was saying. "I'll even help with the tea." Before Jeff or Stella could protest, she swung her legs down and got up from the bed. "See, I'm perfectly fine."

"It's a miracle," Jeff said, and there was genuine relief in his voice. "You really did have me worried."

"A cup of tea, and I'll be ready for anything," Ronnie vowed.

"I'll join you in a moment," Jeff said as he walked with them down the stairs. He turned left into a doorway that revealed a library. "I have a few calls to return."

"Okay," Ronnie said. She would have an opportunity t talk with Stella alone.

While Stella put the kettle of water on, Ronnie prepare the cups and tea. Stella chatted about the kitchen, an Ronnie waited for an opportunity to turn the conversatio back to Jeff.

"Have you ever been to a horse race?" Ronnie suddenl asked. Time was running out and she had to have some an swers.

"Me?" Stella asked, surprised. "Never. A waste c money."

"A few moments ago you said something about mone and Jeff. About the bad men?" Ronnie opened the pack of tea bags and held her breath.

"Mr. Jeff has much business," Stella said slowly. ' spoke out of turn when I mentioned his business. This hous is expensive to run, and Mr. Jeff bought much new furn ture. I'm afraid I am old and too fearful. That is none of m concern, and I know really nothing about it." There was degree of formality in her voice that let Ronnie know th subject was closed.

"I'm sure you didn't mean to interfere in Jeff's bus ness," Ronnie said.

"As I said, I spoke without thought. Forget what I said."

Ronnie almost cursed aloud. She was closer than she' ever been to something that had to be important. She kne it. And now Stella had become cautious.

"Please go and tell Mr. Jeff the tea is ready," Stella sai "I'll serve it in the den."

"Sure," Ronnie said. She backed away slowly, hopin that some other opportunity for questions would aris Stella carefully kept her face turned away as she worked ove the tea and some small cakes.

Ronnie left the kitchen, turning back to the library.

"You're insane! If your carelessness doesn't stop, I'm going to pull out!" Jeff's voice carried easily into the hall where she stood. "I mean it, Carlisle. One more mistake and you can find someone else to be your tethered goat. She knows too much already. It's only a question of time before she finds out the whole thing, and then we'll be forced to act." He slammed down the phone and burst through the door, knocking solidly into Ronnie before she could make another move.

Chapter Eight

"Stella made the preserves herself," Jeff said, handing the small jar to Ronnie. Her hand shook so that the spoon rattled against the glass as she accepted it.

"Stella runs this house like an old-fashioned estate, and Earl takes care of the grounds, even the birds," Jeff said.

"Birds?" Ronnie asked feebly, trying to force her voice around the fear she felt in her throat. Once again, the night had turned upside down.

"My mother had a fascination with feathered creatures," Jeff said. "At one time, we had all sorts of birds, big and little." He chuckled. "It was something, wasn't it Stella?"

"Those were good days," Stella said flatly. She didn't have to add that they were long gone; her tone of voice said it.

Ronnie and Jeff sat at a small table in the black and white tile kitchen, while Stella busied herself putting hot tea and buttered cakes before them. The older woman avoided Ronnie's eyes. Her face was a mask as she poured the tea.

"Eat something, Ronnie," Jeff insisted. "We could go down the coast for dinner."

"No thank you," she said, too quickly. "I really want to slip into bed and sleep. I feel like I've been up for days."

That wasn't exactly an exaggeration. Her body ached with fatigue, but more than anything else she needed time to think. She nibbled at the cake and gratefully drank the hot, soothing tea. She couldn't bring herself to look at Jeff, even when she felt him watching her.

"If you don't need anything else, I think I'll go to bed also," Stella said softly. Her eyes were directed at the floor.

"Certainly," Jeff said, putting his arm around her for a hug. "Thanks for taking care of this. Tomorrow Ronnie has an appointment out at Ann Tate's so you don't worry about cooking breakfast. Get a good night's sleep."

Ronnie's first thought was to ask the other woman to stay. The idea of being alone in the house with Jeff made her want to run as fast as she could in any direction. Damn her car. Mechanical things were always giving out when they were most needed.

"Stella," Ronnie began, then paused. She wasn't certain, but she thought she detected more tears in Stella's eyes as she turned away. She felt a pang of sympathy. Stella felt disloyal, she'd confided her fears to a stranger, and those fears certainly put Jeff Stuart in a bad light. "Have a good rest," she finished, pushing the telephone conversation she'd overheard out of her mind. When he'd come out of the library suddenly, and then gotten all concerned that he'd accidentally knocked into her, there had been no sign of the anger she'd heard in his voice, no indication he had anything to hide. He'd been considerate, caring and charming. She watched him carefully as he locked the back door after Stella.

"I think I'll get some sleep, too," she said, muffling a yawn.

The look Jeff gave her was questioning. Before he could say anything, she was moving away.

"It's really been too exhausting." She spoke as she walked, a sideways movement that readily betrayed her nervousness.

Watching her carefully, he couldn't help but think that it was too bad she was so damned attractive, even when her fear was transparent. He started to reach out to her, but his motion made her start. Calling good-night over her shoulder, she turned and ran up the stairs. He didn't have to listen to know she shut the door firmly behind her.

THE HOUSE WAS CLOAKED in midnight silence when he went to her bedroom door. Putting his hand roughly on the knob, he turned it quickly. It rotated in his hand, but the door failed to open. She'd locked it from the inside. He wanted to talk to her, wanted to feel her melt against him once more. Her look when he came out of the library had been one of a trapped animal. It was madness, but he couldn't escape the memory of her lips, her body against his in the magnolia grove. Turning on his heel he walked down the hall to his own room.

Flinging off his clothes, he walked to the window and threw it open wide to let the cold winter air flow about his body. The lawn was bathed in brilliant moonlight. In the distance, the howl of a dog drifted on the wind. Jeff smiled grimly. "I know, fella," he said softly. "I know."

He strained his eyes in the darkness, examining the grounds. After talking to Carlisle on the phone, he was still angry, but not as nervous. At last he saw the man hidden carefully in the dogwood trees and azaleas, about twenty yards from the house. Jeff waved and after a moment, the man signaled back.

THE FIRST SCREAM was like a distant siren, long and wailing, breaking through the deep sleep that had fallen over

Ronnie as soon as her head touched the pillow. She woke slowly, the scream pulling at her. When at last her eyes were open, there was nothing, just the empty silence of the night.

Tossing her silky hair to one side, she dived back into the pillows and snuggled deeper beneath the blanket. She was just drifting off when the anguished scream echoed again. Wide-awake, she sat in the bed, hugging the covers to her chest. The sound was one of undisguised pain, mingled with madness. Her heart thudded loudly against her ribs. Where had it come from? The question raced through her mind, bouncing and echoing like the scream. Had it been the last remnants of a nightmare?

She forced herself to take several deep breaths. The serene and comfortable bedroom was suddenly strange, unfamiliar. Slipping out of bed she found the long, silky nightgown she'd left over the arm of a chair. The satiny material slithered down her body, hugging every curve. Though it was sheer, the gown somehow made her feel safer, less exposed. She tucked herself back beneath the covers and forced herself to lie down.

"I have an overactive imagination," she said, relieved to hear her own voice in the blackness. She wanted to snap on the bedside light, but something held her back. Instead, she waited. Just when she was about to chalk up the strange noise to a case of silly jitters, a scream cut through the night once again. Long, low and intensely mad, it invaded her room, making the skin down her back prickle with fright.

"My God!" she whispered. Very slowly she got out of bed. Whoever had made the noise was in terrible trouble. She had to find her, for there was no doubt that the screamer was a woman.

Ronnie's sense of direction was usually sharp, and she could have sworn that the scream didn't come from an upper floor. Still, Magnolia Point was an enormous old house

with three stories and an attic. Also there were other build
ings on the grounds. Could someone have strayed into one
trying to escape the bitter chill of the night? The though
made her hurry as she ran down the stairs.

Cracking the front door, she listened, ignoring the brisk
night air that swirled around her almost nude body. The
only sound was the creaking of the oak limbs whipped by
the wind. Though she was shaking with cold, she concen
trated. What if the noise had come from upstairs? she
thought with a jolt. Turning from the door she let it shut
softly. The house was in darkness, its rooms unfamiliar to
her. Her blood pounded against her temples, and she had to
fight back the panic that threatened to rise in a black tide
The scream came again and she jumped backward, striking
the door with her shoulders.

The noise definitely came from the back, outside the main
house. She tiptoed into the sunroom, hoping to catch a
glimpse through the windows of some nighttime move
ment. What about Stella and Earl? Her panic almost over
whelmed her. And the scream could be either madness or
terrible suffering. She pressed against the window, trying to
find a distant light or some other sign of life.

In the bright glow of the moon, the yard looked peaceful
and quiet. The wind moved among the trees, creating sin
ister shadows. Ronnie held her breath, hoping that the
scream would not come again. Maybe it was all a night
mare. Maybe she was asleep in her bed, struggling against
the weight of the covers. She tried desperately to calm her
self. If she heard it one more time, she'd have to call the
police. If Stella and Earl were in danger, then she had to act
fast.

Standing at the window, hugging her elbows tightly
against her side to ward off panic and cold, she was unpre
pared for the next scream. It seemed to come from above her

now, somewhere in the oak trees. She swallowed her own cry and forced herself to look into the night.

"Ronnie, what are you doing?"

Jeff's voice was too much of a shock. She turned slowly, as if she were falling, and a muffled scream slipped from between her tight lips. Before she could completely lose her balance, he was at her side, pulling her against the warmth and strength of his chest.

"You're half frozen," he said, sweeping her into his arms. He wore only a pair of soft, faded jeans.

"Put me down," she said, trying to free herself. "We have to see about Stella and Earl."

"Stella and Earl? What are you talking about?" He held her tightly, refusing to yield to her struggles. "You must be out of your mind with cold."

"There's someone out there, Jeff," she said, fighting back her fright. She had never felt so alone in her life, or so vulnerable. "There was this terrible scream. It woke me, and I came down to see what it was. There's a madwoman out here."

Jeff's grip suddenly lightened, and he swung her into his arms more firmly before he sat down on the sofa with her. "Oh, Ronnie," he said softly, "I should have told you sooner."

"Told me what?" she asked, hardly daring to breathe.

He looked out the window, as if thinking through what he wanted to say. "About Katie."

His words were chilling. Ronnie's head involuntarily turned toward the staircase, and her mind mentally tracked to the third floor.

"What about Katie?"

"It's such a sad story," Jeff said. His face was close to hers, and she couldn't see a single feature. But her body was

becoming more and more aware of his warmth, the rough
texture of his hands on her cold skin.

"I think you'd better tell me about this, Jeff," she said
quickly. She fought to retain control of her logic. The fear,
the security of his arms around her, all worked to create
confusion. She had to listen carefully, to understand.

"Well, she's my only cousin. A beautiful girl, with long
blond curls and the biggest blue eyes you've ever seen. A
perfect picture, but that was all a long time ago. Before..." He broke off.

"She's here, in this house?" Ronnie couldn't help the
shudder that trembled down her back.

"She has her own room, and we take the best possible
care of her. But after the accident, when her boyfriend, well
she's just never been right."

"Oh, Jeff," Ronnie said on a sudden intake of air. "Why
in the world didn't you tell me? I was frightened nearly out
of my mind."

"To be honest, Ronnie, I try to forget about it. I've done
everything there is to be done. It's hard to keep someone you
love a virtual prisoner. But there's no telling what she would
do if she got loose."

"What about doctors? There's all types of new medica-
tions." Ronnie's mind whirled with possibilities. Her fear
was disappearing, lulled by Jeff's gentle voice, his obvious
pain and the feel of his powerful arms holding her securely.

"We've tried everything," he whispered.

"I'm sorry, Jeff," she said. "I only wish you'd told me
before tonight. I would have understood."

"It's just so much like something you'd read about in a
horror novel about an old Southern family. You know, Aunt
Betty or Cousin Sue, locked away in the attic."

For the first time, there was something other than sadness in Jeff's voice. She couldn't put her finger on it ex-

actly, but she turned to face him, her eyes searching in the darkness for some hint. With his head bent over hers, she couldn't see him clearly. The moonlight touched his hair with a halo of highlights.

As he told her about Katie, Jeff deliberately kept his face hidden. As soon as Ronnie discovered the truth, he'd have the devil to pay, he knew.

When she turned her compassionate eyes up to him, he forgot all about his mischief. Her bare arm was pressed against his chest, his hand supporting her long, slender, exposed back. When she had been standing at the full-length window, searching the night for a madwoman, he'd had a clear view of her lithe body, silhouetted in the moonlight. Fire surged through his veins at the memory of the image. His hands tightened on her back, and he felt her involuntary response. She curled slightly into his chest, the smallest movement of encouragement. Slowly he brought his lips down over hers. He had the sensation of dancing on ice, but then her soft lips parted, inviting him to explore further.

The sudden power of his kiss was overwhelming as all rational thought was turned aside. Ronnie's arms moved up his neck, clinging in the tide of desire that united them. With each sensuous probe of his tongue, he pulled her deeper and deeper into a feeling like waves swelling on a wild ocean. She pressed herself against him, then felt his hands follow the firm outline of her muscles down her back.

His touch was electric, sending high voltage shocks through her in a way she'd never experienced before. She gave herself to his kisses, knitting her fingers in his thick hair to anchor herself to him. She felt that if she let go, she'd be cast relentlessly about by the stormy desire that now ruled her body. Whatever concerns she felt, they were swept away in a moment. She wanted nothing more than to feel him against her, taking her with him on the wild journey of pleasure.

His hand moved up her ribs to cover her breast, and she arched against him. Her need for him had blocked everything else from her mind. There was no turning back.

Suddenly, the wild, maddened scream once again split the night.

Ronnie froze, her body growing instantly rigid. The sound was so unexpected, so wild and insane, that she felt paralyzed.

Jeff cursed angrily under his breath. He tightened his hold on her.

"It's Katie," she said breathlessly. "Maybe she's sick or hurt or something. We should go check on her."

Jeff turned slightly away, fingers circling her arms. "Ronnie, I have to tell you something," he said softly.

There was an edge of remorse in his voice, and she reached up a hand to brush his cheek. "It's okay, Jeff. I don't want to pry into your personal family business. Just go take a look at her, make sure she isn't hurt. I'll even wait here for you."

The depth of her compassion made him feel worse. His hands roved down her back once more, stroking gently. "There isn't a Katie," he said very low.

At first, she thought she'd misunderstood. "No Katie? Then what?"

"Ronnie, I shouldn't have started this. Oh, hell, that noise was made by one of the peacocks. I told you that Mother raised birds. Well, now there's peacocks on the property and sometimes they scream like that. I meant to tell you before, but we never had a chance to go out to look at them. Tonight I just wanted to tease you a little, but I got carried away."

It took a moment for the full impact of what he said to sink in. "You mean that awful noise is made by a bird, not a mad person in terrible anguish?" Her breathing was shallow.

"I know it was rotten of me to make up such a thing, but I just..."

"I can't believe you've done this to me!" she said. The anger whipped through her body like a burning wind. "I just can't believe it!" She struggled to sit up, but he held her tightly, letting his strong arms form an iron band. "Let me go this instant," she said, trying to wriggle free of him.

"Ronnie, just calm down a minute. I know you're mad, and you have every right to be, but give me a minute, please."

"Jeff Stuart, the only thing I'd like to give you is a black eye! I've had enough of your tricks and jokes. I was frightened half out of my mind earlier tonight, and then you had to go and pull a story on me about your mad cousin, implying all sorts of dreadful tragedies. And I believed it. I was such a sucker that I swallowed the whole thing. Let me go!"

"I'll let you go, as soon as you calm down," Jeff said, trying to contain her flailing legs. Her strength was surprising, but he easily held her back. "Ronnie, I only meant to..."

"Play another trick? Make a fool of me so that I fall into your arms again? Why should I ever believe anything you say?" Her fury was beginning to wear down, and she slowed her struggles. She was panting roughly from the exertion, and she took a deep breath. "You are a snake."

As soon as he felt her relax, Jeff loosened his grip. He cradled her against his chest, feeling her tense body as she took in deep lungfuls of air.

"If I had it to do over, I wouldn't," he said softly. "You were so frightened, I wanted to make you laugh."

"I don't want to hear it," she said coldly. "I'm calm, so let me up."

"In a minute," he insisted, "just another minute." H risked generating new anger, but he didn't want to let her go Once free of his arms, he knew she would stalk out of th room and go straight up to her bedroom.

As the anger faded, Ronnie felt a slow weariness cree over her. Her muscles relaxed, and she allowed his arms t support her weight, shifting to a slightly more comfortabl position.

His hand moved up to stroke her hair, pushing a tangle strand from her cheek. She turned a cold profile to him, ig noring the tenderness of his touch. Her attraction to hin was dulling her senses. The business with the peacocks migh be funny in the light of day, but there were many othe things that held no element of humor, only danger. And sh had to keep those in mind. She struggled into a sitting po sition.

"You're not going to forgive me?" Jeff asked. The teas ing tone in his voice was almost irresistible.

"You're forgiven," she said quickly. She wanted to avoi any situation where he might try to persuade her to forgiv him. "That was a crummy joke, but I do understand th juvenile tendencies behind it," she added, making her voic as stern as possible.

"Juvenile?" Jeff laughed. "Now I find beneath the re porter's exterior beats the heart of a schoolmarm."

"Jeff," she said with exasperation. "You allow me to ge involved in a tragic story after having been half frightene out of my mind, you tell me the whole setup is a practica joke, then I'm supposed to have a good chuckle and run of to bed!"

She got up from the sofa and walked to the window. Th moon was high in the oaks, riding the graceful branche

The view was the most magnificent she'd ever seen anywhere.

"How about a drink, Ronnie?" Jeff said. "I doubt you'll drift right back to sleep. A little bourbon might be more effective than hot tea."

He was right. After the fright she'd had, sleep wasn't going to be easy to find. A nightcap, even if it was early morning, would help her to relax.

"A very small one," she said. "I'll help you."

"No, that's fine," Jeff said. "Just wait there and I'll bring it to you. Don't move until I get back," he said as he started to leave the room. "I've seen some beautiful sights from those windows, but none to equal the one I'm seeing now."

His words brought a faint blush to her face and she didn't dare turn around. He was so damn charming! The wind pushed against the tree limbs, setting the view in motion. Shadows danced beneath the moon. Her heart halted as something appeared to shift. It was only the wind. For a moment she thought there was someone in the oaks, but it was just a paranoid hallucination. Her nerves were shot. She looked again into the darkness and saw nothing. She forced herself to turn her back on the window and face the door, waiting for Jeff. She couldn't resist the small laugh that escaped her lips. Cousin Katie, indeed. The man was a rascal. Her smile faded. She didn't want to believe that he was anything worse. Yet...

The glimmer of a small, shiny object on the floor caught her eye. It was a cuff link, a button or something like that. She could hear Jeff coming with the drinks.

"A little toddy for a cold night," Jeff said as he walked toward her carrying two glasses. The object caught the light again, and she bent to pick it up. A sharp report sounded just before the glass wall behind her shattered with an explosion. The blasted glass flew in all directions, and Ronnie tumbled to the floor. She lay motionless as shards of glass rained down on her, biting her skin in a thousand places.

Chapter Nine

Beneath the slivers of glass, Ronnie moaned. She tried to lift herself from the floor as a million ant bites of pain stung her back and arms and legs. There was a movement near her, and glass tinkled.

"Don't move," Jeff's voice ordered softly as more glass cascaded in a clinking avalanche. The room was flooded with light, and outside she heard the sound of rushing footsteps coming toward the house. Her body was convulsed with another tidal wave of fear. Then Jeff was at her side, carefully lifting her from the glass.

"Are you hit?" he asked.

"I don't think so," Ronnie managed to answer. She couldn't be certain, her mind was numb. There was no major pain, just the sensation of being immersed in ants.

"Mr. Jeff!" Stella's voice was almost strangled as she hurried up to the shattered window. "What in Heaven's name?"

"Help me, Stella. Ronnie's covered in glass."

"Someone blew out the wall," Stella said in awe as she stepped into the room, glass crackling beneath her shoes.

Jeff's strong hands held Ronnie like a doll, and he gently shook her, sending more glass to the floor. When she tried to walk, he lifted her and moved her across the room.

"You'll cut your feet to pieces," he warned her.

"I'll get some towels, some powder," Stella said, hurry ing from the room.

"I'm okay," Ronnie finally managed to say. At last sh looked up. Blood was dripping from a cut on Jeff's cheek The bright red slash dripped down his jaw and fell un heeded on his jeans. For the first time, Ronnie felt as if sh might cry. She turned away, to the nonexistent glass wal The entire window had been blasted apart.

"My God!" she whispered at the sight of the destruc tion, and the realization how close she'd been to death.

Jeff gently turned her away. "Are you hurt?" he aske again. "When I saw you lying in that glass, I thought for moment..." He didn't finish.

"I don't even know what happened. I was standing there waiting for you. I saw something on the floor, and I bent t pick it up. Then there was glass exploding everywhere." Sh felt a wave of dizziness, and Jeff's hand immediatel touched her elbow.

"Be very still," Stella directed as she arrived and too over. "First the powder—" she dusted Ronnie liberally wit talc "—and then a gentle brush." The stroke of the pea cock feather fan was like the softest whisper. "We'll loose the glass, and then remove the pieces that remain." Stell talked calmly as she worked. "Mr. Jeff, would you get m some antiseptic, tweezers, cotton and bandages?"

"Certainly," Jeff said.

"Get enough for you, too," Stella called after him Turning back to Ronnie, she touched her arm. "This isn' going to be fun," she said. Then she cast a long look at th door. "You must leave here," she whispered to Ronnie "Take Mr. Jeff and leave. It isn't safe."

"Stella, you were going to tell me about the bald man remember?"

"There is no time. It has gone beyond all of that now. You must leave, and take Mr. Jeff with you. They'll be back."

"Here's everything," Jeff said, returning.

She silently took the powder and scattered it, first over Ronnie's back, then Jeff's. "Come with me." Her touch on Ronnie's arm was kind.

She moved Ronnie to a low stool in the kitchen where the lights were brighter. With great care, Stella picked the shards of glass from her back. Ronnie bit her lower lip until she tasted blood, but she refused to signal her discomfort. She was alive. The pain was evidence of that fact. Whenever she thought of the gaping hole in the wall, she knew how easily she could have been dead. Bending over for the cuff link, or whatever it was, had saved her life. A simple movement, unexpected, spontaneous. She felt her body begin to tremble. Standing in the window, she'd been a perfect target. Jeff, too. Or had he been just out of range?

"Only a few more," Stella said patiently. "None of the cuts are bad. The glass must be removed, though. Mr. Jeff, please bring some brandy. I believe we all need a small glass."

Jeff obliged, then watched as the last sliver was removed.

"This is going to sting," Stella warned as she applied the antiseptic to Ronnie's back.

"I feel like I've stepped into a horror movie," Ronnie said dully. "In the span of less than a week, I've been shot at twice, threatened, tricked, lied to, scared out of my wits too many times to count, and now I'm a pincushion for glass." She started laughing, and suddenly found tears running down her cheeks.

"Hush," Stella said softly, pushing the glass of brandy to her lips. "Take a sip of this, very slowly, and swallow. Feel the warmth of the brandy." Her musical voice was soothing, and Ronnie felt the panic pass. "Now you must help me with Mr. Jeff," Stella said, touching her elbow to help her rise. "I am old, and your hands are steadier."

With that, she placed the tweezers in Ronnie's hand. She lifted the fan and gently brushed over Jeff's naked back, sweeping away the loosened glass. There were several pieces still embedded, not deeply, but enough for discomfort as Ronnie carefully clasped the first one with the tweezers and eased it out. A small trickle of blood flowed down the slope of his muscles. Stella dabbed at the wound with antiseptic-soaked cotton, and Jeff flinched.

"This reminds me of scraped knees and bicycle wrecks," Jeff said.

"It reminds me of attempted murder," Ronnie snapped. "As soon as we get this glass out, you should call the police."

Before Jeff could answer, the kitchen door was pushed open and Earl entered, a large spotlight in his hand. "I have searched the grounds, and whoever was here is gone," he said. "There is a place beneath the oaks with some footprints, but they are not clear. There is nothing, not even a shell. From the way the glass shattered, it was a shotgun blast."

"We'll have better luck in the daytime," Jeff said, leaning over more to give Ronnie better access to his broad shoulders.

"This is the last one," she said, easing out the bit of glass. "I'm sure the police will want to secure that area, so they can gather evidence tomorrow. What are you going to do about that wall?"

"I'll get someone to come tomorrow and start work on replacing the glass," Jeff said. "For now, we'll have to lock that room off from the rest of the house." For the first time, e sounded exhausted. Ronnie darted a glance at him, seeing he furrows in his forehead and the grim set of his mouth.

"How fast can the police get here?" Ronnie asked.

"Stella, Earl, thank you," Jeff said. "Ronnie and I are both fine, and I want you to go back to your house. Tomorrow there'll be plenty of time to worry about the hows and whys."

"I'll stay and make coffee. The officers will want something to eat," Stella said, starting toward the stove.

"Stella," Jeff said softly. "No cooking, no coffee. You look worn out, and so does Earl. Now go and get what little sleep you can. And Earl, take the shotgun out of the library," Jeff said softly.

"The police will . . ." Stella began.

"Go!" Jeff interrupted her. "You'd gladly kill yourself feeding strangers, but not tonight."

Earl put his arm around Stella's shoulders and kissed her on the cheek. "Mr. Jeff is no longer a boy in short pants, Stella. He knows the best way. Tomorrow there will be so much to do." He led her from the room.

For a moment, Jeff and Ronnie looked at each other. His face was tired and closed, the mouth narrow and determined.

"What is it?" she asked, feeling fear race through her.

"I'm not going to call the police," he said softly. "I don't want this reported."

"What?" Ronnie couldn't believe her ears.

"Another attempt on my life would make it seem that I'm desperate for public attention, emotional support. This close to the session opening, I can't afford the publicity."

"You can't afford the publicity?" Ronnie almost shouted. "You seem to forget that I was the one who was nearly killed! I was the one standing in the window, a perfect target. I want this investigated by the best damn cops in the state! Neil Brenton's special investigative team needs to know about this!" Her emotions were raging.

"I'll see that Neil hears about this," Jeff said grimly, "if he doesn't already know. Remember, though, you can't afford the publicity either." His voice was cold and harsh. "Think about it, Veronica. A national reporter, in her negligee, shot at in a senator's home on the coast."

The ugly implication made her turn away from him. She wanted to cover her ears with her hands, run from the room and everything that had happened. The night had come very close to being what he described. Only a peacock's scream had saved her.

"Do you still want me to call the police?" Jeff pressed her.

"Do anything you damn well please," she replied, turning to him with angry peaks of color in her pale cheeks. "I've had it. I'm going home even if I have to walk."

"Just a moment," Jeff said softly, but there was an edge of firmness in his voice. "I suggest that you stay."

"I'm not staying in this house another minute," Ronnie flung back at him. "Another hour, and I probably won't be alive."

"I'll take you out to Ann's," Jeff said steadily. "It's almost morning. She's an early riser."

"I'm going home," Ronnie insisted.

"You'll be safe at Ann's, you can get your story, and I'll have your car repaired by tomorrow," Jeff said.

"We can't go rushing out to someone's house in the middle of the night," Ronnie objected. She felt her resolve crumbling. All she really wanted to do was find a nice safe place and sleep for several hours. She had no car, no way to travel. And there were a few things she had to find out before she left Magnolia Point, things she needed daylight to examine.

"Good, then it's settled. Bright and early, I'll take you to Ann's. Now, I promise you, you're safe here for the rest of the night. I'm going to stay up and guard the house."

That thought gave Ronnie no consolation as she climbed the stairs to her bedroom.

THE BAD DREAMS FADED and were replaced by a steady, rhythmic sound that signaled peace and serenity. Ronnie rolled onto her stomach in bed and sighed. The down comforter was warm, and the sheets were soft and silky. The rhythm floated all around her, unidentified yet wonderfully familiar. As she slowly began to wake, she recognized the sound of an ax biting wood. She smiled to herself, her eyes closed, associating the sound with all the mornings she'd awakened to her father's wood chopping. She'd grown up on a small farm, which her family still operated, and the steady sound of work was like a lullaby. For a moment there was no recollection of the past night, no memory of anything except loving parents and safe, warm winter mornings.

At last she opened her eyes, startled into recognition of the fact that she was in a strange bedroom years removed from the safety of her parents' home. Sunlight was streaming through the windows, bright winter light that offset the dark, bare branches of the leafless trees. She slipped from the covers and walked over to the window, expecting to see Earl hard at work. Instead, there was Jeff neatly swinging the ax high above his shoulders, bringing it down on a fat log with expert accuracy. The edge of the blade bit deep into the wood, and with a quick twist, Jeff tore the log apart.

She started to walk away, but the swell of his shoulders as he lifted the ax stopped her short. No matter what she thought of him, she couldn't slow the beat of her heart as she watched his muscles ripple. He bent to the task, tightening the jeans across his strong legs and muscled thighs. Another log was blasted apart. She remembered the feel of his hands, the way the calluses were so rough against her face, along her back and legs. How could hands so strong be so tender? She brushed her own fingertips across her face, reawakening the memory of his touch. But her body shook as she recalled the blast of the gunshot through the window, the echo of the phone threat at the Deadline.

She placed her fingertips against the cold windowpane and watched Jeff work. There was a large stack of wood already. He worked for the exercise, the physical release. Looking closer, she saw the tiny marks along his back where the glass had lodged in his flesh. Whom had the shot been intended for? Was she a victim of circumstances or a target? There were things at Magnolia Point that might give her a clue to those answers. She found her jeans, a sweater and shoes, and was down the stairs in less than three minutes. She moved with the silent footsteps of a thief, holding her breath in fear she'd be discovered.

Contrary to Jeff's orders, Stella was in the kitchen cooking and humming a low, sad song under her breath. Ronnie paused against the doorway, slinking back into the shadows. Stella's information would be the hardest to get. The woman was loyal to Jeff, and very smart. She'd protect him, even if it meant taking the blame for something, assuming Jeff had done anything wrong. That thought made Ronnie shiver again with apprehension.

She slipped around to the front door and left without a sound. The oak trees behind the house were her destination. She tried to walk naturally, just in case Earl or Jeff should happen around a shrub or up a path. Last night, someone had been lurking around. She'd seen him, and he'd come back. Her heart began to beat a wild cadence. What if he were still there? None of the attacks had been in daylight, she argued with herself, forcing one foot in front of another. Not a single one. The threat had come from the restaurant at lunchtime, but it didn't take a lot of nerve to make an anonymous call in daylight. Lurking around in shadows at night was the ticket for these people. She was perfectly safe as long as the sun held out. She tried to soothe her jumpy nerves as she ambled around the house. She focused on the grounds, the beauty of the trees and the elegant splendor of their artful arrangement.

Something was lying in the middle of the drive, and she slowed to examine it. The beautiful colors of the orchid contrasted harshly with the shells, and she picked it up. The stem had been snapped with a deliberate stroke. Someone had picked it and then thrown it down. She held the delicate flower in her hand. Who could be responsible for such carelessness? Certainly not Earl. His love for the estate was marked in every shrub, every detail. She held the flower in her hand as she made her way back to the oaks.

Several large, magnificent peacocks were strutting among the trees. Looking up, she saw six more perched on the graceful limbs of the oaks. The males were fanning their tails, spreading their exotic colors to the sun. Ronnie exhaled sharply. The colors were iridescent, radiant. In the distance, the gentle lapping noises of the water came to her. Magnolia Point was truly a paradise. Was Jeff a guardian of paradise, or a criminal?

The birds moved regally away as she sauntered into the oaks. Looking toward the house, the sight of the blasted glass wall made her want to cry out, but she held back the sound and began a careful examination of the ground. Earl had said footprints were to be found in the oaks. She looked back at the house again, gauging the place where the gunman must have stood.

She moved west, her feet barely inching along as her eyes scoured the ground. When she saw them, she felt nothing at all. She'd expected to find the overly large prints of a big man. Leaning against the tree for support she braced her trembling knees and automatically looked toward the house to make sure no one was watching. As soon as she caught her breath, she went back to the side door. Just before she entered, she remembered the orchid, clutched so tightly in her hand that the delicate petals were crushed. The sight made her cry out, a low startled sound, and she dropped the flower into the shrubs and hurried back inside.

"Something smells good," she said, forcing lightness into her voice as she entered the kitchen.

"French toast, bacon, hot coffee," Stella said. Though she, too, tried to sound normal, there was worry and pain in her voice.

"Jeff's chopping wood. He'll be ravenous," Ronnie observed, taking a seat at the small table in the kitchen. "Anything I can do?"

"No thank you," Stella said formally. "What did the police say?"

"Jeff wouldn't call them," she said, watching the older woman carefully for any clues. "He says it would be bad publicity."

"He doesn't want the publicity? Does he think you will ignore this story, an eyewitness?" Stella's green eyes were quick. She watched Ronnie as eagerly as Ronnie watched her.

"I haven't decided what to do," Ronnie said, but she knew her decision had been made the night before. If she'd been going to report the shooting, she'd have done so immediately. Now too much time had passed. Stella knew it, too.

"So, the fact that you and Mr. Jeff both were nearly killed will never be known, not to the police or to the public," Stella said with an edge of anger.

"Jeff said he'd report it to Neil Brenton," Ronnie pointed out.

"Mr. Neil?" Stella's intake of breath was sharp.

"Isn't he head of the investigation?" Ronnie asked.

"Yes. Yes he is," Stella said, too quickly.

"Stella, what is it?" Ronnie pressed.

"I heard Mr. Jeff on the phone. He was saying that Mr. Neil is trying to frame him for something terrible." Large, silent tears hung in Stella's eyes. "It is killing Mr. Jeff. Mr. Neil is like a father to him."

"Stella, this can't be true!" Ronnie exclaimed. "You have to tell me what you know about the bald man. He fits into this somewhere. I just know it."

Still gripping the spatula, Stella left the stove and came to her. "There is a man who calls here. He and Mr. Jeff talk about money, large sums. I do not know what he looks like, but I know that he is a bad man." She laid her hand on top of Ronnie's. "You must help Mr. Jeff. If Mr. Neil has turned his back on him, then he is all alone." She turned away and Ronnie rose and left the kitchen to give Stella time to compose herself before Jeff came in.

The door to the sun room was firmly shut, but Ronnie opened it with a determined twist of the handle. The place was a shambles. She picked her way through the glass and went to stand beside the shattered wall. This was where she'd stood as she waited for Jeff to return. She remembered his words; he'd said she was the loveliest view he'd seen from the window. He'd asked her to wait there for him. And she had. Perfectly framed in the window as a target, until she'd bent to retrieve something from the rug.

Using the toe of her shoe, she pushed the glass around. There was so much rubble, so much destruction. She hunted, moving as fast as she could. The sun's rays glinted off the glass, making it almost impossible to find what she'd seen the night before in the moonlight. But she continued to search, shifting the glass until she saw the glimmer of gold. She pushed the glass away, bent down and picked up a gold foil band embossed with a horse's head and the lettering, Mr. D's. Holding it in her fingers, she felt certain it could tell her more about last night's shooting, maybe more than she wanted to know.

Her fingers were calm and steady as she slid the paper to the very bottom of her jeans pocket. She needed longer to study it for significance. Walking back to the kitchen and the sounds of Jeff and Stella talking, she had the peculiar feeling that the lettering was pressing into her thigh, branding her flesh with its unique stamp.

Chapter Ten

Ronnie was waiting on the front steps when Jeff pulled the truck around to pick her up. The breakfast scene in the kitchen had gone without a hitch, but tension had lodged in Ronnie's throat, making it difficult for her to swallow the delicious French toast, bacon and hot coffee Stella had served. Hungry from his early morning workout with the ax, Jeff had devoured his food, keeping up a casual flow of easy conversation about horses and racing in general. Ronnie felt his eyes on her, thoughtful and curious, before he turned to Stella and gave her the same penetrating look. But he'd said nothing to either of them about their strained faces, the awkward silences that he filled with casual talk. Ronnie had the uncomfortable feeling that he was deliberately ignoring the danger she felt closing in around them.

"Earl is looking at your car now," Jeff said. "The motor seems to be okay, so maybe it isn't anything serious."

"I'm a little attached to that car," Ronnie said as she slammed the truck door and settled against the old leather seat. "I know it doesn't make any sense, but I do get attached to cars, purses, even old shoes." She laughed, still trying to shake the sense of confusion that had begun to dominate her life. Though she was determined to cool her feelings for Jeff, she couldn't avoid looking at him with a

quick glance. In a flannel shirt and soft, old jeans, he was
handsome. He wore none of the politician's slickness that
was so obvious in Neil Brenton. She closed her eyes in weariness at the thought of the attorney general. She had to find
out what was going on between the two of them, before
someone got hurt in the conflict.

"I know what you mean," Jeff said. "Attachments, no
matter how illogical, are hard to break."

There was an undercurrent of unhappiness in his words,
and Ronnie opened her eyes to find him staring straight
ahead, all attention focused on the road as he left the oak-
shaded drive and took Highway 90 that paralleled the beach.

Ronnie watched the few sailboats in the Saturday morning sun. The beach was almost deserted, sparkling white
sand against the dark blue water, a contrast of elements, just
like Jeff. Turning left again, Jeff took a narrow two-lane
road into the heart of the state. They drove in silence, the
peaceful scenery flashing by the passenger window. Twenty
minutes passed, and the small yards gave way to larger
farms.

"Tell me a little about Ann," she finally said, digging in
her purse for her notebook. So many questions had to be
asked, and she had to admit to herself that she was afraid of
some of the answers.

"She's been completely on her own at the ranch now for
about two years," Jeff said. If he saw her nervousness, he
ignored it. "She has a lot invested in her stallion, a young
fellow with good blood lines and the ability to throw foals
with potential to run."

"Divorced?"

Jeff gave her a curious look. "What makes you ask?"

"You said she's been on her own for about two years."

"She is divorced, but that isn't what I meant. Her father
died recently. He was a breeder in Kentucky with a family

adition in horses. I believe he came South for his health nd couldn't get over his dream of racehorses. He brought >me mares with him and Easy Dancer is a foal from his fa->rite mare."

"Easy Dancer?" The name was vivid, creating a picture f flashing hooves and graceful speed. The image of the lasted wall at last receded as she visualized the horse; swept way by Jeff's enthusiasm.

"That's the stud. And I have to tell you, he's something ·ry special."

"Jeff, I don't want to imply anything, but I have to ask iis question. Do you have any financial interest in the horse the farm?" Ronnie watched carefully as he answered. His ce didn't change at all.

"None whatsoever, Ronnie. I know it's part of your job · ask those questions, and I want to make it very clear. My andfather won and lost a lot of money on horses. In fact, : won Magnolia Point on a bet. But his luck wasn't passed >wn in the family gene pool. I've made a few wagers at the acks around the country, and I've lost some money. But I >n't have any financial interest in the horse business."

The sincerity in his voice rang true. Ronnie scrawled a few ·breviated notes, then tucked the pad away. "I guess that's until we get there. How much money have you lost on agers?" She spoke casually, but he turned to her for a oment.

"Not enough to worry about. I haven't mortgaged the rm or gotten into bank robbery to pay my gambling ·bts," he said, almost laughing.

"How much farther?" Ronnie asked. Jeff's response was sy, unworried. Was it the truth? The load of doubt lifted, d she smiled at him. Jeff Stuart was many things, but not crook.

"That's the first smile I've seen today," Jeff said, brush
ing the backs of his fingers along her soft cheek. "Are you
okay?"

"Physically, I'm fine," Ronnie said. "The cuts were lit
tle more than scratches. Emotionally, though, I'm very
confused." She looked straight at him. Now was the mo
ment, the time for candor.

"Confused?" Jeff asked, a degree of caution creeping
into his words. "About what?"

"Exactly how you fit into this puzzle of racing, payoffs,
wild bullets and politics." She felt the truck slowing until
they came to a stop.

"The ranch is around the bend," he explained, "and I
want this settled before we get there." The look he gave her
was direct, searching, as if he sought the truth in her eyes.
"An old friend of mine is in serious trouble, Ronnie. Don't
ask who, because I can't tell you. I'm working to help him.
That's all I can say." The blue blaze of his eyes fixed her
with open honesty.

"What kind of trouble?" she asked, her mouth dry from
tension.

"I don't even know all the details myself, but it is seri
ous. I've seen enough evidence to know that he may be
guilty, but I don't believe it. This man would never sell out
his convictions. Never." A dark anger burned in Jeff's eyes,
fused with a deep pain. That more than anything made
Ronnie reach across the seat and brush a strand of brown
hair from his forehead.

"Why is someone trying to hurt you?" she asked.

"Hurt or frighten?" Jeff countered. "And there's the
possibility both assaults were directed at you."

The fear that made her spine tingle had become an old,
familiar friend, but Ronnie forced a smile. "Me? That's
absurd. Why would anyone want to hurt me?"

"Maybe they think you know something," Jeff said, putting the truck in gear and moving forward again. "That's one reason I'm glad we're going out to Ann's today. No one will ever find you there."

His words sent a small shudder through her body, and Jeff pulled her to his side. "No more of this for now," he said softly against her hair. "We're almost there, and I want to have today for us. No danger, no tensions, just us."

Pressed close to his side, Ronnie felt her rigid body begin to relax. Was it unreasonable to want one day with Jeff? One day of winter sun and pleasure? She sighed and leaned her head on his shoulder, delighted to be near him and at peace. When they rounded the curve, Ronnie was immediately struck by a vast expanse of winter pasture bordered with neat white fences that stretched to the horizon. A large barn dominated the property, and she could make out the roof of a gracious frame house tucked among a grove of live oak trees.

They followed the fence line for over a mile, then turned down a shell drive to the house. A large sign bearing the emblem of a galloping steed carried the inscription Dancing Water Ranch.

"It's beautiful," Ronnie said simply.

"Ann works hard. This place is her life."

Before the truck could coast to a stop, three large German shepherds circled the cab, barking furiously. As soon as Jeff stepped to the ground, the barks changed to whimpers of welcome. The dogs crowded against his legs, licking his hands and demanding attention. Coming around the truck, Ronnie couldn't help smiling.

"You seem to be regarded as a friend."

"I've known Shadow and Shasta since they were pups. Luna's a little older, but she's grown fond of me in the past few years."

The sound of a door slamming alerted Ronnie. A tall, slender woman dashed down the porch steps, a smile of welcome on her face.

"Jeff," she cried, running into his arms and offering her lips for a kiss, "where have you been, you devil?"

"Working hard, Ann, just like you. The last time I was out here you had more interest in mucking out stalls than in talking with me." He was laughing, holding her firmly in his arms. "All this manual labor agrees with you. You look terrific."

A pang of jealousy swept through Ronnie like a knife. Standing to one side of the intimate scene, she had plenty of time to notice Ann's shiny dark hair, cut in an efficient yet very feminine bob. Her clear skin was bronzed from the sun and belied every doctor's report that a healthy tan would bring wrinkles. Pale blue eyes twinkled merrily in a face filled with humor and warmth.

"Ann, this is Veronica Sheffield, the reporter I told you about." Jeff loosened his grip long enough to make the introduction. Then his hand went possessively back to Ann's waist. "I told her you could feed her the straight facts about the racing industry."

"I'm ready with more facts than she'll ever want to hear," Ann said, breaking free of Jeff's grip and extending a long-fingered hand to Ronnie. "I'm very glad you decided to come. This is the first chance I've had to really talk from a breeder's point of view, and I can tell you, the free publicity won't hurt." She laughed warmly.

"I hope Jeff told you that my job is to present a balanced story," Ronnie said cautiously.

"Of course. I wouldn't expect anything else. But at least I'll have an opportunity to have my say, and as Jeff will tell you, I always have plenty to say." She grabbed his arm and gave it a warm squeeze. "You look like you've been run over y a train," she commented dryly. "Having a hard time leeping?" There was a teasing edge to her voice, and she urned a warm smile on Ronnie.

"That's my business," Jeff said too quickly, cutting off ny response Ronnie might have wanted to offer about the ast night.

"Well, we'll discuss your vices and bad sleeping habits a ttle later. Come on in and I'll give you a cup of coffee. Mannie's off today, but I can brew up a pot without the hreat of botulism."

They entered the house across a large shady porch that verlooked the precisely manicured pastures. A swing and ocker stood there, and a large yellow tomcat slept in a patch f sun. Ann herded them through a long, very masculine en into a kitchen that could have been lifted from a Norman Rockwell painting. Ronnie felt at home immediately as he took a seat in a straw-bottomed chair around a large oval able.

"I do a lot of business in this kitchen," Ann said. "That vay I can eat and succeed at the same time."

She put the coffee on and started setting cups around the able. "Freddie came in this morning to feed up and turn ut so I could rest and look presentable for my interview," he said as she worked. "Usually I'm up at six, feeding, urning out, doctoring, grooming and riding. By this time I ook and feel like a throwaway scarecrow."

"That's the first lie I've ever heard you tell," Jeff said uickly, his face alive with warm feelings. "Ann looks great, ven after a day that would kill six stout timbermen."

They laughed together, Jeff's low rumble seeming to upport and encourage Ann's lighter tones. Ronnie manged a smile, but her anguish was growing stronger with ach word. Jeff might not have an interest in Ann's horses, ut he obviously had a big one in her.

"Let's get on with the tour," Ann said when they fin
ished their coffee. "I'm glad to see you wore sensibl
clothes," she commented to Ronnie.

"One thing about Veronica, she's a sensible lady," Jef
said. There was no inflection in his voice, but Ann quickl
caught his eye.

After a brief overview of the ranch, including acreage
stalls, horses and employees, Ann led the way to the stal
lion barn.

"Before Mannie left yesterday, she did bake a chocolat
cake," she said temptingly to Jeff. Then she turned to Ron
nie. "With men you have to make them work for dessert,'
she said, winking, "especially Jeff. Underneath that ster
ling exterior is the heart of a slug."

"Thanks, Ann, impress my friend for me," Jeff re
torted.

"I don't want to impress her, I want to warn her," Ann
said. "In case Stella hasn't told you, this man is a devil."

"Can I quote you on that?" Ronnie asked.

"Enough, enough," Jeff said. "The two of you will have
me ruined in no time. I can see that. Ann, why don't you
show Ronnie the office? I'm going to earn some cake."

Leading the way, Ann ushered Ronnie into a tidy room
lined with ribbons, trophies and photographs. Some of the
pictures featured a young, pigtailed girl astride powerfu
horses.

"Is that you?" Ronnie asked.

"My father liked to have the pictures up. Since his death
I'm afraid I haven't cleaned as thoroughly as I'd like."

"They're very nice," Ronnie said, feeling Ann's loss ir
her voice. "You must have been on a horse from the tim
you could walk."

"Even before." Ann laughed. "My mother died when
was very young, so Dad just took me with him when he ha

o work a horse. I literally learned to ride before I could walk. But that's enough about the past. Let's talk about the future.''

For the next hour, they went over figures and facts, Ronnie taking meticulous notes. At last, Ronnie closed the notebook. "These figures are impressive. I never believed horse breeding could employ so many people, involve so much.''

"These animals require a great deal of care and attention o detail. It isn't a gigantic factory that would employ thousands in one location, but it is a viable industry. And it's a beautiful industry. You're from Kentucky. You must know.''

"Yes,'' Ronnie agreed. "I'm afraid I ignored horse racing as a sport, but the farms are indeed magnificent.''

They walked slowly down the hallway until they found Jeff grooming a tremendous sorrel stallion. The horse danced in the cross ties at the sight of Ann, demanding attention and a carrot from her back pocket.

"This horse is one smart cookie. Ann's had him since the day his tiny little hooves touched the ground,'' Jeff said.

"I'm afraid he's a trifle spoiled.'' Ann shrugged. "He likes Jeff fairly well, but he doesn't much take up with strangers.''

Ronnie kept a respectful distance from the enormous golden animal, but she noted the loving way Jeff stroked his glistening hide. Easy Dancer threw his head, nosing out toward Ronnie.

"He wants you to come a little closer,'' Ann said. "He wants to tell if you're friend or foe.''

Ronnie boldly stepped forward, noticing the fleeting look of approval that touched Jeff's features. Stretching her hand out to the horse, she let his sensitive nostrils sniff her wrist and palm. Unexpectedly he burrowed his muzzle into her hand.

"He likes you," Ann said with pleasure. "Dancer's an excellent judge of character, too."

"How about a ride, Ronnie?" Jeff offered, looking at Ann as he spoke. She nodded agreeably.

"Maybe for a short while," Ronnie said. "I don't want you two to make me so saddle sore I can't walk." The idea of a ride with Jeff was exhilarating, and Ann Tate was a woman she liked, someone she would one day like to know as a friend.

"Betta and Duke are both trustworthy mounts," Ann assured her.

"Aren't you coming?" Ronnie asked.

"I do have work," Ann said, laughing. "I realize it's a cruel act to throw you out in the woods alone with Jefferson Stuart. But you seem to be a big girl, able to take care of yourself and defend your virtue. Just remember—" she grinned wickedly "—devil," and she pointed to Jeff.

"Get out of here and check on Tango," Jeff said, pushing at her. "Can I see her when we get back?"

"I'll have Freddie bring her back in from pasture," Ann said. "She needs a good grooming, and I'm glad you're here to do some work."

"Tango?" Ronnie asked.

"She's the most beautiful mare in the world," Jeff said quickly.

"I bred her to Easy Dancer last spring, and she's due to foal in late January or early February," Ann explained. "When the foal drops, he or she will belong to Jeff. It's my repayment for the insurance premium Jeff loaned me last year."

They shared a look, and Ann reached out a hand to touch Jeff's face. "I like to tease this guy a lot, but I have to admit that he has a heart of gold, Ronnie. If it hadn't been for Jeff, I would have come very close to losing this place. Without insurance I couldn't operate. As I showed you earlier, there's liability, medical, life insurance on Easy Dancer and the other horses, all the facilities. You name it, it all costs big money.''

Ronnie remembered the allocations for expenses, and the figures had struck her as very large. Until she'd looked at Ann's books, she'd never realized the unseen costs. Jeff had come up with a pretty penny, that was for certain.

"Saddle up, you two," Ann said. "Work up an appetite for Mannie's cake." She walked off, leaving them to get on with it.

The horses were just as Ann promised, trustworthy and easygoing with a spark of healthy frolic. The winter sun, the motion of the horse, everything was magical. Jeff knew several wooded trails, and they cantered side by side. Ronnie couldn't keep herself from looking at him. His legs around the horse were powerful, well defined. He sat at ease in the saddle, shoulders straight and graceful. The sight of him made her want to feel his lips on hers, feel his hands roving down her body with the touch she remembered only too well from the night before.

Feeling her eyes on him, Jeff slowed and watched her as her mount, Duke, settled back into an easy walk. "I've learned never to believe a woman who says she can't ride," Jeff said. "You have an excellent seat, good hands and—" he grinned wolfishly "—magnificent legs."

The fact that she'd been thinking along similar lines about him put a new gleam of color in her cheeks.

"Let's race," she said, wanting to escape the thoughts his words and presence were putting in her mind. She didn't trust herself with him. Before he could answer, she closed her legs around Duke's sides and he burst forward, only too eager to show some spirit on a crisp, bright day.

The wind tore around her face, sending her hair behind her like a banner. Jeff laughed, clucking to his horse to catch up.

Ronnie cast a look over her shoulder to see his smiling face leaning into the horse's mane as he urged Betta forward. He was gaining, and she leaned forward into Duke's neck and lifted herself out of the saddle to free his back. "Go, boy, go," she whispered.

Duke stretched, giving his heart to the game, but Betta was gradually gaining ground. Ronnie felt the wild laughter in her throat; the excitement made her want to dance and sing. Her hair tangled about her face, and she turned to see Jeff drawing up on Duke's flank.

"I'm going to get you," he warned her, his blue eyes fired with the fun of the day. "Spitfire!" The word was a challenge and he threw it at her.

A small log lay across the path in front of her. Before she had time to think, Duke pushed off his hind legs and sailed over the log. Landing on the other side without breaking his stride, he continued pell-mell down the path. The sensation was exhilarating, and she pressed her body as close to Duke's as she could. Still, Betta's hooves were pounding only inches behind her. She heard Jeff's laughter, and saw his hand reach out to her reins. With care, he gently pulled both horses to a trot, and then a walk.

"Caught you," he said, breathing deeply from the excitement and exertion. "That was some jump."

"More than I expected," Ronnie said with a laugh. She hadn't felt so young and alive in years. Jeff's hand was still on her reins, and before she could anticipate his action, he lifted it to her thigh.

"I thought you were beautiful on the dance floor," he said, "but on a horse, you're incredible." His hand lifted and brushed a few disordered locks from her face. Then he reached behind her head and slowly pulled her to him.

Ronnie caught the scent of his cologne, the tang of spice. His face rubbed against her cheek and he kissed her cold nose lightly. "I'd say you're healthy," he teased before his lips came down on hers. Duke shifted beneath her, and Jeff released his hold as the horses moved them apart. Slinging her head, Betta asked for more galloping. Jeff laid a calming hand on the mare's neck, but he looked at Ronnie.

"Easy, girl," he murmured. "There'll be other times."

Hearing the sound of another horse coming through the woods, Jeff turned in the saddle. "Must be someone from Dancing Water," he remarked. "No one else around has horses, and this is private property." There was a flash of red as Ann cleared the log and cantered to their side.

"I should have known Jeff would try to go parking, but it isn't as easy on horseback," she laughed. "Stay mounted and Duke will take care of you," she told Ronnie.

"I thought you had work to do," Jeff retorted.

"I did. Exercising Krista is one of the things I have to do. But I came out to tell you that Earl called. He seemed a little upset about a car."

"My car?" Ronnie asked. For a few hours she'd managed to forget everything except Jeff, the way he made her feel.

"He didn't say whose it was," Ann continued, unaware of the tension in Ronnie's face. "He said it was a 280Z, and he said the gas line had deliberately been cut. He's looking for a part."

"I see," Jeff said, his voice also filled with tension.

"What's going on here?" Ann asked, looking from one tight face to the other.

"It's my car," Ronnie said slowly.

"So why would someone want to cut your gas line, and where was the car when it happened? Let's head back to the house while we talk. These animals are too hot to stand around." She nudged Krista into the lead, leaving Ronnie and Jeff to walk side by side.

"Ronnie's car was at Magnolia Point," Jeff said. His voice was now flat and unemotional, giving none of his feelings away. "Someone must have broken into the garage and done it."

"Not really!" Ann said, shocked. "You've never had any difficulty with vandalism there, Jeff. This is terrible." She turned and gave Ronnie a sympathetic look. "I'm so sorry, but Earl will fix it right up. There isn't anything that runs that he can't repair."

"I'm sure," Ronnie responded dully. Jeff rode beside her and refused to even look at her. The bald man had done it. He'd been sneaking around the estate. But why? To keep her at Magnolia Point? For what reason? Unless it was to deliver the shotgun blast through the window.

"What did the police say?" Ann asked.

"We didn't call them," Jeff said before Ronnie could speak. "At the time I thought it was simply a malfunction."

"Who would ever think someone was up to no good?" Ronnie asked bitterly. Jeff's face was stony with anger, and he flashed her a warning look that stopped her short.

"Here's the shortcut back to the farm," Ann said, unaware of the play of emotions between them. In the distance, the paved road was visible and the white fences of the farm lay just beyond. When they were off the path, they rode three abreast. Jeff moved so that Ann was in the middle, and he rode closest to the ditch.

The day was still beautiful with perfect blue skies and bright sun, but for Ronnie, the outing had been robbed of its fun. Fear weighed her down in the saddle.

"I think I'll canter ahead a bit," she said. "I may not get to ride again for another fifteen years, and I'd like to take advantage of it."

"Go on," Ann said. "Don't forget to cool Duke when you get to the barn."

"Sure thing," Ronnie said as she lightly applied her legs to Duke's sides. Once again he moved off at an easy lope. She didn't look over her shoulder, but she felt Jeff's eyes on her. The road ahead was clear, and she closed her eyes, losing herself in the rocking motion of the horse. She opened them again and saw a car approaching in the distance. Slowing Duke to a walk, she pulled over to the ditch. The gate to the farm was only two hundred yards ahead. As soon as the car passed, she'd gallop again.

Her mind was on the events of the past night and Jeff's unexpected admission that he was involved in something to help an anonymous friend. Who could it be? A man of conviction, he'd said. Surely someone in power. Neil Brenton's face flashed into her mind and she straightened so suddenly in the saddle that Duke came to a complete halt. Glancing at the road, Ronnie saw that the driver of the big car had slowed to a near stop. He was being courteous, taking it easy so as not to startle her mount. She lifted a hand to wave her appreciation when her heart stood still. The man behind the wheel was big, hidden behind dark sunglasses. He shifted slightly and the midday sun glinted from his shiny scalp. Before she could even scream, the car shot forward.

Ronnie dug her heels into Duke's side, and he responded like a loaded spring. Blindly she pointed the horse at the white wooden fence and then leaned forward on her knees, doing her best to imitate every jumping event she'd ever witnessed on television. With a surge of power, Duke cleared the top rail just as the car skidded in the gravel at the side of the road, almost crashing into the fence.

Ronnie had no time to look back or think. Duke was running wild, flying across the pasture for all he was worth. Gradually she eased back on the reins and regained enough of her seat so that she could calm him. Reluctantly he dropped back to a trot and at last stopped. Unable to control the shaking in her legs, Ronnie slid to the ground and finally turned to look at the road.

Ann and Jeff were racing toward her as fast as their horses could go. There was no sign of the car, but there was a trail of light dust where he'd turned in the gravel and headed back the way he came.

Ann's face was white with concern but Jeff's wore a look of anger.

Ronnie leaned into Duke's neck and took in his clean, horsey smell. Somehow it helped, and she stood up and patted him on the shoulder.

"Ronnie, are you okay?" Ann called as she flung herself from the saddle and draped Krista's reins over the white fence. She was over the rail in a flash and dashing across the pasture, Jeff not far behind her.

"I'm fine," Ronnie said, still too shocked to feel the fear."

"What the hell was that all about?" Ann demanded. One look at Ronnie's face, and she turned the question to Jeff. "What's going on here? I want to know right now."

"Ronnie," Jeff said, grabbing both of her shoulders and pulling her against his chest. She could hear his heart pounding. "Are you okay?"

"It was the bald man," Ronnie said, unable to stop the tremble in her voice. "It was the man from the party. The same man that shot at ...." She stopped herself. The same man who was at Magnolia Point the night before, the night

he was nearly killed by a shotgun blast. Looking into Jeff's
blue eyes, she saw the terrible truth. Somehow in the crazy
game Jeff was playing, she'd become the real target, not
him. His plan to save a friend had endangered her life.

"It's okay," Jeff said, crushing her to him, "it's okay."

"Was that the man who tried to kill you, Jeff?" Ann said.

"We've had a series of accidents," Jeff answered tightly.
'Would you mind if Ronnie stayed with you tonight?
Magnolia Point may not be safe."

"You're both welcome to stay," Ann said quickly. She
put her hand on Ronnie's shoulders and gave her a squeeze.
'Listen, Ronnie, if you ever get tired of newspaper reporting, I think I could get you a job jumping horses."

"Thanks," Ronnie said, stepping back from Jeff. "At
his moment, the offer sounds almost too good to turn
down." She forced herself to stand away from Jeff, away
from the haven of his arms. Another moment of weakness,
and she might be crying.

"I'll put Ronnie in the blue guest room, and Jeff, you can
have the gray one that opens onto the veranda. You always
liked that room."

"I won't be staying," Jeff said. His eyes were back on the
roadway, and the anger on his face had returned. "I have
some business to finish in town."

"Surely it can wait," Ann said. "Ronnie's nearly been
killed."

Jeff looked into Ronnie's wide eyes before he grimly replied, "This business can't wait, not for even an hour."

"What are you going to do?" Ronnie asked. The expression on his face was chilling. She'd never seen a man look
so cold, so capable of violent action.

"Don't call the police," he ordered. "I promise you that
I will report this incident, but not to the local police."

"Jeff," Ann interrupted, "Ronnie's car has been vandalized and now some maniac in a black car tried to run down her and one of my best horses. I want to make a report of this. If we call right away, they may be able to capture that man."

Jeff's eyes bored into her. "Stay out of it, Ann. For your own sake. For your own safety."

Chapter Eleven

Shooting home the bolt on the stall, Ronnie hung the halter on the hook by the door. Visions of chocolate cake danced in her head and she wiped a hand across her forehead.

"Thanks for the help," Ann said, grinning.

"You do this every day?" Ronnie asked, amazed.

"Every day, rain or shine. Unless it's too cold to turn out, that is, but down here along the coast those cold days only come once or twice a year." Ann snapped off the lights as they walked toward the house.

The moon had crested over the oaks, and Ronnie noticed that it was waning. Hanging above the old limbs, it looked older and wiser than she'd ever seen it. She couldn't hold back the sigh that escaped her lips. If only she had a little more wisdom. Maybe then she'd know what to think about Jeff. So many strange things had happened in the last few days. He'd torn out of the ranch as though devils were biting his heels. And his concern had been frozen in anger, an anger that Ronnie didn't understand. Someone had tried to hurt her, and Jeff was angry at her. Nothing made sense, and now she was hiding at a horse ranch because Jeff told her to.

"How about a drink?" Ann asked as they trudged up the steps.

"I'd really like some of that chocolate cake," Ronnie said, "and even more than that, a cigarette."

Ann laughed quickly, throwing open the door. "I can help you with the cake, but I don't smoke. In fact, I don't have anyone working here who does. Barn fires are too easy to start, and too hard to finish."

"I'll settle for a piece of cake and some coffee, then," Ronnie said. "Better for my health, if not my waistline."

"Jeff seems to approve of your waistline just as it is," Ann replied, grinning.

Ronnie felt her smile tighten into a hard, artificial mask.

"Did I say something wrong?" Ann asked.

"No, I just think you're mistaken."

"Are you telling me you two aren't romantically involved?" There was doubt in Ann's voice.

"What makes you ask?" Ronnie countered, jockeying for time. Ann's questions were not unreasonable, but the answers were so unclear. When Jeff held her in his arms, she felt romantically involved. But when she thought about recent events, she didn't know what to think.

"I see the way he looks at you when you aren't looking at him. There's something there I've never seen before," Ann said.

"I don't know what you mean. Jeff's actions toward me have always been... I mean Jeff's famous for his interest in women." She winced at her openness. She couldn't hide her feelings for Jeff from herself, or from anyone else.

"Jeff has never been a man to ignore his own passions, that's a fact," Ann said. "But that has nothing to do with romantic involvement." Ann put a huge piece of cake in front of Ronnie while the coffee dripped.

"I don't think Jeff has time for or thoughts of any involvement other than a political one." Ann's words had sen her heart racing and she spoke in an effort to calm her emotions.

"I thought that, too," Ann said. "You know, the two of us have been friends for a long time. When I was married my whole future turned toward children and a home. Then things changed—" she shrugged away the pain that still touched her eyes "—but I've always hoped that Jeff could one day find the right woman to settle down with. He's promised me that I can be the official aunt to all of his children, and I'm ready."

"You two have been close," Ronnie said.

"Like brother and sister. By the way, I need to ask a favor."

"Sure," Ronnie said.

Ann poured two mugs of coffee and put them on the table. "I mentioned that insurance money earlier. Please don't put that in the paper. It might look funny for Jeff, but it was a legitimate loan."

Ann came around the table and sat beside Ronnie, sipping her coffee. "Because of my father's death and the legal complications involved with the inheritance, all of the money here was tied up. A bank might have loaned me the funds, but it would have taken forever and there wasn't a guarantee. Jeff stepped in and paid the insurance and I insisted he take a foal in return. It was a wonderful deal for me, and one day Jeff will have a horse that will be worth a lot more than what he paid, whether racing ever comes to Mississippi or not. But it would look funny in print, especially with this horse racing thing already creating such a fuss."

"It would look bad, for both of you," Ronnie said, wishing she'd never been given the information.

"I'm telling you the truth," Ann said. "I care too much bout Jeff to see him hurt because he's kindhearted and generous. A man shouldn't be punished because he does the right thing, even if it looks funny."

"You're right," Ronnie finally agreed, smiling at last at Ann. "I guess I don't have to include that."

"I know Jeff better than anyone," Ann said, "and when he looks at you, he has a strange look in his eyes."

"That's because I'm a reporter and he wants to make sure I write nice things about him," Ronnie parried.

"It's because he has begun to care about you. I saw his face when that car swerved toward you. He was terrified."

"Terrified, or angry?" Ronnie asked.

"Both, I suppose," Ann said. "What are you getting at?"

"I don't know," Ronnie finished lamely. There was no reason to involve Ann. She remembered Jeff's quick efforts to keep her from talking about the gunshot at Magnolia Point, his direct order for Ann to stay uninvolved. If he was protecting Ann, then there was no point in dragging her into the trouble. Ronnie tried to find another topic of conversation, but all she could think about was Jeff's role in the events. She toyed with her cake and avoided Ann's look.

"Ronnie, why didn't you report that car to the police?" Ann's voice was casual, but she put her cup down and waited for the answer.

"I didn't get the license. Neither of you did either."

"Are you certain it was the man you saw at the ball?"

Ronnie felt her skin begin to chill. She'd only caught a glimpse of the man's broad shoulders and the hint of baldness. Everything had happened so fast; there'd been no chance to get a good look at him with Duke spinning beneath her. Gathering details had been the last thing on her mind when she'd aimed the horse at the fence and hoped

he'd be able to clear it without killing the animal and her-
elf.

"The truth is," she said, shrugging her shoulders, "just
is Jeff pointed out, I didn't get a really good look at him,
iot any of the times." Ronnie put her cup down to still her
haking hand.

"What other times?" Ann asked.

"You'd make a good reporter."

"I'm not interested in becoming a reporter, but I am de-
ermined to help an old friend, and someone I hope will be
. new friend."

The warm words almost brought tears to Ronnie's eyes.
t would be so nice to confide in someone, but now wasn't
he right time. "You have helped," she said, smiling across
he table at Ann's worried face. "More than you'll know."

"I'll make some supper, and then I think you should get
ome rest. You look like you've been up for days."

"Can I help?"

"You ask after bringing in twenty horses and putting out
ver a hundred pounds of feed? You go take a bath, relax.
 have some great old cotton shirts to sleep in and I think
ou can probably wear a pair of my jeans and a flannel
hirt."

"That sounds wonderful."

"Soak," Ann urged her. "Tomorrow you may be sore
rom that fantastic ride you took today."

Ronnie already felt the beginnings of sore muscles as she
ot to her feet. The bathroom was off her bedroom, and she
illed the tub with hot water and immersed her body, think-
ig again of the black car coming down the road. This at-
:mpt was made in broad daylight, before witnesses, and it
adn't been directed toward Jeff. There was no denying that
he was the intended victim, yet Jeff had been reluctant to
all the police. When he'd left the ranch, his jaw had been

rigid with anger. She slipped into the water up to her chin. If Jeff was protecting someone, say Neil, where did she figure in the story? Had Neil been right? Was Jeff so ambitious that her death would be the price he'd pay for... for what? For a payoff from a crime boss? She didn't understand. There was so much she didn't understand.

Getting out of the tub she found a long cotton T-shirt on the bed and gratefully pulled it over her head. Barefoot, she padded back into the kitchen where Ann had prepared a hot meal.

As soon as the dishes were washed, Ronnie excused herself, eager for the feel of warm blankets and a bed. As plagued by her thoughts as she was, sleep eluded all of her efforts.

The night sounds of the ranch were strange. Horses galloped across the pastures, and the dogs seemed to be chasing something out by the barns. Minutes ticked by, and Ronnie tried to force herself to sleep to stop the churning of her heart. Uttering a moan of aggravation, Ronnie finally threw back the covers and dressed in the warm clothes Ann had given her. Trying to sleep was pointless with the jumble of thoughts and doubts that were assailing her. More than anything she wanted to hear Jeff's voice, to see the truth shining in his eyes. He hadn't come back to the ranch, though. He hadn't even called. Hurrying away from her own doubts, she slipped out of the house and walked toward the barn.

She'd gone half the distance before she noticed the dogs were nowhere to be found. All evening they'd been right at her heels. She started to whistle, then stopped. Ann was asleep.

Away from the city, the night sky was blacker than anything Ronnie had ever remembered. Spotting constellations had once been a minor interest, and she looked up to see what she could remember. Then she heard a low moan from the shrubbery near the stallion barn. She walked closer, then paused. There was a whimper, then another moan coming from deep within the shrubs. Wishing she had a flashlight, she dropped to her knees and began searching the darkness with her hands. The moan grew louder. The darkness was impenetrable, and she was forced to crawl slowly, sweeping one hand in front of her. When she touched the warm fur of an animal, she almost screamed. There was the softest moan, and she recognized the thick fur and short muzzle of the animal as Shasta's. She shook the dog lightly. "Come on, girl," she urged softly. "Come on now, let's get up." Shasta refused to move, only giving another soft moan and whimper.

"What's wrong, girl?" Ronnie urged her. "Get up."

The hands that closed over her mouth were hard and calloused, smelling slightly of old leather and tobacco. She arched her body, trying to break away, but she was drawn from the shrubs as easily as a child in the grip of an angry adult.

"So, the little reporter's out looking for clues. Forget the doggie. She's in dreamland with a large dose of sedative." His hands held her harshly as he laughed. "When she wakes up, she'll be toasted nicely." He laughed again. "And so will you."

Without any warning, he jerked her abruptly, snapping her head painfully against the wall. Twisting in the man's grip, Ronnie fought for her freedom until his savage hold shut off her air. Effortlessly he hauled her into a small tack room in the stallion barn.

His fingers dug into her face, and though she tried to look up at him, she could see nothing. Pointing her at the floor, he waited until she saw the ten gallons of gasoline.

It took only a second for the sight to register, then Ronnie fought with all of her strength. He was going to burn down the barn. He'd sedated the dogs, and now he was going to kill her and burn the place. She twisted her chin and finally captured one of his fingers in her mouth. With every ounce of strength, she bit down on it.

"You nosy bitch!" The man spat the words at her, slapping her with his free hand across the jaw. "You couldn't stay away. You had to keep snooping. Well, this is a present from the senator."

The blow was hard. Ronnie felt herself falling to her knees as the blackness became total.

WHEN SHE TRIED to lift her head, the pain was nauseating. But the cement floor was cold and rough against her face, and by sheer will, Ronnie forced her arms straight and lifted her upper body. An acrid smell drifted toward her, bringing back the horror of her abduction.

"Damn!" she whispered, pulling her hand away from a sticky spot on the side of her head. She was bleeding, but she was still alive. She crawled to the door and grasped the knob. It turned in her hand, but the door didn't move. The knowledge that she was locked in came fast and hard, almost making her stumble to the floor again. The smell of smoke was stronger near the door. In his stall, Easy Dancer snorted nervously.

She was a prisoner in a barn that would soon be a roaring oven, and there was no one to help her.

Saddle racks lined the windowless walls, and Ronnie remembered that there was an opening in the ceiling that gave access to the hayloft. But there was no ladder. Somehow she had to find a way to climb out! Taking a few deep breaths she found a secure saddle rack and started up. The wooden rack was firmly mounted to the wall and she moved from the irst rack to the second climbing gradually higher. At last, er head bumped against the ceiling. In the smoky dark- ess her hands searched for the loft opening as she bal- nced precariously on the wooden rack and leaned against ie wall. At last her fingers found the edge of the loft floor nd she pulled herself, inch by inch, up into the hay. The limb hadn't been that difficult, a fact that made her be- eve the man who struck her intended that she'd never wake p.

In the loft, the smoke was beginning to curl in small wisps om the feed room. The drop was fifteen feet to the dirt oor, but there was no choice. Crouching, the better to ab- orb the shock of landing, she dropped over the edge and to the hallway of the barn.

Ronnie didn't wait to see if she was hurt. As soon as her et touched the ground, she was off and running to the ouse.

"Ann! Wake up! Someone's set the barn on fire!"

Ann came out of her room already half dressed. She fin- hed pulling on her boots at the door, her face white and nse. "Call the fire department!" she yelled as she dashed utside.

The blackness of the night was fractured by the wild range blaze springing from the roof of the stallion barn as onnie watched, telephone in her hand. A sleep-muffled ice finally answered.

"There's a fire at Dancing Water Ranch," Ronnie said, calmly as she could. The words themselves were angry ings of panic. "Please hurry!" she begged.

Ann was nowhere in sight, and Ronnie knew she must be side the building, trying to rescue Easy Dancer.

Flames leaped across the roof in a mad ritualistic dance. he sound of the fire was terrifying, but Ronnie forced rself to remain calm. If Ann was in the barn, she had to

get inside and help. Easy Dancer was Ann's dream, an
Ronnie knew she would risk her life to try and save the stal
lion.

Running to the side door, she slipped into the smoke-fille
barn. Its stout timbers looked solid, but she didn't wast
time trying to ascertain their sturdiness.

In the glow of the fire, she saw Ann in the stallion's sta
trying to catch the frightened animal's halter. Easy Dance
rose on his hind legs and pawed the air, striking at the flame
induced shadows that danced across his stall.

"Come on fella," Ann coaxed. "Come on." There wa
desperation in her voice.

Ronnie grabbed a lead rope from the side of the barn an
walked slowly to the stall door. Wordlessly she entered
holding the hook at the ready. Ann's hand shot quickly t
the stallion's head. This time she caught the nylon halter. H
reared, but she held on and Ronnie, too, grabbed the ha
ter. Together, they held long enough to get the lead snapped

"Give me your shirt," Ann ordered, and Ronnie tore ot
the warm flannel and handed it over. With a quick lunge
Ann wrapped the shirt over the stallion's eyes and held it.

"I've only seen this in movies, and I hope to God
works," she said as she motioned for Ronnie to throw ope
the stall door.

The frightened stallion danced and tossed his head, bu
Ann kept a firm grip, easing him steadily toward the ope
doorway. Flames had darted to the rafters overhead, an
Ronnie held her breath as she walked on the other side of th
horse. They were ten feet from the door when a loud crac
signaled that the overhead timbers were giving.

"Run!" Ann commanded, and together they trotted th
stallion out of the barn.

The air was freezing, so as soon as they were clear, An
untied the shirt and tossed it back at Ronnie.

"You'll catch your death," she said, trying for a grim humor that only confirmed her nervous exhaustion.

"Is he hurt?" Ronnie asked, running her eyes over the horse.

"Not burned. I don't know about smoke," Ann replied, trying to keep the tremor out of her voice. "Thanks for coming. Not many people would have walked into a burning barn to save an animal."

"I came after you," Ronnie said dryly. "I knew you wouldn't leave without that horse."

The sound of the fire trucks echoed dimly in the night. Ann walked Easy Dancer slowly in circles, her practiced eye making sure that nothing was amiss.

"I'll get us some coats," Ronnie said. "Were there any other horses . . . ?"

"No," Ann said. "I only kept Easy in the stallion barn. But the office, all of my papers and records. I hope the safe doesn't melt."

"They'll put it out," Ronnie said as the fire trucks pulled into the yard. Her teeth chattering from the combination of fear and cold, Ronnie hurried to the side of the barn and grasped the big dog. A fireman hurried to her side, helping her lift Shasta away from the now hot flames.

"Are you hurt?" The fireman wiped a drop of blood from her cheek.

"No," she whispered. "I just hit my head." Shasta made movements of recovery on the ground.

"Bad fire," the man said slowly, shaking his head. "If it wasn't the hay, then it was set."

"Deliberately set." Spoken aloud, the words were the vilest thing she'd ever said.

"Ann's lucky she caught the fire so soon. Another ten minutes and the whole thing would have been gone."

The sound of high pressure water hitting the roof took the fireman back to his job. Hugging her arms, Ronnie watched the jets of water fight the flames. Another ten minutes. She bent down to help Shasta rise shakily to her feet. The man who'd hit her had said something, but she couldn't remember exactly what it was. He'd known she was a reporter, made several references to her nosiness. Rubbing her smarting head, Ronnie was mesmerized by the fire. Another ten minutes. The phrase echoed again and again. "A present from the senator." The words came back unbidden. Ronnie turned away from the sight of the fire and went into the house for coats. She knew if she stopped moving, she'd collapse completely. Who so wanted her dead that he'd burn down the barn? And why? The only man who could possibly know the answer to that was Jeff.

Chapter Twelve

For a long moment, Jeff stood in the small parking lot looking across the highway at the blue water of the sound and the white strip of empty sand. The day was sunny and bright, a perfect afternoon for sailing with a warm coat and a drop of brandy. But he turned from the beach, his eyes hard and angry, and searched the highway in both directions. The traffic was slow, leisurely. There was no sign of the car he sought and he turned to the weathered wooden door in front of the small, dark building. Jeff entered the gloomy bar and went to the end of the counter. There was no other customer in sight.

"Bourbon and water," he ordered absently.

"Lucky for you this is a resort," the bartender said, grinning. "It's the off-season—" he nodded toward the empty room "—but no matter. It's still resort hours, even on Sunday."

Jeff didn't reply. His eyes were riveted on the door. The smell of smoke still clung to his flannel shirt and down jacket. When the college-age bartender placed the drink in front of him, he closed his fingers around it, but made no attempt to drink. Leaning one elbow on top of the bar, he waited.

"Something wrong with your drink?" the barkeep asked. He draped his towel over his shoulder and leaned across the bar toward Jeff. "It's hard to mess up bourbon and water."

"The drink is fine," Jeff said, but his eyes never left the door. "I'm waiting for someone."

"Yeah, that's the life. Most of the guys who come in here are waiting for someone. Course she don't usually show up." He laughed, and slapped the bar with his palm.

Without a word, Jeff took his drink over to a table in the far corner. The lighting was even dimmer, but the rigid outline of his jaw was still evident. His blue eyes were almost black with anger.

Five minutes passed, and Jeff finally sipped his drink. There was a small circle of water on the table and he brushed it away with his hand. When the door opened, he gave no signal of interest. But in the darkness of the room, his eyes bored into the heavyset man who slowly came over to his table and sat down.

"What'll it be?" the bartender asked.

"Budweiser," Carlisle said, easing himself into a chair opposite Jeff. A cloud of smoke from a neat cigar circled his head.

No other words were spoken until the beer was served and the bartender had gone back to his post.

"I'm finished," Jeff said very softly.

"Too late for that now," the other man said just as softly. "There was a time to pull out, but that was before you got in this deep."

"Listen, Carlisle, you've broken more promises to me than you've kept. I don't owe you anything." Jeff spat out the words.

"You haven't been so damn careful yourself," Carlisle said, lunging forward in his chair and reaching both big hands across the table at Jeff. "Where's that reporter?"

"On her way home!" Jeff said quickly. "I couldn't keep her here any longer. Not after everything that happened." No matter how hard he tried, he'd never erase the memory of the complete lack of emotion in Ronnie's face. Beneath her carefully composed mask of professionalism lay anger, loathing and pain. Ann wept in his arms at the terror of the fire, but Ronnie had stood her distance, watching with a disbelief that mirrored his own worst fears.

"We needed her snooping around like we needed a hole in our heads," Carlisle continued angrily. "If Mr. D had any idea some news shark was on you like a shadow, he'd pull out of this...."

"You could have killed her!" Jeff said, barely able to control his temper. "What if the horse had hit the fence! You're stupid, Carlisle. And then the barn fire! I thought you were watching her. I never objected to taking the money. I thought it would be worth the risk. Now, though, things have changed."

"Nothing has changed," Carlisle insisted. "Nothing except your nerve. And don't forget, I have a lot at stake in this too. It isn't just your little game. I wanted to scare her off, but it was your friend who set the fire. Just remember that!"

Jeff moved slowly, but with precision. His hands were at Carlisle's throat before the other man even knew what was happening.

"I don't believe that! In fact, I'm getting to the point where I don't believe anything you say. You promised me Ann wouldn't get pulled into this. When I agreed to use her to get Ronnie down here, you swore to me that she wouldn't get drawn into this. My God, man! Both of them were almost killed.''

"It's not my fault neither of them has common sense," the other man retorted contemptuously. "Anyway, you heard the fire report. There was plenty of time for her to get out. The barn wasn't even destroyed." He rubbed his hands together, grimacing slightly.

"I thought you were a professional," Jeff said coldly.

"It doesn't matter a damn what you think," Carlisle said evenly. "The woman is okay and that reporter is still on the loose. Now she's the one I'm worried about. Whatever possessed you to pay the insurance on that barn?" Carlisle asked, a sudden smile tightening the corners of his mouth. He brushed a lock of black hair from his forehead.

Jeff almost started, and let his hands fall to the table. "She needed the money. She'd have lost the farm without the premium. I didn't give her the money, I loaned it to her. She'll repay me."

"That might wash with the Goody Two Shoes, but it looks as suspicious as hell," Carlisle said, but he was not displeased. "Did Neil Brenton know about the insurance?"

Jeff paused a moment. "At one time, I shared almost everything with Neil. Why?" Something changed in Jeff's face. The anger was slowly defusing as a deep sadness settled into the lines beside his mouth.

"Think about it," Carlisle said. "I'd call it a professional frame."

"I didn't come here to listen to you allude to plans and designs," Jeff said. His voice was weighted with weariness. "I was serious when I said I wanted out. Someone is going to get hurt, and I don't want that responsibility."

"If you pull out, several people will get hurt," Carlisle said softly. "Things haven't gone exactly as planned, but so

r no one has really been harmed. Things are okay. There's
o real damage done. If you pull out, several people will
e."

The words hit him like bullets, and Jeff listened to them
ithout changing expression.

"You have to make that warehouse meeting Tuesday
ght," Carlisle said. "Without the money, we have abso-
tely nothing. Just do that, and then get out. Whatever
appens from there, it'll be fine. But you make the contact,
ey'll give you the money. That's all I really need. Then I'll
e gone out of your life forever."

Jeff swallowed and clenched his jaw again. "Okay, Car-
le, but if anything else happens, I won't be a part of this
y longer. Involving and jeopardizing innocent people isn't
actly my idea of how this should be handled."

"Maybe someone should call the cops?" Carlisle sug-
sted, grinning from ear to ear. "But that's even too late.
our old buddy Neil Brenton is trying to pin the rap on you.
e called the FBI."

Jeff recoiled at the sight of the other man's gleeful
pression.

"Neil reported me to the FBI?" Jeff asked incredu-
usly.

"That's right. Now that's the pot calling the kettle black
I've ever seen it." Carlisle laughed. "I just wanted to
epare you for the news before you got back to Jackson. I
n't know how public the facts will be, but you should be
epared to make a statement that refutes all of his accusa-
ons."

"This had better work," Jeff said, rising slowly. "Neil
ed to be a good man. Just remember that." He walked out
the bar, leaving his drink and a five-dollar bill on the ta-
etop.

"Hey!" Carlisle called after him. "Better keep Lois Lan
out of our hair for the next two days or she's liable to fin
that a little scare is nothing compared to what could hap
pen to her. That's a warning, not a threat, Senator. Deluck
plays for keeps."

RONNIE HELD THE TELEPHONE tightly to her ear. Wher
ever she closed her eyes she was confronted with a sicker
ing montage of flames and Easy Dancer rearing, Ann'
white and worried face—and Jeff's angry and accusing eyes
As she waited for Kurt to resume the call, she reached up t
touch the cut on her head, shutting her eyes against the tear
that threatened to escape. For reasons she didn't even ur
derstand, she hadn't reported the attack on her to anyone

"I got a printout of the conversation," Kurt said. "Wan
to hear it word for word?"

"Yes," Ronnie said quietly. "When did he call?"

"Neil made the call this afternoon, to my house," Kur
said. "He said he'd been looking for you but couldn't fin
you." There was a question hanging at the end of the ser
tence, but Ronnie ignored it.

"Read me the transcript," she said. "It's a good thin
you got the conversation recorded."

"I won't give you the whole thing, but here's the pas
sage. 'I never would have believed that Jeff was involved i
taking a payoff, but now I don't know what to think. M
men have been searching for any other possibility, but ther
doesn't seem to be one. And now this business about th
barn fire and the fact that Jeff paid the insurance. It's to
much to ignore, although I'm pursuing one other angle.' "

"Okay," Ronnie said. "So Neil Brenton thinks that Je
is behind the fire and the scheme to kill the horse racin
bill."

"Brenton has some tip that the payoff money is coming real soon," Kurt said. "What's your reading of all this?"

This was the question Ronnie had been dreading to hear, the question she'd fought with herself not to consider. Sally Duvall's words still made her heart constrict, but they were true. No one else but Jeff and Ann knew she was at the horse ranch. "How could Jeff benefit from killing the bill he created and introduced?" she asked. "I'm not really clear how this would help him."

"Brenton figures that Jeff initiated the bill to gain a populist base of support when he campaigns for higher office. Then he engineered an almost assured passage, but sold out to someone with interest in other tracks. Now he has the popular support and the money for a national campaign." Kurt was talking around the stubby old pipe that was a part of his working life, and Ronnie felt a twinge of longing for a cigarette. She reached in the desk drawer and found a portion of a chocolate bar. Breaking off a small piece, she put it in her mouth.

"Why would someone from another track want to kill the Mississippi track?" Ronnie asked.

"Clean tracks can be a problem, especially if it's a track that won't come into line. Races can't be fixed, horses can't be pulled up. It makes gambling a real, serious gamble," Kurt said, laughing at his pun.

"Do you have a fix on who's supplying the money?"

Kurt paused and Ronnie could easily imagine him chewing the stem of his pipe as he shifted the phone from hand to hand, trying to decide what to tell her.

"There's this guy, big into gambling. Johnny Deluchi. Brenton thinks he's the man behind the deal. He's a real heavy. Has a private gaming club in Vegas with all of the amenities, even personal keys, private stock wine, tobacco, women and horses. All first-class, except for the clientele."

"Deluchi," Ronnie whispered. "Chicago, Miami, tha Deluchi." The man had connections everywhere. Was possible he was involved in a potential horse track in Mi sissippi?

"None other. It's sort of crazy, I know, but these guys lik to protect their business interests, and they have the mone to pay to make sure that it happens like they want it."

"Yeah," Ronnie said tonelessly. "By the way, I'm ge ting ready to send up the story on that barn fire."

"Eyewitness account," Kurt said proudly.

"That's right," Ronnie answered, trying to hide th grimness in her voice. She'd almost been an eyewitness t death.

"Did you know Stuart paid the insurance on Tate barn?" Kurt asked suddenly.

Ronnie hesitated. She'd promised Ann, but after the fir and everything else that had happened, there seemed to b no point in keeping this secret. "Ann told me that before th fire. She said Jeff had helped her out when she needed th premium, and in return she'd promised him a foal. Jeff ever mentioned the foal." She saw him in the barn, brush in han as he groomed Easy Dancer's glistening hide. He couldn' have started the fire. It was impossible that he would bur to death something he cared for as much as that horse. No to mention Ann. And herself? Once again her fingers fe for, and found, the cut on her head.

"That's odd," Kurt said thoughtfully. "He's either a foo or extremely arrogant. A man doesn't call attention to th fact he holds the insurance on something he intends to se fire to."

Ronnie lowered her head and rubbed the bridge of he nose with her fingers. "Jeff didn't tell me, Ann did."

"You never told me what your reading on all of this is," Kurt said. "And how did you happen to be at that farm overnight?"

"I'm not sure about the first point, and it's too long a story to go into on the second. I have to write up the barn fire and get it turned in to this slave-driving editor before tomorrow's deadline," Ronnie said quickly. "I'll tell you more when I have time."

"Okay," Kurt agreed reluctantly. "But I'm interested in your opinion. You know you have the best intuition in the business. Send up the story and give me a call when you get a break."

"Fine," Ronnie said, replacing the receiver and pinching her nose to relieve the headache that suddenly sprang upon her.

Her house was too silent. She stood, walked to the windows and looked out at the sunny Sunday afternoon that was getting ready to fade into dusk. Her car was parked in the drive, good as new with Earl's repairs. Funny, she didn't even remember the long drive back to Jackson. She'd left the farm in a state of total shock, sickened by the sight of the ravaged barn, by the thought of what could have happened.

Ann had bucked up like a real trouper after one teary scene with Jeff. It was that scene more than anything that had driven her back to Jackson. She couldn't stand the sight of Ann relying on Jeff, taking comfort from him when there was a very good possibility that Jeff had sent someone out to the barn with gasoline and matches. If only she'd been able to get a glimpse of her attacker. If only all the evidence didn't point to Jeff.

"No," she said sharply, walking away from the window. "That can't be." Kurt had told her to trust her intuition. She always had before, but this time, her feelings for Jeff were clouding her ability to analyze the facts. No matter how hard she tried, she could not picture Jeff as the man who would destroy Ann's barn. And no matter how hard she tried, she couldn't ignore the growing evidence that he was involved in something far beyond legislative duties. Even his best friend, Neil Brenton, had called a newspaper editor and confessed his suspicions. Brenton, who'd tried to warn her at the party. She sighed and hurried to the phone. He was the man she needed to talk with. Maybe he could help straighten out the tangle of her thoughts.

"I'm sorry to disturb you on a Sunday afternoon," she said as soon as he came to the phone. "I was wondering if might come to talk with you, in a couple of hours maybe."

"It's about Jeff, isn't it?" he asked. His voice sounded old.

"Yes," she replied.

"I suppose it's unavoidable," Brenton said quietly. "I have something for you, some information that you'll find useful. Jeff's financial statements. Before I release them to other members of the press, you might want to take a look. I'm not playing favorites, but I know you have more than a professional interest in Jeff. I want you to be prepared."

Ronnie's heart pulsed. Brenton's tone of voice was ominous. There had been the faintest hope that the attorney general might be able to throw some light on Jeff's behavior, another reason for the suspicious events that seemed to mark him as a criminal. The tone of voice he was using, though, was one of utter disillusionment.

"Would six o'clock be a good time?" she asked.

"Yes." He paused. "Veronica, I'm sorry about all of it."

Ronnie replaced the receiver and forced herself back to the computer on her desk to finish writing the story about the barn fire. With each sentence, the horror returned, and only sheer determination and necessity saw her to the end

When the last paragraph had been sent to her paper, she leaned back, exhausted.

The computer screen was blissfully blank. She had almost two hours before she had to be at Brenton's, and she wanted to be strong, calm and professional. That was going to take all of the inner strength she had left.

There was a short knock on the front door. She got up slowly, dreading the interruption. Probably the paperboy collecting, she thought, something of that nature. She sighed.

When Jeff Stuart filled the doorway, the acid odor of smoke still clinging to his clothes, her body automatically reacted by stepping back.

"I have to see you," he said, lingering in the doorway and looking around to make sure no one else was on the street. "May I come in?"

Ronnie nodded, stepping back even farther to allow him to enter. "What do you want?" she asked.

As he walked into the house, his gaze never left her face. "I had to see you, Ronnie. One more time."

The words struck her with fear. *One more time.*

"A drink?" she asked, playing for time to gather her wits. Had he really tried to kill her?

"Yes," he said slowly. "You're afraid of me, aren't you?" He reached a hand out to touch her, and she pulled back once more. "You don't even have to answer. That told me enough."

He looked away from her around the room. "You've almost gotten unpacked," he commented.

Ronnie's hands shook slightly as she poured the bourbon over ice. Instead of handing it to him, she placed it on the table in front of the sofa. After he took a seat, she curled into a chair opposite him. Looking at him was difficult enough. If she sat near him, would she be able to control her emotions? His face was chapped from the cold wind, the hours of talking with the firemen, comforting Ann and hunting for clues. She felt the tears behind her eyes and tried to look away, but his face was haunted by fatigue and something else. He looked positively driven, and his eyes searched hers for some reaction. She knew the feel of his skin against hers, the clean smell of his cologne, now hidden by the acrid odor of smoke.

"What do you want, Jeff?" she asked softly.

"What happened last night?" he asked. "Ann wasn't in any condition to be coherent, and I had to get back here." He noticed the cut on her head and started. "What happened to your head?"

"I think you're the man who could answer that question better than me." Accusation was in her voice, if not her words.

"I got there after the fire. Did you see anyone, anything odd?"

"That's a strange question. Remember, I'd never been to the ranch before. How would I know what was odd or not? I do find it a little strange that someone tried to run me down, and then that Ann's barn was burned." As she spoke her anger returned, helping her keep her back straight and her voice level. Was Jeff's surprise at her cut real? It seemed to be, but he could be pretending.

"Ronnie," Jeff said softly. "Things are happening that shouldn't. I shouldn't even be here now."

"Then why are you here?" she asked.

"You have to leave the state, just for a day or two."

"Leave?" Ronnie asked, amazement in her voice. "You want me to leave? Have you forgotten that I'm down here to work? This isn't a lark, a vacation that I can cancel on a whim." The night of panic, the fear and pain combined to make her furious. She stood, hands on hips as she glared down at him. "What makes you think you can tell me to leave?"

Jeff stood, too, slowly rising to his feet. Each confronted the other, only a yard apart. "You have to leave, because I'm telling you that it's important."

"Forget it, Jeff," she said bluntly. "I have a job to do." She turned away, unable to bear any longer the deep gaze of his eyes that stirred her, no matter how wrong things were. She didn't understand why he wanted her to leave, but she could no longer trust his motives.

His hand was on her wrist, holding with a gentle pressure. "Ronnie, please, this isn't a game. I wouldn't ask it if it weren't important."

She tried to tug free, but he held her securely. "Let me go, Jeff, and forget it. I'm not leaving. Not until my job is finished."

The force he used to pull her to him was sudden and sharp. She stumbled awkwardly against his chest, but he clasped her back with both hands, holding her safely.

"Look at me," he said softly, his breath warm against her temple as she held herself aloof.

"Let me go," she repeated, keeping her voice as calm as possible.

"Remember our first evening in Magnolia Point?" Jeff said. The tenderness of his kiss was in his voice, caressing her.

Those were exactly the moments she didn't need to remember.

"Yes," she forced herself to say coldly. "As I recall, that was the only moment my life wasn't in danger the whole time I was your reluctant guest."

Instead of relaxing his grip, he tightened his arms around her. "I know what you think," he said, loosening one hand long enough to turn her face to his. "Now look at me."

There was no escaping his hand. Her eyes found his, and she saw the clear depths of the sea, the same look of passion and caring that she remembered from the dusky evening among the magnolia trees on his estate. His lips touched hers softly. Against all her better judgment, Ronnie did not struggle. The sensations he created in her were too strong. This man could not hurt a friend.

"I couldn't stand the way you looked at me at Ann's," he said, drawing back an inch or two so that he was whispering against the soft skin of her cheek. "You acted as if you thought I was somehow responsible."

"Who is responsible, Jeff?" she asked, and there was no demand, only a desperate need to know.

"Mississippi isn't safe for you," he said, nuzzling her cheek with his lips. "Two days is all I'm asking. Leave for two days." His lips returned to hers, and this kiss was more demanding.

His body against hers was hard, strange yet terribly familiar. Ronnie responded to his kiss with all the turmoil of emotion that had tormented her since she first arrived in Jackson. Everything was confused, and the only certainty was her feeling for Jeff. She'd tried to deny it, tried to kill it, but the fact was that she was falling in love with him.

Gently he moved her to the sofa so that she rested against the strength of his chest. His hand stroked her hair, comforting her, stopping at the cut.

"What happened?"

The terrible story poured from her as Jeff's arms held her safe. When she finished, his face was etched with deep sadness.

"You didn't tell anyone, because you knew that a charge of attempted murder would get me arrested. With arson, I'd have time . . . to clear myself."

Ronnie nodded. "I still don't know what I believe."

His eyes narrowed with pain, and Ronnie couldn't stop herself from reaching up to stroke his face. The skin was rough with a faint stubble of beard because he'd had no time to shave.

"I sent a story about the barn fire, about the insurance," she said, watching him closely.

Surprise registered in his face, but not the anger she had dreaded.

"The business with the insurance will look bad."

"Ann asked me not to mention it, and I wasn't going to. But then someone called Kurt and told him. He knew about it before I even wrote the story."

"Kurt Chambliss?" Jeff asked. "He used to be editor down at the *Sentinel* during the sixties. The paper went downhill when he left."

"That's my boss," Ronnie said, surprised that Jeff knew something of the newspaper's history. "How did you know?"

"Neil used to talk about him a lot. It seems that Kurt was Neil's only supporter during some of those times, the protests, the marches. Neil wasn't a popular man when he upheld civil rights, and Kurt wasn't a popular editor."

"I know," Ronnie said. She was interested in the history, but far more interested in the anguish that filled Jeff's voice at each mention of Neil's name.

"Neil Brenton called Kurt and told him about the insurance," she said softly. The reaction was expected. Now Jeff turned away to hide his hurt. "I thought he was your friend."

"We go back a long way," Jeff said. "Neil taught me a great deal, about politics and life. I hope to return the favor."

"Why is he trying to hurt you now?" Ronnie asked. She was onto something, something important. Her suspicions that Jeff might be protecting Neil were right.

Jeff leveled a direct gaze at her. "Neil may be in trouble," he said softly. "I can't say any more, but you have to be careful around him. Stay away from him, Ronnie. Promise me. Stay away from Neil, or you might regret the consequences."

Chapter Thirteen

Neil Brenton answered the doorbell after the first ring. Quickly he drew Ronnie inside and shut the door.

"Would you care for something to eat?" he asked as he led her into a book-lined den with a nice fire. "Martha left plenty of ham and potato salad before she took off," he said.

"No, thank you. Mrs. Brenton is out?" Ronnie asked quickly. Jeff's dire warning made her nervous about every little detail.

"Yes. Under the circumstances I felt it might be better if she were out of town," Neil said. The phrase echoed in Ronnie's mind. Out of town. Safe.

"What circumstances?" she asked, settling into the wing chair beside her host.

Brenton's brown eyes were as assessing as they'd ever been. He coolly took in her face, the nervousness in her hands as she fumbled for her notebook and pen.

"Someone is trying to frame me," he said.

His words were shocking. Ronnie stopped in the act of opening her notebook and looked at him. There was no jest in his face, no humor in his gaze.

"Frame you for what?" she asked.

"Payoffs, bribery, even worse. Attempted murder, arson." He gave the list as if he were ordering groceries, without any hint of emotion.

The list matched Ronnie's experience. The coincidence was too close for comfort. Neil Brenton was the attorney general, but how much did he know from his investigation, and how much because he was behind it all? She looked down at her notebook to hide the thoughts she feared were too transparent on her face.

"Who would try and frame you for such things, and why?" she asked in her best professional voice. When she raised her eyes to his, she was confident and calm.

"Jefferson Stuart."

His reply blew away her veneer of confidence. She started forward, then forced herself to remain seated. "Jeff?" she asked.

"I know," Brenton said. "The thought has driven me crazy for the past week, but there's no way around it. No one else could know the things he knows, do the things that have happened." He put his hand over his face to shield his emotions from her.

"What are you talking about?" Ronnie asked. Her heart was thudding, and she thought of Jeff's accusation. Both men were pointing the finger at each other. Which one was innocent?

The attorney general stood, lighting a cigarette with deft, graceful gestures. "The night of the party—the random shooting—I was responsible for that," he said. "I know it was illegal, but I was making one last desperate attempt to save a man I've considered a son. I thought I could frighten Jeff away from the men he'd started getting involved with. I know Johnny Deluchi, perhaps better than anyone would ever want to. Jeff's a brilliant man, but he isn't cunning like

Deluchi. Jeff wouldn't last ten minutes against that man. I was only trying to warn him."

"And my purse?" Ronnie asked, still struggling to accept the fact that a state official had just confessed to a crime.

"What purse?" Brenton countered.

"The one that was thrown down into the garden to tie me to the gunshots."

Her host's face was a convincing blank. "We had nothing to do with that. It was never reported."

"That's true," Ronnie said.

"I begged Jeff to let this horse racing thing drop," Neil Brenton hurried on. "But he won't. And now this!" He took a folder from the mantel and brought it to Ronnie. Before he handed it to her, he said; "I called you because of your boss. Kurt earned my respect years ago, and whatever your personal involvement with Jeff, you wouldn't work for Kurt if you weren't the best damn reporter around." He dropped the manila folder into her hands.

She opened the folder and quickly scanned the front page. Somehow, the news wasn't as big a shock as she'd first thought it would be. There, in neat columns and rows, was a red river of capital deficits that led directly to the Mississippi Sound and Magnolia Point. Jeff was in over his head, way over his head.

"How did this happen?" she asked.

"The only thing I can figure is gambling," Brenton said. "I've known Jeff all his life, and I never knew he had such a problem. He's certainly covered it well, except here—" he nodded at the financial statement "—where no amount of acting can hide the truth."

"Where did you get this information?" Ronnie asked, closing the folder carefully. On the drive to Dancing Water Ranch, Jeff had mentioned a small interest in gambling.

He'd emphasized that he wasn't lucky. But he'd also pointed out that he wasn't a gambler. She tried to recall his exact words. Something about losing a little money but not mortgaging the farm. The folder in her hand showed the exact opposite. Unless Jeff came up with some money fast, he would lose Magnolia Point, the exact horrible scenario Stella had mentioned to her.

Brenton returned to his cigarette, thumping the ash nervously into an enameled ashtray. "This was left by the FBI this afternoon when I got back from taking Martha to the airport. It confirms all of my suspicions, and now I'm going to have to act."

"By doing what? Arresting Jeff?"

"Not yet," the attorney general said. "The fact that he's in debt isn't criminal. But I'll be ready when he makes his move."

"Move for what?" Ronnie pressed.

"My bet is that Jeff will kill the horse racing bill," Neil Brenton said. "Kill it and take a quick payoff. There could be a handsome profit in such a move, enough to clear up his debts and finance a campaign for the U.S. Senate."

"That's only speculation," Ronnie said. She rose from her chair and paced the room. "As you said, debt isn't a criminal act. The rest is simply coincidence and guessing." She fought her own doubts as much as Neil Brenton's accusations. If this man, Jeff's lifelong friend, believed him capable of illegal behavior, how could she fail to see his guilt? Was she blinded by a few kisses, a few looks into his eyes?

"He's guilty," Brenton said, his voice cold and unforgiving. "He's damn guilty, and he's trying to frame me to take the heat off him."

"Frame you?" Ronnie asked.

He smiled, but the curve of his lips didn't match the coldness of his eyes. "When it happens, don't say I didn't warn you."

"Before I do anything with these figures," Ronnie said, "can your office confirm them?"

"By Wednesday," the attorney general said. "I was going to caution you to hang on to them until then. It'll take some checking, but we should have it straight by then. We're checking one other possibility, but it's a long shot."

"I'll give you a call Wednesday afternoon," Ronnie said.

"The session starts tomorrow," her host said. "If I'm right, and I know I am, things should begin to heat up quickly. Jeff's debts, as you can see, are pressing. If he takes money for killing the bill, he's going to have to do it soon. Let me get an envelope for that material," he said, walking out of the room.

"Thank you," Ronnie replied. As soon as he was gone, she turned her attention back to the ashtray. A small piece of gold paper had caught her eye, and she plucked it from the ashes. Her fingers quickly unrolled the crumpled paper to reveal a familiar design, a horse's head with the inscription, Mr. D's. "I'll bet you know Johnny Deluchi," she whispered to herself, stashing the paper in her purse before Neil Brenton returned.

"Thanks for coming," he said, walking her to the door. "I'm sorry to have to tell you this. I think you, too, care a great deal for Jeff."

"Yes," she said, keeping her voice flat. Unable to meet his eyes, she hurried down the steps to her car and drove straight to Sally's.

It took Ronnie three hours to fill Sally in on the past three days, but when she left for home, still nothing was resolved.

Monday morning, she went to the Capitol and spent the day learning new faces, committees and the flurry of legislative work that made every new assignment a nightmare. Though she watched carefully, there was no sign of Jeff. Her story about the barn fire had created a sensation in the local media, and by the end of the day, she was too exhausted to even stop for a drink with Sally. She went straight home to bed.

Tuesday was the same, work and hurry. Jeff made a brief appearance in the Senate, but the barrage of reporters asking him questions prevented her from catching his eye. He made no effort to see her or call. Ronnie watched from the background, and hoped that he would search for her. But he didn't, and she just had to talk with him. She'd left a dozen messages at his office and on his answering machine.

"Go on home," Sally said gently, slipping to her side. "Get some rest and I'll see you Wednesday morning. There's really nothing else to be done here today."

Ronnie left the pressroom feeling a hundred years old. She stopped by the attorney general's office, but he was gone for the day. On an impulse, she stopped at Jeff's office, but Margaret, his young secretary, said he, too, had left. As she drove home, a small determined thought was growing in Ronnie's mind.

All through dinner and several vain attempts to relax with a book or watch television, the need to see Jeff grew. Again she flipped through the folder Neil Brenton had given her. The debts were staggering. Her mind checked off the events that had happened, the accusations Brenton had made against Jeff.

At last she closed the folder and threw on a pair of jeans and a dark, heavy sweater. She'd made up her mind to confront Jeff with this evidence and the tiny pieces of foil, the one from Jeff's house, and the one from Neil's. It wasn't the

)est journalistic move, but then she had a lot more than a
story riding on the outcome. She checked her watch, know-
ng it was late, but that didn't matter now. If Jeff was asleep,
hen he could damn well wake up and answer her ques-
ions. She walked into the night, feeling better that at last
he'd decided on some action.

Her car purred softly as she turned the corner to Jeff's
apartment. Headlights were coming out of the parking lot,
and she slowed as her low beam picked out the shape of
Jeff's truck. He turned in front of her and drove away.
Easing her car into second, she followed, careful to stay
several blocks behind him. The traffic was sparse, and she
allowed him to lead her back downtown, past the Capitol
and toward the old business section, toward the small café
and the alley where she and Sally had lost him the week before. With each passing block, she felt her fear grow. There
was no time to stop and call Sally or anyone else. If she
hesitated, she'd lose sight of him. That was the one thing she
couldn't afford to do.

Jeff's truck pulled into the alley, and Ronnie parked down
the street. She held her breath, hoping that there was some
logical explanation for what was happening right in front of
her eyes. She cut her lights and ducked as low in her seat as
she could.

N THE DARKENED WAREHOUSE, Jeff tried to get his bear-
ngs. Every noise seemed to echo against the metal walls, as
f the building rejected each sound again and again. Now
hat he was inside and the moment was upon him, he felt no
ear. He was perfectly calm. Either months of preparation
and groundwork would pay off tonight, or he would be
ruined, possibly dead.

He looked at his watch, exactly one minute until midnight. The dim glow of the dial was reassuring. He dropped

his hands, leaving them free of his pockets so that no gesture could be misinterpreted. When the warehouse door groaned open, he took a deep breath and relaxed. As the high beam of the armored Mercedes hit his face, he was smiling confidently with just the vaguest hint of arrogance.

The car came to a stop and the warehouse door was pushed shut by some unknown person. Jeff walked casually to the car. Above the door handle was embossed a gold horse's head. A black window came down and a voice from deep within the recesses of the car said, "So, Senator, even the most idealistic men have their price." There was a low chuckle.

"I've always heard that everyone has their price; some are just higher than others," Jeff replied, laughing also.

"Then let's get down to business and talk money. For a small favor, I'm prepared to offer you half a million. Surely your debts couldn't exceed that amount?"

"My debts are my business," Jeff said quickly. "But what you're asking me to do is worth much more than that. You see, you are buying an honest man. The price for my soul is much higher." He laughed bitterly. "Surely a soul is worth more than half a million? I'm sure Neil Brenton's cost you more than that!"

The chuckle from inside the car was low and dangerous. "I don't give a damn for your soul, Senator. What I want is action. For half a million all I'm asking you to do is kill one single piece of legislation. We don't want legalized racing here, and we're willing to pay the price. To whoever. This doesn't involve souls. It is a simple piece of business. I was given to understand that you were a businessman, not a theologian." The speaker paused. "If you aren't interested, there are other ways to gain my desires. Some are rather messy, but they are just as effective."

The anger that ran through Jeff was like a current. He wanted to reach into the window and smash the face, feeling the crunch of bone beneath his fist. But he reined in his temper and forced another laugh. "You drive a hard bargain, Deluchi. Let's say three-quarters of a million."

The low laugh came again from the darkened car. "So, you have at last named the price. Now you have lost your soul, whether you take the money or not." The man's laughter was cruel and filled with pleasure. "You will get your money, Senator Stuart, and I will get what I want. My people will be in touch with you to establish the delivery."

The car window came up and the engine cranked. As if by magic, the warehouse door moaned again, opening on the black night. The Mercedes backed out slowly, the lights illuminating Jeff in the dismal emptiness of the warehouse.

RONNIE SLUMPED LOW in the car seat as headlights came out of the alley. She peeked up in time to see the Mercedes again, leaving. She checked her watch. The car had been in there less than five minutes. Jeff had arrived only a few moments before. The car cruised out of sight, and Ronnie was torn between following the Mercedes or waiting for Jeff. The red taillights disappeared, and her decision was made. Jeff's truck came out, taking the same path as the other car. Ronnie started up her car, praying that Jeff would be too preoccupied to notice the headlights following him at a distance.

He drove for several blocks, taking an aimless course that forced Ronnie to use all of her driving skills. When he stopped in front of a small café with a glaring neon sign that flashed an Open All Night guarantee, Ronnie stopped three blocks back. She watched him get out of the truck, his muscular body walking with a tense stance. He entered the diner and didn't come out.

Fifteen, twenty minutes passed, and nothing happened. The night seemed to close down around her, and Ronnie turned on the motor for a little heat.

What could Jeff be doing? Drinking coffee? Reading an early edition newspaper? No. None of that made sense. He could do all of those things at home with a lot more comfort and convenience.

Her questions were answered when another car cruised the block in front of the café. At the dark outline of the big car, Ronnie felt a real chill of fear. Sure, there were thousands of big, dark cars in Jackson, but this one looked familiar. The car drifted down two blocks from the café and the front door swung open. A big, heavyset man stepped out into the street. He looked in both directions and pulled his hat farther down on his head. Even though Ronnie knew the distance was too far for him to see her, she ducked beneath the dash. When she looked up again, he was entering the café.

Another ten minutes elapsed, and Ronnie could stand it no longer. She had two choices. She could drive by the restaurant and try and see what was happening, or she could sneak down the street and chance catching a glimpse through the window. The latter seemed to be the wisest, since she knew Jeff was familiar with her car. She cranked the motor and backed up, finding a darkened alley where she could park and escape detection if either man happened to glance down the street.

She left the car, dodging quickly among the shadows cast by the building fronts, hiding for a moment behind a column to catch her erratic breath. She was almost there. The café was the next building. Dropping to her knees she offered a wordless thanks that the streets were truly deserted and no one had driven by to find her crawling along the sidewalk. When she calculated, she reached the harbor of a small doorway.

Jeff and the heavy man were in a back booth, talking. They appeared angry, upset. The tension in Jeff's face made her chest squeeze shut. What was happening? The heavy man leaned forward and removed his hat. The sight of a thick shock of black hair made her duck down to the pavement again. He wasn't bald! He drove a black car, but he wasn't bald! She'd been mistaken. Relief made her almost weak, and she crawled back to the safety of the other buildings. She'd reached the safety of a small doorway when she heard the café door thrust open. Angry voices spilled into the night.

"I finished my part," Jeff said. "The money will be delivered tomorrow night. Be there, because I'm through."

"You have to make the pickup," the other man said. "You can't back out now, Stuart. This has gone too far."

"I'll make the contact, Carlisle. Don't worry. Then once you have the money in your hands, that's all I need to do, right?"

"Don't you want to be in on the action when your old buddy Brenton takes the fall?" Carlisle taunted.

"No," Jeff said quietly. "Watching Neil ruined won't give me any pleasure at all."

Ronnie heard footsteps coming toward her. They stopped at the truck and Jeff got in, revved the engine angrily and tore away from the curb. There was no sound from the other man, and she held her breath for what seemed like twenty minutes before she risked looking down the street. There was only blackness and night. The neon sign of the café flashed on and off, on and off, but the streets were completely empty, as if she'd imagined the whole scene.

Chapter Fourteen

The newsroom was in a state of complete chaos when Ronnie walked into the Capitol the next morning, half an hour late and dark-eyed from a sleepless night. Jeff had gone home after the meeting with the man in the diner, but it had been too late to confront him. Besides, his meetings with the people in the Mercedes and the man at the diner had put a new complexion on the entire situation. Jeff was involved in something, she just wasn't certain what. The big man had made reference to Neil's fall. Was it a frame? What about the foil wrappers? Brenton smoked, but Jeff didn't. Was one a plant, or had the attorney general left the small wrapper on a visit to Jeff's home? What was Mr. D's? She went into the Senate coffee room and poured a cup of black coffee, but the sight and smell of it made her stomach lurch.

"Where have you been?" Sally said behind her, almost making her jump out of her skin.

"Working," she said.

"What happened to you?" Sally's voice registered alarm. "Is skin and bones some new fashion fad I haven't heard about? And you look like someone slugged you in both eyes. Maybe sleep is passé too?"

"Thanks a million," Ronnie said, trying for a smile. "I've been too busy." She'd looked forward all night to talking with Sally about what she'd seen, but now, in daylight with the Senate humming around her, she was reluctant to begin.

"How long have you been here?" Sally asked, caution adding an edge to her voice.

"Just walked into the pressroom and it looked like five pounds of sugar had been dropped on an anthill. I couldn't take the excitement, so I came down for a cup of coffee." She sipped the hot liquid, forcing herself to keep it down.

"You haven't heard, then?" Sally asked. Her voice had become gentle and worried.

"Heard what?"

"Jeff killed the horse racing bill this morning."

The cup was at her lips, but Ronnie couldn't move. She couldn't swallow and she couldn't put the cup down. Sally took it from her hand and set it on a table, then grasped her elbow.

"Let's get out of here," she said. Several senators were looking in their direction.

"Anything wrong?" one man asked.

"Touch of the flu," Sally said, guiding Ronnie out the door. "She should have stayed home, but you know us reporters, we never quit."

"Don't I know it!" The man laughed. "Our life would be easier if you all took a sick leave and let us conduct the business of this state."

"Dream on," Sally shot back at him, laughing too. "Someone has to protect the public from you guys." Gripping Ronnie's arm, she said, "Keep walking; we're almost here."

They stopped in a foyer outside the Senate chambers and Sally pushed Ronnie onto a bench. "What is wrong with you?" she asked.

"Jeff killed the bill?" Ronnie questioned.

"Just like that!" Sally snapped her fingers. "The whole place is in complete turmoil. I filed a very brief story with Kurt. That should hold him until tomorrow, but I know him, and he's going to want an exclusive interview with Jeff about the hows and whys of this. Can you swing it?"

"Kurt isn't the only one with some unanswered questions," Ronnie said. "And, yes, I can swing it. In fact, the sooner the better." She stood up and started out of the foyer, narrowly missing a large man wearing bifocals who pushed through the door taking up both aisles. In his hurry, the man dropped a briefcase, and papers spilled across the floor.

"Excuse me," Ronnie said automatically. "Let me give you a hand." She bent to pick up the papers.

"Get away from those," the man said, stamping his foot near her fingers. "I know you reporters and your tricks. Get away from my papers."

Torn between amusement and anger, Ronnie stood catching the glint of laughter in Sally's eyes.

"Veronica, this is Senator Homer Fogle. His briefcase is loaded with valuable, secret information."

There was little respect in Sally's voice, and the tone of devilment was the nudge needed to push Ronnie into laughter.

"What's so funny?" the man demanded, straightening up. "You reporters are all over the Capitol, making trouble for us lawmakers. You shouldn't get in the way of our work."

"I'll keep that in mind, Senator," Ronnie said, shaking her head in disbelief at Sally as they escaped the foyer and the angry man.

"What a character," Ronnie said.

"This is politics, my dear. The public will elect anyone."

The short encounter with Fogle was enough to help Ronnie regain her balance. She followed Sally to the snack bar where the older woman forced a Danish on her.

"Not exactly nutrition, but it's better than nothing," Sally commented. "Now let's see what we can find out."

They spent the day hunting for facts, and following leads that took them nowhere. By six o'clock, they were both tired and frustrated, and no closer to what "Mr. D's" could mean. All efforts to find Jeff had also failed.

"Jeff is gone, of course," Sally said. "And Neil Brenton is conveniently 'out of town.' What's a working girl supposed to do?"

"Strike when least expected," Ronnie said, a light growing in her eyes.

"You're going to his house?" Sally asked, her excitement tempered by caution. "Is that smart?"

"The worst he can do is slam the door in my face," Ronnie said. Actually, the worst he could do was look at her with that strange power of his eyes. Why had he killed his own bill? Neil Brenton thought he was guilty of bribery. So did Kurt. And Sally was leaning more in that direction with each passing hour. To judge by the gossip in the pressroom, every reporter in town had changed his or her mind about Jeff Stuart. He'd gone from being the best man in politics to the biggest scoundrel around. And Brenton had yet to release the facts about Jeff's financial status.

But mulishly, Ronnie refused to accept the facts. She'd started once to give Jeff a chance to explain, and she'd wound up chasing him into an alley and an incriminating conversation with another man. Would he simply admit his crime tonight? Or would he explain?

"Oh, Jeff, you've got to tell me the truth," she whispered to herself.

"If you're going out sleuthing tonight, better get some rest first," Sally suggested. "Promise you'll call if any thing goes on?"

"Word of honor," Ronnie said, picking up her things a she started out the door and headed for home.

THE MINUTES SLIPPED AWAY so slowly that Ronnie change clothes three times before it was late enough to leave he house. With a final glance in the mirror, she sighed at he reflection. The black sweater matched her hair and made he face a pale oval surrounded by a silky curtain. With quic motions she deftly repaired her makeup, found her coat an hurried out.

The street was empty, the lights casting undisturbe shadows onto the asphalt. For a moment she paused an took in a breath of the clean, cold air. On a night very sim ilar to this at Magnolia Point, she had begun to fall in lov with Jeff Stuart. The spontaneous intimacy that had devel oped between them was one of the most wonderful thing that had ever happened to her, and now she was shut of from him. Whatever was behind Jeff's decision to kill hi own bill, she wanted to know.

The night was crystal clear as she drove slowly to th Capitol. The small tape recorder she needed was still in he desk at the pressroom office. She'd been in such a hurry she'd forgotten it that afternoon. A tape wasn't evidence but it certainly made it easier for a reporter to get accurat quotes.

At the beginning of the long, tree-lined driveway up to th Capitol parking lot, she suddenly decided to park the ca and walk. The fresh air was exhilarating, and she felt bette than she had in a week. A short walk would be just the thin to completely help shake her feelings of confusion.

Her flat shoes were comfortable, and the brisk feel of the night was both stimulating and calming. As she expected, there were no other cars parked by the large, old building, and she skipped up the steps and into the warmth with a little relief. The night was lovely, but the cold was harsher than she'd expected. She went straight to the third floor and sat down at her typewriter. The tape recorder was in the right-hand drawer, and she tucked it into her purse. Several stories she'd started lay beside the computer, and she looked over them, sighing at the mental state that was affecting her work, her entire life. Checking her watch, she saw that she had time to work before going to Jeff's.

Fifteen minutes later she was half finished. Sally had told her that sometimes the janitors kept a pot of fresh coffee going all night in the Senate chambers. A good cup of coffee would certainly make the rest of the job easier.

An unusual silence filled the Capitol as she stepped outside the pressroom and closed the door on the clacking teletype machine. She leaned over the banister and looked straight down to the first-floor rotunda. The pattern of the tile was beautiful from her vantage point. In fact, there were many beautiful things about the old building. She took her time, wandering along the corridors and taking in the graceful arches and columns that she seldom had time to see. There was a narrow stairway that led down to the second floor, and she took it, taking care not to trip.

On the second floor, she had the strongest temptation to go to Jeff's office, maybe wait there all night until he came in the next morning. She smiled grimly at the thought. Already Margaret, Jeff's secretary, was embarrassed whenever Ronnie appeared at the door. Jeff was obviously avoiding her, and the situation was awkward.

She strolled down to the Senate chamber, eyeing the rows of dark mahogany desks, all empty. In only a few hours, the place would be filled with men and women, each trying to pass new laws or amend old ones. The process was endlessly fascinating.

The coffee room was empty, but she checked each silver urn, shaking them slightly. They were cold to the touch, and she shrugged. Coffee would just have to wait; she had no intention of walking back down the drive to her car and going to a fast-food place. There was one last pot in the corner, a small percolator. To her delight, she found it hot and freshly perked. As the coffee struck the Styrofoam cup, there was a sound of muffled voices in the chambers. She paused, then finished filling her cup. The janitors were obviously back on the job.

JEFF SAT PERFECTLY STILL at his desk. Margaret was many hours gone and the new moon was coasting high overhead. Only one lamp burned, a clear signal on the west side of the Capitol that he was working late. The pile of paperwork at his left hand remained untouched. Occasionally he lifted a sheaf of documents, only to drop them back unread. Every few minutes he looked at his watch, as if painstakingly marking time. At a quarter to midnight, the phone rang.

He answered quickly, gripping the receiver in his strong hand. "Tonight?" he said, lacing his voice with daredevil nonchalance. "Of course that's fine with me. The sooner the better." He laughed slowly. "You have my word, don't you? Isn't that enough?" There was a longer pause as he listened. "I don't think that's such a good idea. The Capitol isn't a good meeting place. Anyone could walk in."

There was another pause as concern gave way to anger on his rugged features. "I have more to lose than you, and I'd like another meeting place." He waited, his knuckles turning white with anger. "If you insist," he said coldly. "When?" He glanced at his watch. "Midnight is perfect, since I'm already here." He replaced the receiver and sat back in his chair, taking a deep breath. There was no time to call Carlisle. Things had suddenly moved into high gear, and he knew he was on his own.

He picked up the telephone and started to dial another number, but replaced the receiver once again. There was too great a possibility that someone was already in the Capitol watching him closely. Johnny Deluchi, the man who had just called, was a very smart character. Too smart to set up a meeting in a public building unless he could make certain of his own safety.

The thought that he was being watched made him nervous. He stood, gathered up the papers on his desk and stacked them neatly before he walked away.

Outside his second-floor office he listened to the sounds of the old building settling. For many years, he'd spent innumerable nights in the Capitol, toiling over bills and compromises. The work had always been hard, but very satisfying. He walked over to the banister and looked down at the rotunda. He could only hope that he'd made the right decision. Maybe he should have gone to Neil, but it was too late now. The ball was rolling.

He checked his watch again, taking a long time to read the distinct numbers. In exactly four minutes, he would walk into the Senate chamber and accept a large amount of money. The Capitol was a safe meeting place if no one stumbled in, but there was little danger of that happening. The corridors had been silent for the past three hours.

When another three minutes had passed, he walked briskly into the Senate anteroom. The post where the sergeant at arms normally stood was vacant. The richly upholstered seats where legislators entertained visitors or gathered for a quick, presession discussion were bare of occupants. There was not a sound or movement to indicate that anyone would ever return. It was as if the Capitol had been put soundly to sleep and he were the only person awake.

As he rounded the door, there was the movement of a shadow at the back of the chamber. The room was darkened, the lights lowered for the night. He couldn't be certain, but instinct told him that his contact waited beneath the huge marble columns that supported the east gallery. Without any hesitation he walked to the back of the room, the sound of his footsteps completely muffled by the carpet.

As he drew near the other man, Jeff saw the large black valise. A calculating smile touched his lips, giving him a cruel and ruthless look. "I hope you have it all," he said slowly.

The other man, a few inches shorter than Jeff and dressed in a dark coat and hat, simply grinned. "Johnny couldn't make it," he said, his hard eyes never leaving Jeff's face. "But he did send a message for you. If you don't come through, you're a dead man. And Johnny always means what he says."

Jeff's smile tightened, but he chuckled softly. "You can tell your boss that I also mean what I say. The bill is dead. Now why don't we see what's in that little black bag of yours and cut out the amiable chatter?"

RONNIE STARTED OUT the door with her coffee, but the low intensity of the voices in the distance aroused her curiosity. She slowed, walking around the corner with only mild interest. It took a moment for her eyes to find the two darkly dressed figures at the back of the Senate chamber. They were almost hidden by the shadows cast by the gallery, both men rigidly confronting each other. Their voices were low, giv-

ıg off a sense of danger. Instinctively, she drew back and
eered around the door.

At first, Jeff's figure was only vaguely familiar. Distance
ınd darkness made it hard for her to distinguish anything
xactly, but as she watched, she recognized his back, the
ɔng, powerful legs. Their voices came to her only as a very
ıerce undertone.

As her eyes adjusted to the dim lighting, she was able to
ıake out a shorter man holding up a large black case. He
ipped the latches and lifted the lid, showing Jeff what was
ıside. Then he closed it and offered the case to Jeff. With
ɔmplete authority, Jeff took the valise and turned on his
eel, striding out of the chamber without a backward
lance. The other man looked around the room and then
:arted walking directly toward her.

There was something in the man's walk, the way he held
is head, that made her certain he was dangerous. Her in-
inct, her ability to sense when people were truthful or not,
ad always been her best tool as a reporter. And now a clear
arning was singing through her veins.

From the shadows on the opposite side of the room, there
as another movement. Ronnie bit her fist when a heavyset
ıan stepped out of the darkness. As he walked past a win-
ow, a streetlight was reflected from his bald head.

"He got the money?" the bald man asked, laughter rip-
ling under his voice. "Won't he be surprised. He sells out
is principles, himself and his state, and then winds up
olding an empty bag." He laughed, and the other man
ɔined in.

"Johnny wants to thank you personally," the first man
ıid.

"He'll have his chance," the bald man answered, "just as
ɔon as we put Senator Stuart to rest. We have to move fast,
ıough, before Stuart finds out who's really employing me."

"Don't worry about Brenton," the other man said. "He'
wedged in this tight. Now you'd better get out of here be
fore somebody spots you."

"Right," the bald man agreed. "I'm glad this is through
Framing a politician isn't all it's cracked up to be." H
started walking directly toward the coffee room.

During the conversation, Ronnie had been frozen to th
spot, but her faculties returned immediately as she pulle
back into the small room. She hurriedly scanned the area fo
a hiding place. There were three shoe-shine chairs that of
fered no protection at all, and a couple of tables she migh
hide under, though there were no tablecloths or anything t
duck behind. She felt her panic building, but she kept con
trol. Off to the right was the door to the men's rest room
Without another thought, she darted inside and went to th
stall at the far end. Barely able to breathe, she quietl
latched the door and waited.

Hours seemed to pass, but she knew it was really onl
seconds. She pressed herself against the wall, feeling th
smooth marble against her sweater. The main door creake
open with sudden force, and she had to stifle the scream tha
rose in her throat. Jeff was somewhere in the Capitol. If sh
could only reach him, he would...what? She thrust th
question aside and tuned her ears to the slightest noise
There was someone in the rest room; footsteps were walk
ing on the tile with a soft, easy stride.

They came toward her, stopping in front of the stall wher
she was hiding. With nowhere to go, Ronnie clenched he
fists and prepared for the worst. The footsteps retreated
going to the end of the room, to the door. She was going t
be okay. They stopped, then started back her way, mor
slowly this time, as if sensing her presence.

Relief quickly gave way to anxiety as the footsteps paused. But after an agonizing moment they started up again and soon the door of the rest room slammed shut.

Squaring her shoulders, Ronnie flung the door open and ran out of the rest room. She had to follow Jeff and find out what was happening.

Never breaking her stride, she pushed the outer door and stepped back into the coffee room. Quickly scanning the chamber, she saw it was completely empty. There was no sign of Jeff, the stranger or the bald man. The whole scene might have taken place only in her mind, yet she knew that less than five minutes before, Jeff had accepted a black valise from some sinister man.

Chapter Fifteen

"Sally, listen," Ronnie commanded. "I haven't got but a minute, but I wanted someone to know what was happening, just in case."

"What in the world are you up to Ronnie? It's two a.m.," Sally answered in a disgruntled voice.

"I'm at home," Ronnie said, "but not for long. I have to get into Jeff's office. Tonight."

"It's only six hours until the place opens. Couldn't i wait?" Sally answered dryly. "What's so important that you think you want to sneak in there at night?"

"I saw something tonight," Ronnie said. Her breathing was short and shallow. She smothered her thoughts about Jeff, the painful throb whenever she considered the question of his guilt, and told Sally everything. "And I was almost caught by the bald man. He was the man at the Dennisons', the man at Jeff's the night I was shot at, and the same man in the black car that tried to run me down when was riding," she concluded.

There was no longer any sign of sleep in Sally's voice "You aren't going into that office, Veronica Sheffield. forbid it. We'll call the police or get a search warrant There's ways to do this."

"No warrant!" Ronnie declared. She took a deep breath. "I don't want the law involved until I can see what is in that valise myself. It's something I have to do."

There was a pause on the other end of the line. "He doesn't sound very innocent to me, not since he killed his own racing bill this morning. You know it sounds like a payoff."

"I know," Ronnie said. But no matter how it looked, something in her held back from accepting Jeff's actions at face value. "Isn't it possible Jeff could resubmit the bill?"

"It's possible, but unlikely," Sally said. "Look. I've admired Jeff Stuart for as many years as he's been in office. This is hard for me to believe, too. But we'd better call the police and let the law decide right or wrong. That's the sensible thing."

"I'm afraid I can't be sensible about Jeff," Ronnie said, at last admitting her feelings. "Don't worry about me."

"Sure. When pigs can fly I'll quit worrying," Sally remarked. "If you get caught, don't call me for bond money until after eight. I run a legitimate household."

Ronnie was smiling when she hung up the telephone. Sally's support was comforting, especially in view of what she was about to do.

THE GUARDS STOOD near the steps, their breath pluming out in front of them as they talked. Since both of them were in sight, Ronnie knew the guard office was empty. Now she had to decide what to do.

She watched the two men, unable to recognize the burly figures in their winter clothes. Dark hats were pulled down low to protect their faces from the harsh wind, and they moved restlessly from one foot to the other as they talked. Soon they would seek the warmth of their office.

Ronnie bolted across the grass, keeping low and using the shadows cast by the Capitol lights to hide. Rather than endanger the men's jobs, she was going to try and lift the key. If she got caught, she would involve no one but herself.

The guards' office was on the far side of the south doors, a small glass-enclosed space where the entrance to the Capitol could be kept under constant surveillance. Ronnie shuddered at the thought that she might well be the first person ever charged with burglary in the Capitol. *Won't that look great on my employment record?* she thought, trying to keep her spirits up.

As she moved to the office door, she kept one eye on the guards. Even if she got inside, how would she find a key she couldn't possibly recognize? The pressure and fear made her flush with tension.

She ran her tongue across her dry lips and gripped the knob. The door swung open with a small creak, but to Ronnie it sounded like an earthquake. On the steps, the guards continued to talk. Football scores drifted toward her and were somehow reassuring. If they were like most men who enjoyed the ball games, they could talk forever.

Looking into the room she saw three desks, standard black telephones, a radio, a stack of old newspapers and the casual clutter associated with any office. There were hardback chairs, typing tables, two typewriters and several rifles in a locked cabinet. Nowhere was there a clue to where the keys were kept.

She slipped inside, shutting the door to keep in the heat. After the brisk air outside, it felt good to be indoors. Trying to keep her body from trembling, she went to the first desk. She reached out for the top drawer, her hand shaking in midair. Never before had she opened someone else's drawer with the intention of stealing something. What if Jeff was guilty? Grasping the back of a chair she waited until the izzy spell passed—a matter of seconds. If he was guilty, then he was no different from others who broke the law. He would be prosecuted. But deep inside she knew better. Jeff *was* different; she loved him. No man had touched her as he had. Jeff had tapped the inner reserves that she never before knew existed. He was a part of her now in a unique and marvelous way that she could accept, even if it still didn't make sense.

Her slender fingers touched the metal drawer, feeling the coldness with a sense of shock. She pulled it open and looked inside. There were only paper clips, rubber bands, ticket stubs to a hundred things, pencils and some rumpled documents. She went down the drawers on the left side, then the right. Not a single key.

Moving on to the next desk, she hurried through the search. Her hands were shaking and her breathing grew rapid as she began to fear that the keys weren't in the office. Maybe the guards carried them at all times.

The idea sent a flood of panic through her, making her fumble as she went to the third desk. In the middle drawer she finally hit pay dirt. There were at least fifty keys, all with coded tags on them. Her heart, excited first with the discovery, sank as she realized that sorting the keys would take at least thirty minutes—even then there was no guarantee that she could figure out the codes properly. She'd just about have to scoop up all the keys and try them one by one.

Her fingers closed around a fistful. She held them up, the tags and keys dangling down her arm. An unreasonable anger grew, and she had a strong impulse to hurl the keys across the room at the wall. She knew it was an absurd thought, but the release would be wonderful. Also very stupid.

She lowered them back into the drawer, letting them slide through her fingers as if a very important treasure were cascading away. There was no way she could find the right key. There just wasn't enough time. She had to get out of the guard office, and figure out a way to get the guards to give her a master key. At the moment, the idea seemed too far-fetched to even consider. How had she ever hatched such a harebrained scheme?

She was closing the drawer when a single red tag caught her eye. She flipped it over to find a 111 code listing. She had no idea what it meant, but she had to try, at least once. With a new surge of hope she pocketed the key and hurried out of the office.

Outside the door, she paused, making sure that both guards were still engrossed in conversation. To her horror, she saw that one sentry stood alone. She quickly scanned the front steps, but there was no sign of the other. To the right of the door, she heard a rustling, then a whistle. The other guard was coming up to the office.

Holding her breath and running hard, Ronnie tore across the lawn. She kept low and never looked back. At any moment she expected to feel the strong grip of the guard around one ankle or on her shoulders. Or worse, the sound of a shot echoing through the night. But there was nothing, just the sound of her harsh breathing and the tearing of tree and shrub limbs across her jacket. When she was on the other side of the Capitol, she slumped to the ground, panting. She couldn't believe she'd actually gotten away with the key!

After she caught her breath, she circled back to the door. Summoning all her dignity, she walked up the steps and gave both guards a friendly greeting. They smiled at her as she walked by, and she suppressed a pang of guilt. She went straight to the pressroom and started typing frantically. After fifteen minutes, she pushed back from the desk. The key was firmly tucked in her pocket. Her nimble fingers pulled it out and held it up to the light. She had to give it a try.

She turned out the lights in the pressroom. If the guards came up that far, she wanted them to think she'd already left. Then she went down the back stairs to the second floor and confronted the solid oak door to Jeff's reception area.

The Capitol was perfectly silent as she palmed the key, feeling the ridges and forcing her hands to remain steady. Slowly she inserted the key and turned. The tumblers rolled and the lock opened. For a moment she couldn't believe her luck. Then she darted in the door and closed it softly behind her.

The lights were out and the office unfamiliar as she felt her way to Margaret's desk. The smooth wood was a relief as she found the edge of the desk and worked her way behind it. It was too risky to turn on the lamp, so she felt in the dark, pulling open the top drawer. She had to keep reminding herself that she had plenty of time. Now that she was inside, her only goals were to use caution and patience. She was too close to let panic ruin her victory.

She felt in the drawer, fumbling over pens and small bottles. In the darkness she sought the hard edges of a key, yet she could find nothing that resembled one. Her heart pounded in her chest, and she had to fight back the fear that stalked her. She told herself she had time to search carefully. The panic, though, made her want to dump the contents of the drawer on the floor, to scatter them across the carpet so that she could better examine them.

Once again she roved through the drawer, letting her fingers touch and experience the strange objects. In the light, the small vial she grasped would be Liquid Paper. In the darkness, it was an object of mystery. She started at the front, working back. There were papers, a letter opener, each object an obstacle in her path.

At the back of the drawer she finally found a small compartment, almost hidden behind a stack of papers. She reached out forcing her long fingers back into the recess, and was rewarded with the cold feel of metal. Her fingers captured the key and brought it forward.

There was no way to straighten the desk in the darkness, so she simply closed the drawer. Taking great care, she made her way to the door of Jeff's office and tried the lock. Once again, the tumblers rolled and the door silently coasted. For a moment she leaned against the door frame and held her breath. Whatever she found, she had to be calm and observant. There was little chance that the valise would still be there, but if it was . . .

Jeff's office was partially lighted by the window. The outdoor lights and a half moon cast enough illumination for her to make out the desk and the larger pieces of office furniture. Pulling a small penlight from her pocket she searched methodically. When she found the black valise by the desk, her heart almost stopped.

She lifted it, feeling the weight with a slight sense of sickness. Placing it on the desk, she tried to find the lock using the small rays of light from the window, afraid to use even the tiny beam of her flashlight now. The silver gleamed, but she couldn't be certain how the lock worked. There was no key, and the valise looked very sturdy and ruggedly made.

She thought of taking it out with her but rejected that idea. It was too big, too awkward. The guards would notice her leaving with it. The memory of the black sedan, the determined attempts on her life were like a cold wave of caution. She didn't want it at her house; she only wanted to see the payoff money with her own eyes, so there could be no doubt.

Her fingers fumbled with the lock, slipping over the smooth leather of the valise. She was so close, but now it seemed as if she would fail. She thought about the scene between Jeff and the stranger. No matter what it cost, she had to find out the truth—for herself, and for Jeff. She couldn't continue in limbo. In the past, she'd always trusted her instinct. Now she knew that only the sight of the money would make her believe Jeff was guilty of taking a payoff.

She lifted the bag and shook it. It was heavy. "I have to see for myself." She spoke the words aloud to bolster her courage. "I'm going to open this thing if I have to blow it up."

She didn't hear the office door silently glide open several inches. A tall, dark form appeared, watching her intently as she talked.

From the desk she took a letter opener. She'd have to pry open the lock.

Slipping the metal opener down beside the lock, she pressed with all her strength. The leather creaked, but the lock did not give.

"Damn," she said, pushing the opener against the lock. Once again she pressed with all her strength. The valise shifted on the desk, but the lock held.

"Open, damn you," she ordered, using her whole body against the stubborn lock.

"A key would help."

The dark, forceful voice cut across the room. Ronnie felt the air leave her lungs, and she almost collapsed onto the carpet. But she steadied herself and quickly swung around.

Jeff stood in the open door, hands on hips. In the poor lighting, she couldn't see his face, but his voice was anything but friendly.

"You seem to make a habit of breaking and entering," he said. "Were you looking for something specific?"

Ronnie had visualized being caught either by the guards or the men from the black sedan, but never by Jeff. The possibility that he might return to his office had never occurred to her. The sight of him, angry and cold, was more

than she had bargained for when she started her adventure.
She'd rather have faced a jail sentence.

"I'm looking for... I'm looking for the truth. Nothing
more." She held herself rigidly at the desk.

"Get out of my office, before I call the guards." His voice
was harsh, angry, but she read something else beneath the
surface.

"I'm sorry, I'm not leaving until I see what is inside this
valise." Gripping the edge of the desk, she decided to bluff.

Time had at last run out. If she left now, she'd never see
the valise again. Jeff would never be stupid enough to leave
it in his office, knowing that she was determined to get to it.
He could throw her out, have her arrested, do anything he
wanted, but she was going to open it.

She lifted the letter opener and plunged it into the black
leather, trying with all her might to slash the tough case. But
the dull opener was easily deflected and crashed down onto
the desk.

In a second, Jeff was at her side, his hand capturing her
wrist and holding it straight in the air.

"Stop it! You're going to hurt yourself."

"I don't care. I don't care," she retorted as she struggled. His grip was cutting off the blood to her fingers, and
she felt the letter opener begin to slip from her grasp. She
fought harder, trying to wrench away from his iron grip. His
other arm came around her, the steel power of his muscles
pulling her against the strength of his chest.

"Ronnie, stop," he said. There was a softer note in his
voice. His arms held her, and he couldn't ignore the feminine strength of her body battling against him. He tried to
hold her steady, but she continued to thrash, causing her
firm breasts to press against him as she fought to free her
legs. He knew if he let her go, she would attempt to kick o

bite or run. He had no choice but to hold her until her burst of strength diminished.

"Let me go!" she whispered angrily. "I'll call the guards myself if you don't take your hands off me."

Jeff said nothing. He held her to him, and fought his own battle against his rapidly growing desire for her.

His harsh grip forced her to drop the letter opener, but still he didn't lower her hand. With her wrist firmly in his grasp, he held her close, his other arm a band against her back. She could smell the spice of his cologne, feel the crisp starchiness of his shirt beneath her cheek.

With her free hand, she pushed against his chest, trying again to break away from him. The effort was futile. Jeff's superior strength held her with ease.

"I'll charge you with assault," she threatened, surging against him once again. If she could only get one leg free, she'd kick him if she had to, anything to get away from his body and the memory of the things that he did to make her weak with pleasure.

"Stop struggling," he said, his voice thick and husky. He felt her breath against his chest, the rapid breathing of someone who has struggled almost to the point of exhaustion. Now he supported more than restrained her.

Weakly she brought her free hand to his chest and struck him, but the blow was halfhearted and not intended to hurt. It was more a gesture of frustration.

He lowered her other arm, carefully bringing it down so that both of her hands rested against his chest. His arms encircled her, holding her gently until she regained her composure.

"I won't give up," she promised, holding back the sobs that threatened to break through. "You can tie me up, arrest me, put me in jail, I don't care. But I won't give up. I'm going to find out what you're trying to hide—for both our sakes."

She tilted her head back, seeking his eyes in the near darkness. She wanted him to see that there was more behind her vow than simply words.

When she raised her face, her determined chin jutting out even in the depths of her failure, Jeff's restraint snapped. His lips were on hers before he even considered the act. His large, powerful hands coursed down her body, pulling her against him now with a need that had nothing to do with curbing her flight. He wanted to feel her against him, to delight once again in the sensation of her body pressed as tightly as possible against his.

"Oh, Ronnie, don't you see I'm trying to keep you from getting hurt! Don't you know by now they'll kill you?" The words slipped from him in a soft rasp. He buried his lips in her disheveled hair, taking in the clean smell that reminded him of spring rain.

The gentle tone of his words, the security of his arms around her eased the fear that his words produced. He held her against him until she was steady enough to stand away. When she finally looked up there was no anger in his face, only deep concern. As he reached out his hand and cupped the back of her neck, pulling her against him for a moment longer, she accepted her deep, unexplainable love for him. Right or wrong, it didn't matter now.

Reaching up, she let her fingers gently trail along his face. "This lighting suits you, Jeff. One half of your face is revealed, and I can see into the blue depths of your eyes. But the other side is in darkness, the secret side that comes out when..." She didn't finish, but her fingers stroked once again across the hidden side of his face.

"I see you clearly, though," he answered, brushing his lips across her forehead. "Perhaps too clearly." Then he kissed her, taking her mouth with a fervor that created an instant response. Her arms circled his chest, pulling his weight against her as her fingers kneaded the rippling muscles of his back.

From the first moment when he kissed her, Ronnie halted all efforts to attach her feelings to reality. With Jeff, it was too dangerous, and too confusing. As his lips plundered her mouth, she wanted nothing but the moment.

He pulled back from the kiss. "Make me a promise, Veronica. No matter what happens in the next few days. No matter what you think, or have to write about, meet me a week from tonight at Magnolia Point."

The request left her momentarily stunned. At last she asked, "What's going to happen?"

"Promise me, Ronnie. A week from tonight, in the magnolia grove beside the sound. At midnight."

His words held a lulling promise of romance tinged with a dark, swift edge of danger. Slowly the magic of their kiss began to fade, and Ronnie thought of the leather case.

"Jeff, I don't know what's going on, or even who you are anymore. Like this, when we're together, I know you. But then you change into someone I can't figure out." She started to pull away from him, but he caught her, drawing her back to him.

"Please, Ronnie, just say you'll be there."

The urgency in his voice quelled her misgivings. She could never deny him, whatever he asked.

"I'll be there," she said softly. "At midnight, beneath the magnolias."

Chapter Sixteen

With the promise she'd made still echoing in the room, the quiet was ripped apart by the sound of someone stealthily entering the outer office. Jeff roughly pushed Ronnie behind the desk. She was too astounded to speak, but his fingers clamped across her mouth as a precaution.

"Stay perfectly still." His whisper was threaded with warning as he cautiously moved to her left, his hand on her shoulder, forcing her down.

In a crouching position, he quickly maneuvered the desk drawer open and removed a deadly looking .38 caliber pistol.

Wondering why Jeff had such a weapon, Ronnie gripped the edge of the desk and lifted her head to watch the door for movement.

"Ronnie, please get down," Jeff warned as he eased toward the door. "Hurry!"

As she ducked behind the massive protection of the oak desk, she heard the sounds of the intruder approaching. Had the bald man returned? The thought made her flush with panic, but she held herself motionless, her eyes on Jeff's dark form steeling toward a confrontation.

Her heart was pounding so loudly she couldn't be certain what she was hearing, except for someone rustling papers and bumping lightly into furniture. Unable to remain still, she crept to Jeff's side. "Who is it?" she whispered, but her only reply was an angry wave of his hand for silence. Outside the door there was a muffled curse, and then the sound of someone stumbling toward the door.

Jeff's arm reached back for her, pressing her forcefully against the wall. The gun was pointed at the door, a dull gleam reflecting off it in deadly fashion. Ronnie felt like screaming, but her throat was closed with tension. Had her luck finally run out? Four times her life had been threatened, each time more deadly than the last. Was this the way her life would end? She could only press herself against the wall and wait.

The door opened a crack, and an exclamation of pleased surprise that sounded anything but sinister drifted in to Ronnie. While she tried to sort out why the voice seemed familiar, she put a restraining hand on Jeff's arm.

He, too, sensed the lack of danger and slowly lowered the gun. But every tense line in his body let her know he was ready for anything.

Grabbing the doorknob, he pulled quickly, with all his strength. A small figure dressed in black flew across the room and crashed into his desk, flipping across the broad surface and landing in a heap on the other side.

Jeff jumped on top of the intruder, his strong hands forcing the small figure to the floor.

"Don't make another move," Jeff threatened. "Turn on a light," he ordered Ronnie.

Glad to oblige, Ronnie found the switch and flooded the office with light. With one smooth gesture, Jeff grabbed the black stocking mask that covered the trespasser's face. As he pulled it away, red hair cascaded onto the floor.

"Oh, my God!" Ronnie exclaimed in dismay. Sally Duvall was stretched on the office floor, her pale face twisted in pain and humiliation.

"Get off me you big oaf!" she managed to hiss.

Jeff leaped backward as if he'd been burned. Then he turned from Ronnie to Sally and back again. "I don't believe you two," he said. "Did you plan this together?"

Ronnie didn't bother answering. She was at her friend's side, trying to assist her into a sitting position. "Are you hurt?" she asked, her voice full of concern.

"Only my pride," Sally said, sitting up and rubbing one hip. "I thought I'd been grabbed by a hurricane and thrown into the pits of hell. Is that door spring-loaded?"

"What are you doing here?" Ronnie inquired, standing and helping her friend to her feet.

Sally tried not to limp, but the tumble across the desk had bruised one hip, her elbow and several hundred other small places. "I came to make sure you were okay." She paused, looking from one to the other and finally resting her gaze on the valise. "And I have some bad news. Neil Brenton was shot tonight. Someone broke into his home. They don't expect him to live," she continued slowly. "He's asking for you, Jeff. Most of the city police are looking for you. I'm sorry, but you'd better hurry."

"I have to get to Neil," Jeff said, his anguish exposed. "Neil wasn't supposed to get hurt. It wasn't supposed to happen this way." He touched Ronnie's arm. "Come with me," he said. "We can take care of this other business—" he waved a hand at the valise "—later. It's Neil that I need to see now."

"Can you make it home?" Ronnie asked Sally.

"Sure, but I'm going to take a terrible kidding from my family when I tell them I was beaten black-and-blue by a door, a desk and a floor," Sally said, gingerly rubbing her hip.

"That's the price you pay for being the inimitable Sally Duvall," Ronnie said, smiling encouragement at her friend.

"Go! Before it's too late. Hurry!" Sally said, waving them off.

Jeff grabbed Ronnie's hand and they rushed from the Capitol and into the truck. His jaw was tight with pain as he pressed the accelerator to the floor and let the truck speed toward the hospital.

Ronnie wanted to reach out to him, to touch the warm leg beside hers and offer some comfort, but there was nothing she could do. For such a short time, their lives had seemed to be entwined, linked by an attraction that held the promise of commitment. Now Jeff's life had suddenly gone awry. Whatever he was involved in could cost his future, their relationship—and even an old friend's life.

"He can't die," Jeff said, almost under his breath. "Carlisle promised me he wouldn't let him get hurt."

Ronnie held her breath. Carlisle was the man he'd met in the diner, the big man with the black hair and a black sedan.

"Who is Carlisle?" she asked softly. She knew it wasn't the best time to probe, but that was her job. The two pieces of foil she'd found had been gnawing at her for three days. Somehow she knew they were important, but she hadn't been able to make the connection.

Jeff turned to her and looked as if he barely recognized her. "You don't know about any of it, do you?"

Her heart tripped, and she wanted to tell him no, that she didn't know anything, but whatever he'd done it didn't matter. But she couldn't say those words, because it did matter. It mattered a lot.

She felt Jeff's arm come around her shoulders and hold her easily, but with firm assurance. "Sit by me," he asked softly, and the tenderness in his voice drew her to him. "So much has happened, I don't even know where to begin."

His hand dropped to her shoulder, gently rubbing her arm in a manner that was almost absent. His eyes watched the road, and something else, some internal vista that played before him and gave him a reason for the sadness that she read in every line of his face.

"Start at the beginning," she said softly.

With a sigh he began, as if his need to talk finally matched her need to know.

"Neil Brenton gave me more things, not material things, but important things like time and attention, than my own father did. Dad was always traveling, rushing from one business deal to another. But when I was a teenager, Neil had a law practice in Biloxi. After school, I got in the habit of dropping around there to talk with him about the law. I knew I wanted to be a lawyer, not only to practice law, but to help create better laws. Through high school and college, Neil encouraged me. We read texts together, and he'd illustrate the principles with cases from his law practice. When he was elected attorney general, I spent the summers in Jackson with him, working as a clerk or investigator at whatever job he had open. With each hour, I learned more about the legal system. And my respect for Neil was unlimited." He paused, waiting for a few more blocks to roll away beneath the truck's tires. "This all seems like some terrible nightmare."

Too aware of his pain, and unable to stop herself, Ronnie placed a hand gently on his knee, giving him a squeeze of encouragement.

"When I was first told that Neil was involved with men who wanted to kill the horse racing bill, I didn't believe it.

But when I got hold of some financial statements that showed he was deeply in debt, I had to get involved." Jeff shook his head sadly. "I can't imagine how Neil got into so much trouble, unless it was gambling. I guess that's the bitter irony of the whole mess. He was so outspoken against the idea of legalized racing and pari-mutuel betting, because he'd already lost so much."

Ronnie's hand remained on Jeff's leg, but there was no feeling in her body. His words echoed fuzzily in her head. Jeff was using the same words that Brenton had used when he handed her Jeff's financial statement! The coincidence was positively eerie.

"Where did you get those financial records on Neil?" she asked.

"Why do you ask?"

"I'm curious. It might be important later on."

"I've been living a life of 'classified information,' but I guess it's okay now that it's over. I got them from the FBI."

"Are you sure?" Ronnie asked, her mind reeling. Someone was manufacturing financial statements. If Jeff's was false, couldn't Neil's be also? Or had Neil simply tried to frame Jeff?

"Absolutely. I took them from the agent myself. We discussed the possibilities of someone trying to deliberately set Neil up, but everything checked out. The FBI wanted to release the financial records to the press, but I talked them out of it, hoping that I could prove they were wrong, that Neil was innocent. They finally agreed to let me act as a decoy to try and draw Deluchi out of hiding."

"And did you?" Ronnie asked, holding her breath.

For a long moment, Jeff said nothing. As they pulled under the lights of the hospital, Jeff finally responded. "I proved everything but Neil's innocence. Deluchi paid me off last night. That's what's in the valise, nearly a million dollars." He shook his head bitterly. "I pinned Deluchi, but I never managed to clear Neil's name, and now it may be too late. The FBI promised me that Neil wouldn't get hurt, that he would be arrested and prosecuted, but not injured. See, they wanted Johnny Deluchi, not Neil. Neil was just small potatoes to them, a local politician gone bad. They never knew him when he used to be a man who would die for his principles. To them, he never even really mattered. Once they decided he was bad, they even tried to nail him with setting up the shooting at the Dennison party."

"Oh, Jeff," Ronnie said, putting her arms around his shoulders and holding him. "I'm so sorry, but I have something I have to tell you." She drew a deep breath. "Neil did plan the shooting at the party."

"How do you know?" he asked, anger mingling with disbelief.

"He told me, last Sunday. But he only did it to try and scare you away from the horse racing bill. He said you'd fallen into bad company and he thought you were connected with Deluchi. He thought he could frighten you away from Deluchi." Ronnie stopped, overcome by emotion. "He did it because he loves you." She remembered Neil Brenton's face when they'd spoken, the combination of concern and love.

Jeff turned the truck into the hospital parking lot and stopped by the emergency entrance.

"Go on in and I'll park the truck," she volunteered.

"Leave it," Jeff said. "I want you with me. Thank God I can say that now." He tossed the keys on the seat and shut the door.

The hospital corridors were white and spotless, and seemed to stretch for miles. At last they found Dr. David Morton, the doctor in charge. Neil was waiting for a thoracic surgeon to be flown in from Houston.

"He's too weak for surgery now, anyway," the doctor said. "If he hadn't been asking for you, I wouldn't let you bother him. But he seems determined. We're hoping his wife can get here before..."

"Where's Martha?" Jeff asked, pain reflected in every word.

"Norfolk, visiting relatives. Apparently Mr. Brenton was afraid of an attempt on his life, so he sent his wife away, for safety. And from what the police said his house looked like, it's a good thing, too. He put up a helluva struggle to save himself." Dr. Morton shook his head. "I was in college when Mr. Brenton's hide wasn't worth a plugged nickel, back during the sixties. I admired him so much."

Ronnie felt the tears sting her eyes, but she held them back. Jeff's face was drained of color.

"Can I see him?" Jeff asked softly. "Just for a moment."

"This way," Morton said, leading them down another corridor to double doors that warned away all but authorized personnel. The doctor laid a restraining arm on Ronnie's shoulder. "You'd better wait here, Miss," he said.

"Please," Jeff intervened. "This is important, to all of us."

Morton shrugged, revealing his lack of faith in a positive outcome. "Tell him we have an escort at the airport waiting for his wife."

Jeff could only nod as he took Ronnie's hand and led her into a small room overloaded with tubes and monitoring machines. Neil Brenton looked small and fragile beneath the white sheet, though he managed a shaky smile when he saw Jeff. From beneath the cover he lifted a hand that trembled, and Ronnie couldn't help but remember the assured elegance with which he'd smoked his cigarettes. She choked back her tears as she stood helplessly at the foot of the bed.

"They found you," Neil said, his voice as soft as the flutter of doves' wings.

Jeff leaned down and gently grasped Neil's hand. "Hold on," he whispered. "You can make it."

Neil only smiled. Then the smile faded from his face, and Ronnie could only describe the look in his eyes as fear. "Martha," he whispered.

"There's an escort at the airport waiting for her arrival. She'll be here as soon as possible. She's fine," Jeff assured him.

"I've been framed, Jeff. But I found out who's really running this show, and if I had just a little more time, I could prove it." Neil's voice trailed off, becoming noticeably weaker. His eyes pleaded with Jeff, and Ronnie gripped the foot of the bed to steady herself.

"It doesn't matter," Jeff said calmly. "Nothing matters except that you hang on. The specialist is on his way. After surgery, you'll be stronger and we can talk about this. Now you must rest."

Jeff straightened up and carefully began to extract his hand from Neil's grip. But Neil tightened his fingers, hanging on with the last of his strength.

"Get the nurse, quick!" Jeff said in a low voice to Ronnie.

"No! Wait!" Neil said, and for a moment, the elegant command was back in his voice. Ronnie stopped, looking from one man to the other, undecided what to do.

"Danger," Neil whispered again, knowing the last outburst had been costly. "Danger," he repeated and slowly pointed his finger at Jeff. "Betrayal."

The word was an accusation and a warning, and Ronnie turned slowly back to Neil. His strength was seeping away, but he kept Jeff's hand in his, pressing the fingers with a desperate need.

"Neil, what are you saying?" Ronnie asked. Was he accusing Jeff of betraying him? She looked at Jeff, whose gaze was clouded with pain and remorse.

"I never meant this to happen," Jeff said, leaning down to his friend and gently grasping his shoulder. "Neil, I never believed you were involved. Not even when I started this."

Neil opened his mouth, but no sound came out. He shifted his gaze to Ronnie, then back to Jeff, and they both saw the tremendous effort he was making.

"Check out car," he whispered, an edge of fear in his voice. He couldn't finish and tried again. "Car..." As his mouth slowly went slack the intensity in his eyes dimmed and then disappeared.

"Neil!" Jeff said, tightening his grip and gently shaking him. "Neil!"

Ronnie didn't wait to be told what to do. She fled the room and found the nearest nurse. Within seconds, a medical team rushed into the room and went to work. But the monotonous scream of the flat line on the heart monitor remained unchanged. Dr. Morton put his hand on Jeff's shoulder. "I know you were close, Senator. I'm sorry."

Chapter Seventeen

For a long time Jeff stood in the hospital corridor outside Neil's room. His friend was dead. Ronnie posted herself at his side, offering her presence as silent comfort until Dr. Morton came out of the room and escorted them from the hospital with kind words of condolence that Jeff never heard. He was dazed with grief.

The truck was still parked near the emergency entrance, and without asking permission, Ronnie climbed in behind the wheel. She started up the engine and drove toward her house.

"Judging by the sky, dawn isn't far away," she said softly, to break the painful quiet as she maneuvered down the deserted Jackson streets. "It's hard to believe it's only Thursday morning."

Jeff didn't reply. His eyes were focused out the window, and she could tell by a quick glance at his profile that he was deep in troubled thought.

"Whatever you're thinking, Jeff, don't ever doubt that Neil Brenton loved you like a son." She kept her voice low and steady. "No matter what he did, he loved you. He was concerned for you. When you have to confront the bad things that have happened, you can't forget what a good man Neil was."

"I need to talk with the police," Jeff said.

"You can call them when we get to the house." And I'll call Kurt, she thought to herself, wondering how she'd sort out all the related happenings for a sensible story. She had a front-page headline, but it gave her no satisfaction. The personal suffering was so great that she wished she didn't have to write anything.

"Johnny Deluchi will pay for this," Jeff vowed. His voice was low and the very lack of emotion in his words was frightening.

"I never got a chance to know Neil well," she began softly, "but I am curious about a few things. One of the most important is why Deluchi would want Neil dead." There was so much that needed an explanation. Who was responsible for the shooting at Magnolia Point, the cut gas line, the attempt to hit her and the violent attack on her at the barn fire? Neil had admitted to arranging the shooting at the party, but as she had realized at the time, the bullets were never close to hitting anyone. The other episodes had been too close for comfort, and they were directed at her, not Jeff. "Was Neil behind all of the attempts on my life?" she asked.

Jeff rubbed a hand across his face in a tired gesture. "A lot of this isn't clear to me, except that Neil was desperate. Supposedly he needed money. But he could have come to me and asked for it. I would have given it to him," Jeff said, suddenly very intense. "I would have given him my last dime if he'd only asked."

Ronnie groaned inwardly at Jeff's words. Neil had believed that Jeff was broke. After all, that's what the financial record on Jeff had indicated. "So Neil intended to undermine the horse racing bill, and somehow Deluchi was going to pay him for that?" Ronnie guessed, guiding the car onto the interstate highway.

"Neil created his special investigative team to find corruption in the people who were backing the horse racing issue. He did that with Deluchi's blessing, and when Neil didn't find corruption, he was going to fabricate some." Jeff shook his head sadly. "When Carlisle first told me all of this, I called him a liar."

"Carlisle?" Ronnie asked. His name was everywhere, and so was he, but she couldn't see his role in all of this.

"Jay Carlisle, the FBI agent who's been working with me," Jeff said tiredly.

"Carlisle, the big man from the diner, is FBI?" Ronnie asked as she turned off the highway and onto residential streets.

"Yes, but how did you know about the diner?" Jeff asked, straightening up and looking closely at Ronnie.

"I followed you there one night."

"You could have been hurt!" Jeff exclaimed, remembering some of his more unpleasant meetings in that part of town.

"I was there when you met with the man in the Mercedes," Ronnie continued.

"Deluchi." Jeff exhaled, reaching over to grasp her shoulder. "You're one lucky lady. If he'd even suspected you were there, you'd be dead and gone. Me, too, in all probability." Jeff picked up a strand of her hair, letting it slide through his fingers. "That's the very scene that's tormented me night and day since I met you. I knew you were too smart for your own good."

"I didn't know who the guy was, and I was too far away to get a license number or any positive identification on the car. I was growing worried, Jeff. It looked damned suspicious. And then you killed the racing bill."

"But you never lost faith in me," he said, leaning over to kiss her cheek. "A few moments of doubt, I dare say, but no desertion."

"Almost," Ronnie admitted. "So who is the bald man?"

"That's one for the FBI," Jeff said, shrugging. "He had to work for Neil, but Carlisle could never get a real line on him. He doesn't seem to exist, as far as the FBI is concerned. He'll turn up, though, I'm positive of that. When Deluchi goes to trial, then the whole pyramid will come crashing down."

"You'll have to testify against Deluchi, won't you?"

"I'm afraid so," Jeff answered. "After what he did to Neil, I'd like to send him away for the rest of his life."

She turned the truck into her driveway just as the first pink glow of the sun tinted the eastern horizon. Entering the house, she went straight to the kitchen and started coffee. Jeff looked at the phone, but didn't make a step toward it.

"I want to finish this with you before I do anything else," he said. "I would have told you before, but it was so dangerous. Neil's men were after you on Deluchi's orders as it was, and I thought the less you knew the safer you would be." Once again his hand moved to rub his face in a gesture that encapsulated his weariness and grief.

"My bill to legalize racing was prefiled last fall. I knew by October that I had the backing I needed, so I went ahead with it. About that time, I got a phone call from an agent with the FBI." He stopped long enough to sip the hot, black coffee she handed him in a blue ceramic mug. He smiled his appreciation, then walked over to her and looped his arm around her shoulders, giving them a gentle squeeze.

"Let's go sit down," she suggested. She was bone weary, and Jeff's face registered almost total exhaustion.

With his arm still around her shoulders, they went into the living room and settled on the sofa. He pulled her snugly against him and let his fingers stroke her arm.

"The FBI asked me to prepare myself to receive an offer to kill the horse racing bill. They were expecting that scum, Johnny Deluchi, to push his weight around to stop the bill, because a clean track in Mississippi could prove very damaging to the crooked tracks he monopolized in other areas."

"I understand that," Ronnie said. "And Deluchi's men told you Neil would discredit you if you didn't take the payoff?"

"Yeah," Jeff said, easing her back against his arm. "So I was determined to get Deluchi's hide nailed and at the same time prove Neil would never work against Mississippi."

They were both silent for a moment. Jeff's body was warm and comforting, and Ronnie settled her head on his arm. She could feel the steady beat of his heart. It was so good to be near him. "I still find it hard to believe that Neil Brenton would try to run me down," Ronnie said. Remembering her attack in the barn, she leaned forward. "There's something else you should know, and I hate like hell to be the one to tell you."

"I have to know the truth," Jeff said, softly drawing her back to him. "Go on." He nestled her against him and kissed her encouragingly on the top of the head.

"The night of the barn fire, someone grabbed me and locked me in the tack room." Ronnie couldn't keep the tremor from her voice. Ducking her chin, she grasped the strong hand he held out to her. "When he knocked me out, he said it was a present from the senator," she finished in a near whisper.

Jeff's arms closed around her, enveloping her in a warm embrace. Gently he rocked her until she relaxed against him.

"That explains the cut on your head," he said, tenderly kissing the area. "And your anger."

"It must have been the bald man," she said, her voice much steadier. "He was at Magnolia Point the night we were shot at, and I know he was driving the car that tried to run me down." Shaking her head with bitterness, Ronnie laughed shortly. "When I saw you in the diner with Carlisle, I almost panicked. Then I got close enough to see that Carlisle had a whole headful of hair."

"Oh, Ronnie," Jeff said, holding her tight against him. An edge of anger had crept into his voice. "The most important thing is that you're safe, but I'm going to find this bald man. Neil may have gotten into trouble, but I know he would never have condoned any efforts to harm you, or anyone else."

Jeff tightened his grip and for a moment he held her to him with so much force she almost couldn't breathe. At last he relaxed and kissed her head, his fingers combing through her dark, glossy hair as he continued.

"I tried so hard to keep you safe. I got you to Magnolia Point because I wanted to be with you so much, and because you were in danger. The situation was very hot. Deluchi had agreed to a personal meeting with me, and Carlisle said if you showed up sniffing at my heels, Deluchi wouldn't hesitate to kill you."

"He came close," Ronnie grimly agreed.

"I wanted to protect you, but everywhere you went, danger followed." He kissed her head again. "Now it's all over, Ronnie. Now I can testify against Deluchi and put him away for a long, long time." His voice hollowed out as he added, "The price I pay is that Neil is dead."

"How could a man like Neil go so wrong?" Ronnie asked. "He was such a powerful man, and so steadfast in his concern for other human beings. How could money have done this to him?''

"My guess is that Deluchi threatened Martha or his children. Neil had either to go along with the plan or watch his family get hurt. Hell, I'd make the same decision if you were threatened.''

Looking into his stormy blue eyes, Ronnie couldn't deny that his statement pleased her. They had been through so much in the past twelve hours, and they had survived, together. She tipped back her head, asking for the kiss that came immediately. Jeff's lips were tender, gentle, and the first probing of his tongue made her stretch against him. Their first kiss at Magnolia Point had been colored by her suspicions. This one she gave without any restraint. His warm fingers closed at her back, drawing her even tighter against him until she thought she would melt with happiness. Out of tragedy, they had truly found each other.

Gradually she pulled back, wanting the moment to last forever. She wanted time to talk, to savor the fact that there were no longer any unanswered questions between them. Gazing into his eyes, she saw no dark suspicions, only the future.

"What will happen next?" she asked.

"I haven't thought much beyond this moment," Jeff said, smiling at her. "We have a lot to talk about, if you're interested in discussing what kind of team a reporter and a politician could make. As for the immediate future, I need to get in touch with Carlisle so he can move on Deluchi. Then I have to go by the Capitol and refile the horse racing bill. There's still plenty of time to pass it.''

"Jeff, that's marvelous!" she exclaimed, smiling. "Will they also be able to arrest that heavyset thug who kept trying to kill me?"

"That still puzzles me. Neil was a desperate man, but not desperate enough to take another human life, and especially not the woman I love."

"Oh, Jeff," Ronnie said, throwing her arms around him and kissing him. "That's your first declaration, and I fully intend to quote you on it liberally, so don't try and retract it."

"Not a chance," he replied, laughing as he kissed her long and deeply. "Not a chance." His voice was rough and husky. "Now I could stand a little of that breakfast you offered, and then I really have to get to Carlisle."

"I've got a story to file and a boss to mollify. And gads! Sally must be biting her nails to the quick, waiting for me to call her." Ronnie jumped from the sofa and dashed into the kitchen. "Stella wouldn't be impressed, but I can put together some eggs, bacon, grits and toast."

"If you'll eat with me, it sounds like heaven," Jeff said.

"I do have one little question," Ronnie said as the bacon began to sizzle in the pan.

"What's that?"

"Were you talking with anyone on the patio the night of the party?"

"As you've probably guessed, Carlisle was there. He decided to work security that night for me. He was afraid one of Deluchi's or Neil's men would try and kill me."

"But why would anyone try to kill you?" Ronnie flipped the bacon and poured the grits into the hot water, then turned to butter the toast.

"Carlisle thought that Deluchi might think it was easier to kill me than to pay me off. There was so much talk that the horse racing bill was my personal campaign and that no other politician would be able to get it passed. In other words, it would cost Deluchi a bullet instead of a lot of money."

"How much money did he agree to pay?"

"Don't tell me you're getting greedy," Jeff teased her. "How much would you pay for my soul?"

"Not one single peso, because I already have your heart," Ronnie declared, breaking into laughter as Jeff cracked eggs into a bowl.

"Well, he finally agreed on three-quarters of a million."

Ronnie whistled. "I had no idea. He must want that bill dead in a bad way."

"Bad enough to kill Neil, when he finally quit being useful."

"That was my next question." Ronnie drained the bacon and poured the eggs into the pan. "Neil cooperated. Why did he have to die?"

"Death is the logical end of a relationship to a person like Deluchi," Jeff said. "That's why I was willing to risk everything to get Deluchi. Everything—until I met you."

"Oh, Jeff," Ronnie said, putting down the spatula and giving him a hug.

"I think if Neil was really involved, he decided to blow the whistle. Neil undoubtedly told Deluchi that he was going to the cops, so Deluchi had him killed. That explains why Neil sent Martha away for her own safety. He was expecting something dangerous to happen." Jeff stepped away from her, looking out the kitchen window to hide his emotions.

"Yes," Ronnie said. "That makes perfect sense. He must have had a change of heart, and it cost him his life." She went to him and circled his waist with her arms. "You're having trouble accepting Neil's guilt, aren't you?"

"People are what they are, Ronnie. I knew Neil inside out, and I still can't believe he'd really go wrong."

"You have to trust your instinct, Jeff," Ronnie said, rubbing her forehead against his spine. "I did that with you, and I was right."

"I'm glad you didn't give up on me," Jeff said, turning in her arms to draw her against him. "You're a real gambler, Miss Sheffield."

They carried the breakfast to the table and sat opposite each other. Jeff toyed with his food. "You've gambled on your instinct and won. Now my instinct is telling me that we need to spend some time together. In bed."

His suggestion brought the blood rushing to her face. He'd so accurately reflected her own thoughts that she felt naked, vulnerable. "So this is the silver-tongued Jeff Stuart I heard so much about before I came down here. You aren't very subtle," she said.

"Under less trying circumstances, I might be more delicate, but I've already told you that I love you. Since you never responded to my declaration, I find myself in a position of uncertainty." His blue eyes snapped with mischief and he again became the charming, devilish senator she'd met on her first working night in Mississippi.

"Uncertainty! No response! What did you call that kiss I gave you? A rotten potato?"

"Does that mean you love me?" he asked, wrinkling his face into a frown.

"Do you want me to write it down?" Ronnie inquired, laughing. "Yes, I love you. More than anyone in the world. Almost from the first moment. Even though you've complicated my life, endangered me and driven me nearly mad with suspense, I love you."

"No hesitations?" All teasing was gone from his voice and his hand gently reached across the table to capture hers.

She only shook her head. There was no doubt what the look on his face meant, and she felt her heart respond with a staccato beat. His kisses ignited her blood, and the thought of his body against hers, skin against skin, started slow fingers of desire moving through her limbs.

"Would you like to take a shower with me?"

"What about Carlisle?" she asked.

"I've given him my life for the last three months. He can wait a little longer. How about your boss?"

"My deadline isn't until noon."

He reached across the table and took her hand. They rose simultaneously and he led her down the hallway to the bathroom. With a quick twist of his hand, he sent the hot water shooting into the large tub. Turning to her, he looked at her a moment, a lazy smile dancing across his lips. When he leaned down for a kiss, he pushed the door closed behind her.

The sound of the shower drowned the sudden pounding of Ronnie's heart. Jeff's kiss anchored her against the cool tile, and she lifted her arms around his neck to hold on as they slowly explored each other. She felt his fingers at her back, moving beneath the thick layer of her sweater onto bare skin. He pulled her closer, then continued to explore her back, taking time to follow the clear delineation of her shoulder blades, to touch the erogenous zones along her spine. When he pulled back from the kiss, he simply lifted her sweater over her head.

Nimbly she unbuttoned his shirt, pushing the material off his shoulders and to the floor. Letting her fingers romp across his muscular chest, she met his eyes. The passion that burned within him held her as he unclasped the front hook of her bra.

She kicked off her shoes. As he watched, she undid her slacks and let them fall to the floor, stepping out of them.

"Let me look at you," he said, his voice savage yet tender. "I've imagined this so many times, but I never really knew how beautiful you are."

His eyes, roving down her body, burned like a cold flame. She forced herself to breathe slowly. When at last he touched her, tracing one finger lightly between her full breasts, she rose on tiptoe to meet him, capturing his lips with a fiery kiss.

The steam from the shower filled the room, covering their bodies with a fine mist. Jeff stepped out of his pants and then drew her under the water with him. The hot torrent cascaded over them as they pressed together and kissed again.

Lost in Jeff's embrace beneath the plunging water, Ronnie lost all sense of time and place. Jeff's hard muscles were beneath her hands as she explored the power of his back and the firm muscles of his chest. His hands searched her body, too, lingering at her waist and then rising to cup her breasts. Slowly he turned her until his back took the full force of the water. Then he began an inch by inch massage that began at the tired muscles of her neck. He found the bath soap, and the slippery lather allowed his roughened palms to glide down her body in silken motions that made her tremble with desire.

Reaching for the soap, she saw how his dark hair curled wetly around his eyes as the water sparkled and jumped from his shoulders. She lathered her hands and brought her fingers to play against his chest. In a few moments, they were both covered in white foam, laughing and clinging together until Jeff pulled her back beneath the water and rinsed her clean.

Ronnie reached for the shower with her toe and pressed the lever. Brushing her hair from her face, Jeff traced a finger across her lips.

"You're magnificent," he said. Before she could respond, he wrapped a towel around her shoulders and briskly began to rub her dry. Then he dried himself with a few quick movements.

"Now that we're clean, how about that nap?" he asked, the sparkle in his eyes more relaxed.

Ronnie tried to answer, but there was a lump in her throat. So she took his hand and led him to her bedroom, drawing him down beside her in the cool sheets.

She gave herself totally, letting him guide her through pleasures she'd never known before. Her body responded to him, yielding and seeking, in a pulse as timeless as the tide against the shore. He called upon every ounce of her strength to match his. His strong arms molded her against him, carried her with him as he moved, until at last, she was beyond his control, slipping into a rippling pleasure that built and built to the climax. She felt him, too, yielding at last to the intensity of their lovemaking. Hot and exhausted, they held each other close in the tangled sheets.

Cradled against his chest, Ronnie listened as the beat of his heart gradually began to slow. His fingers lightly ran down her back, a soft, tender motion that made her exhausted muscles melt. Her fingers gently played in the thick hair on his chest. There was no room for thought, only for feelings. She'd never wanted to be with anyone the way she'd wanted Jeff. And lying beside him, she felt as if her life had suddenly become complete.

"Jeff?" she asked softly.

"Uh-huh," he murmured, his fingers stroking her back as she snuggled into his chest.

"Are you going to run for U.S. Senate?"

The question made him lean up on one elbow. "I haven't thought about that in a long time," he said. "What makes you ask now?"

"I don't know," she said. "Lying here beside you, I didn't want anything to change. I know that's foolish, but...anyway, I just wondered if you'd be campaigning next summer for a Washington post."

His chuckle was soft and easy. "At first I thought you were asking for a story. Then it occurred to me you might like the excitement of a national campaign. Now I find that you want to stay in Mississippi." His lips sought hers and he kissed her gently. "Keep it up, Veronica. You show me with every moment that I love you more."

"Then you aren't running?"

"Listen, spitfire, when this horse racing bill is passed, I'm going to retire to Magnolia Point and simply live. In a few months, I may get around to opening a small law office. That's what I'll eventually do, anyway. But politics have lost their appeal."

She looked down, tracing the line of his thigh muscle beneath the sheet.

"What's wrong?" he asked.

"If all of this with Neil hadn't come up, you would have stayed in politics, probably run for Congress, wouldn't you?"

"For a long time that was my plan. But this did come up, and now I've changed. Why are you so sad when it's what you want anyway?"

"I was just thinking about Neil, about the first night I met him. He seemed angry at you, upset. He warned me that you were too ambitious, that you'd ruin yourself with ambition. And now, the way it's ended, his words were like a premonition of his own death."

Jeff pulled her into his arms and held her tightly, kissing her lightly over her face and neck and arms.

"Remember the promise you made me?" he asked.

"To meet you at Magnolia Point," Ronnie said. "It was only last night, and yet it seems like a lifetime ago."

"I want a revision of that promise," he said.

"What kind?"

"I want you to meet me at Magnolia Point as soon as Neil's funeral is over. I want to go home for a few days, and I want you to be with me during that time. Will you come?"

"Yes," she said. "I'm sure Magnolia Point is safe again, for both of us."

Chapter Eighteen

Ronnie held Jeff's hand as the minister concluded the last prayer at the small Jackson cemetery. In the glare of the midday sun the mourners turned solemnly to leave as Jeff stopped beside Martha Brenton, hugging her gently against his broad chest.

"I'm sorry," he whispered.

"I know, Jeff," she said, then returned to her family, her face buried in a handkerchief to hide her tears.

Sally Duvall stood beside Ronnie, her red hair covered with a black hat. Ronnie's own hair, neatly pulled back in a French braid, glistened in the sunlight. So did her eyes as she watched Martha Brenton's tearful exchange with Jeff. After a moment, Jeff returned to her side, giving Sally a warm hug.

"I still can't believe it," Jeff said, guiding Ronnie and Sally down the narrow road to their cars. "Now it's all over. I can't wait to get home. Kurt didn't complain about giving you a few days off?"

"He was relieved," Ronnie said. "Besides, Sally's here. She's more than capable of handling anything that comes up."

They were almost at the car when Jeff slowed. Parked behind him was a black sedan. The heavyset man Ronnie knew as Carlisle stepped out from behind the wheel, crushed a cigar beneath his heel and headed toward them.

"Damn!" Jeff muttered. "He's the last person I want to see now. I guess he wants the money. It's funny, but with everything else that happened, no one ever bothered to pick it up."

"Jeff!" Ronnie said, shock evident in her face. "You just left it lying around your office?"

"I put it in a safe place," he assured her.

The man stopped a short distance from them and waited. When they were close, Jeff stopped, stepping slightly forward.

"Veronica, Sally, this is Jay Carlisle, the FBI agent I've been working with. Jay, Veronica Sheffield and Sally Duvall."

"I know. Miss Sheffield, you got more lives than a cat," Carlisle said quickly. His brown eyes examined her, but there was no reading the look on his face. Ronnie felt her temper ignite. He was the man who had jeopardized Jeff's career, and ultimately allowed Neil Brenton to be killed. He might be an FBI agent, but he was certainly not a very good one.

"Have the police identified the killer yet?" she asked, a little too brusquely.

"The case is still under investigation, Miss Sheffield. Perhaps you should speak with them," he said. "Jeff, I need to talk with you. Alone." He acted as if Ronnie and Sally were no longer present.

"This isn't the time," Jeff said. "When you need me to testify against Deluchi, I'll be there. Right now, though, I'm going to the Capitol to reintroduce the racing bill, and then I'm going home."

"Mr. D's going to be history, Senator, so what's the hurry on the racing bill?" Carlisle asked.

"No hurry. But there's no reason to delay, either. You have the goods on Deluchi. I'd like to get as much publicity on the bill as possible between now and the vote. After all of this, I'm going to need all the help I can raise to get it passed."

Carlisle seemed deep in thought and strangely nervous. "I need to talk with you. Now, Senator."

"Listen, Carlisle. I never liked working with you. Your carelessness almost cost Ronnie her life, more than once. And Neil Brenton is dead. You were supposed to give him protection." Anger simmered beneath the forced calm of Jeff's manner. "Just get out of our way and leave us alone. You have what you want, and I want some privacy to get on with my life."

"It isn't that easy, Senator," Carlisle said, blocking the path. "We have a few details to work out. Then, I promise, the rest of your life is your own."

Jeff turned to Ronnie, anger and frustration on his face. "Take my car and go home. Get packed and I'll be by to get you—" he looked at Carlisle "—in no more than twenty minutes."

"Sure," Ronnie said, standing on tiptoe for a kiss. "I'll be waiting. Remember, we have a promise to keep."

Jeff and Carlisle walked away, each silent. When they were out of earshot, Ronnie turned to Sally. "I don't like Jay Carlisle. He's just plain rude. Maybe it comes with the job," she said with a sigh, watching them cross the street. Jeff walked around the car to get in the passenger seat.

"Jeff doesn't like him much either," Sally observed. Her eyes followed them as the two men entered the car. "By the way, remember the pieces of foil you found? Mr. D's is the name of Deluchi's gaming joint in Las Vegas. The foil was apparently from some of his private cigars. Pretty fancy, huh? Embossed cigars, cars, his own wine label. He's going to miss all that in prison.''

"Yeah," Ronnie said, watching Jeff and Carlisle pull away. "But I won't miss him. Neil's death really hit Jeff hard.''

"Let me treat you to a cup of coffee," Sally offered, starting toward the other cars lined up outside the cemetery.

"No thanks," Ronnie answered, forcing a smile. "I'll be going to Biloxi with Jeff, and I want to be packed when he comes for me." The incident with Carlisle had unsettled her, and she couldn't explain the need to be alone.

"Something wrong?" Sally asked.

Ronnie shook her head, upset by her own erratic moods. "Not really. It's just a feeling I have that something very obvious has been overlooked. For some crazy reason, I don't believe Neil Brenton sold out." She laughed shakily. "I'm beginning to sound like Jeff."

"Neil was a very dynamic man," Sally said. "I spent most of last night recalling his work for the state. I guess I find it hard to swallow, too. But facts are facts."

"I know," Ronnie said. "Facts are our business. I'll call you from Biloxi. Thanks, pal, for filling in for me with the paper."

"My pleasure," Sally said, "especially when I see the way Jeff looks at you. Reminds me of my younger days with Frank." She waved cheerfully as she went to her car. Ronnie turned slowly and got into Jeff's car.

Her body functioned automatically at the wheel as she tried to pinpoint the source of her uneasiness. The funeral had been very emotional as Neil's family struggled to bear up under the pain of his loss—and guilt.

Neil! Her mind flashed back to the hospital, to the struggle against death Neil Brenton had fought. He'd said somehing. "Danger. Betrayal. Car." The words had seemed nonsensical at the time, as the last wandering words of a man about to die. At first she'd thought Neil was even trying to say that Jeff had betrayed him, but that didn't make sense either.

"Danger. Betrayal. Car," she whispered to herself as she drove toward her house.

"Danger. Betrayal. Car." Her eyes widened in horror. "Carlisle!" she whispered. Neil had been trying to say Carlisle! The certainty of the knowledge was like a body blow. Heat rushed over her, and she stomped too hard on the brakes at a red light, almost spinning the car into the intersection.

There was something else nagging at the back of her mind. She fast-shifted her memory back through the funeral, then hit pay dirt. Sharp as a picture, she saw the shiny black toe of Carlisle's shoe grinding down the end of a slender cigar. Neil didn't smoke cigars, and neither did Jeff! But Carlisle had been smoking cigars at both their homes. He'd given Neil the false information about Jeff, and he'd gone back again one last time, to kill Neil. She was certain of it. Throwing caution to the wind, Ronnie pressed the accelerator and shot through the intersection, horns blaring at her and drivers rolling down their windows to hurl curses after her. It didn't matter. Jeff was with Carlisle, and Jeff was the only person who could testify against Johnny Deuchi, now that Neil Brenton was dead. Somehow Ronnie had to find them and warn Jeff!

Grasping the wheel in both hands, she cut a sharp U-turn on Willingsby Street and headed for Jeff's condo. "Be there, be there," she whispered. With the realization that Jay Carlisle was "part of the nightmare" came a whole flood of proof. For a nauseating second, Ronnie could smell the smoke on the hands of the man who'd attacked her in the barn. Cigar smoke. Expensive tobacco, unlike cigarettes. It was so plain now, yet she'd missed it.

Scouting the parking lot at the condo, she saw no car resembling Carlisle's. She didn't bother to stop but drove straight to the Capitol. They had to be there, somewhere. And she had to find them.

She counted six black sedans in the Capitol parking areas, but not one was Carlisle's. At the small guardhouse she stopped a moment and frantically signaled one of the men to her side.

"Senator Stuart is in serious trouble," she said clearly. "You must notify the police, and you have to call my boss and ask him to run a check on an FBI agent named Jay Carlisle. I believe the senator has been abducted by this man."

The guard looked at her as if she were crazy, but he took one card with Kurt's number and another with Sally's title and number nonetheless.

"Call Sally Duvall and tell her exactly what I told you," Ronnie said. "I promise you this isn't a joke, and Senator Stuart's life is at stake. Now I'm going to look for them."

Before he could ask any questions, she stamped on the gas and shot down the driveway. Where could they be? The money was obviously what Carlisle wanted before he killed Jeff. If it wasn't at Jeff's home or at the Capitol, where was it? She remembered Jeff saying he'd put it someplace safe.

"Magnolia Point!" she yelled. She knew it in her bones. For one last time she had to trust her intuition. Turning the car toward the interstate highway, she bore down on the gas pedal with everything she had in her. Let the cops chase her! For once she'd gladly pay a hundred tickets. Carlisle had a twenty-minute lead on her, but he didn't want to draw attention to himself, Ronnie calculated as she pushed the car into the nineties. She could make it; she had to.

I CAN'T SAY that it's going to grieve me to kill you," Carlie said with a grin. "You were nothing but a pain the hole time, talking to me like I was some kinda creep. Now t out and let's find that money."

"How long have you been on Deluchi's payroll?" Jeff ked. There was no fear in his voice as he coolly eyed the n Carlisle held pointed at his heart. Carefully he eased out f the car and felt the familiar crunch of the shell driveway eneath his feet. He could only pray that Stella and Earl ere still visiting relatives in Louisiana. Carlisle had caught im by surprise, but on the long drive from Jackson to Bi->xi, he'd learned the one fact he needed to know. Neil renton was innocent.

"Seven, maybe eight years, but this is my first big job, nd I must say, he's going to be very proud of me. I got into little trouble with the ponies, and Mr. D got me out. At rst I didn't think too highly of paying my debt to him, but ith each year it got a little easier, and a lot more profit-ble."

"What's he paying you, Carlisle?" Jeff asked, his tone rrogant and contemptuous.

"Enough. But I'll get a little bonus for killing your friend. Ie was a tough old bird. Put up something of a struggle. I as a little worried when he lived to make it to the hospital, ut then he died without blowing my cover." Carlisle started o laugh, but the sound was cut short when Jeff uttered a urse. "Easy, Senator," Carlisle warned him. "This gun is air-trigger, you know. I might have to wreck your house, ut I'd find the money, and I got a little suicide note al-eady penned for you. Now open that door!"

With the barrel of the pistol pressed into his back, Jeff led ie way into the house. "The last time you were here, you ied to convince me that a good man was a criminal. This me you're here to kill me," Jeff said, casting about the

room for some weapon. His lean body was tensed for ac
tion, but the constant pressure of the gun prevented hir
from making a move.

"Not the last time, Senator," Carlisle said. "I was her
the night your girlfriend stayed. I told you to keep that nos
reporter out of the way, and when you couldn't, I decide
to do it myself. If she hadn't moved away from that wir
dow, I'd have put an end to her prying questions."

"The money's in the library, in the safe," Jeff said.

"So get it!" Carlisle ordered, the greed showing in hi
voice.

"This way," Jeff said. Out of the corner of his eye he saw
a movement near the open front door. Whoever it wa
moved too fast to be Stella or Earl. He shifted slightly to ge
a better view.

"Hurry up!" Carlisle snapped. "I got to get out of town
Not much chance of staying in the FBI after this."

The slender form moved soundlessly in the front door an
blended into the darkness of the dining room. Jeff drew
sharp breath as he recognized Ronnie.

"The safe is at the back of the library," he said. "Nea
the fireplace. If I could get to the gun in my bedside table
I'd kill you."

"Brave talk for a condemned man," Carlisle said with
harsh laugh. "The only problem is that I've got the gun an
you're gonna get the bullet. So quit trying to kill time an
move." He shoved Jeff roughly through the library door.

Jeff went to the safe and slowly began to work the com
bination. He fumbled, then started again.

"Quit stalling!" Carlisle said harshly. "A few second
won't matter, Senator."

"I almost have it," Jeff said, pulling down on the han
dle. When the door came open, Jeff's hand smashed up int

Carlisle's face. The heavy man stumbled backward, pointing the gun at Jeff as he regained his balance.

"I hope you enjoyed that, Senator, because you're a dead man."

"I don't think so," Ronnie said, stepping into the room with Jeff's .38 pistol cocked. The barrel was pressed firmly into Carlisle's back. "Drop it, Carlisle."

The gun slipped from Carlisle's hand and struck the carpet. In a second, Jeff had it in his hand. "Thanks, Ronnie," he said. "I don't know how you got here, but am I glad to see you!" Easing around Carlisle, he went to Ronnie's side and hugged her to him. Ronnie lowered her gun, finally letting out her breath in a long sigh.

"I was afraid I'd be too late," she said, her voice little more than a whisper.

"You were right on time. Another minute and our friend the FBI agent would have killed me and left a suicide note. All very neat. He framed Neil and then me. If you hadn't come along, it would have been a perfect crime."

"Only one thing is still bothering me," Ronnie said, strength returning to her voice. "Just how thick is Mr. Carlisle's hair?" With a sudden movement, she grasped the black locks in both hands and jerked. The entire scalp lifted from Carlisle's head and hung free from her hands.

"I'll be damned! It's a toupee!" Jeff exclaimed as the sound of sirens echoed down the long driveway.

"I THINK MAY would be the best month, when all the magnolias are in bloom and my friends have had time to recover from the shock," Ronnie said.

"Miss Ronnie needs time, Mr. Jeff," Stella interjected. "She is right. If we hurry the wedding, then it will be a slipshod affair."

"I think she's getting cold feet," Jeff said.

"May will give me enough time to try to help her get cold feet," Ann Tate said. "If she insists on marrying you, I want to have enough time to tell her the true facts about your character."

"I thought you wanted me to get married," Jeff said, pouring more glasses of wine for everyone as they sat around the den in Magnolia Point. A blazing fire was going and from the window a half moon gleamed through the tree branches over the roof. Ronnie sat on the floor beside Jeff's legs so she could rest her cheek on his thigh and feel his fingers in her hair. She'd never been so happy, and the easy bantering around her made her feel secure.

"I do want you to get married," Ann countered. "But I've really grown to like Ronnie, and I'm not so sure I want her to be the sacrifice for the effort to civilize you."

Everyone laughed, and Stella brought in a tray of freshly roasted pecans.

"Mr. Jeff, are they teasing you too much?" she asked.

"Stella, they're being perfectly awful to me. Come and make them behave."

"I'm sorry, Mr. Jeff, but I have seen you in action. Even as a boy you were full of the devil, and now your past has caught up with you."

"Maybe we should ask Cousin Katie to be the maid of honor," Ronnie said, a twinkle of mischief in her crystal-gray eyes.

Ann laughed delightedly, and Jeff leaned down to Ronnie. "Don't tell them about that," he begged. "I'll never hear the end of it." That brought additional laughter, but Ann did move to Jeff's side and gave him a hug.

"Contrary to my earlier comments, I'm delighted at the wedding announcement, but I think you should let Ronnie set the date. Stella's right; women have a lot to do when it comes to a wedding," she said.

"There's something none of you appreciate," Jeff said seriously. "My reputation, such as it is these days, is at stake."

His words were so earnest that all humor died, and Ronnie sat up to look into his eyes. In the flickering light, they were inscrutable.

"Carlisle turned state's evidence. Deluchi is behind bars, the horse racing bill is all but voted into passage; what's wrong with your reputation?" she asked.

"Well, there's this little matter of offspring. I'd like to be married before the birth, and May will be too late. I'd like someone to make an honest father of me."

For a moment, Ronnie, Ann and Stella looked at each other, then Ann burst out laughing.

"Tango's due to foal in late February or early March. That's the baby he's talking about."

"You are worse than a devil," Stella said sternly. "You are a fool, Jefferson Stuart, talking like that and scaring an old woman like me."

Ronnie laughed, hugging Jeff's knees, feeling the texture of his slacks and the muscles beneath. In the past few days she'd grown to be quite fond of—and very familiar with his legs. She ran her hand down his calf in an easy, loving manner.

"I'm sorry, Jeff, but I won't rush my wedding just to give your foal a name," she said with a laugh.

"I've already got the name," Jeff said slyly. "The Fourth Estate. After all, journalism has been pretty lucky for me."

"You can't give a horse that name," Ann said, slightly horrified. "At least not one of *my* horses!"

"Then you'd better get on my team and persuade this lady to marry me next week. I can't make it through this session without her."

"That's it, Ronnie," Ann said. "He finally twisted my arm. Marry him next week, and then have the reception in May. That's it: a secret wedding with just a few close friends, then make the announcement in the spring."

"Perfect!" Jeff agreed. "How about it, Veronica?"

"I suppose our meeting was accidental, since my presence at the ball was something of a secret. So why not a secret wedding? And that way, Kurt will have a little time to adjust to the idea that I'm actually going to marry."

"He's just upset at the thought that you might quit," Jeff said, "especially after that dynamite story you did on Carlisle. It was something of a coup."

"Well, after a brief vacation, Kurt can content himself with the fact that he now has a resident Mississippi reporter. He sent me down here as something of a vacation treat, you know—a little visit home after some difficult assignments. Little did he know that this trip would be the most dangerous, and the most wonderful of all."

"So, I have witnesses that you've agreed to a wedding next week?" Jeff teased her, putting his hands under her arms and lifting her from the floor onto the sofa beside him. "There's only one thing that has me worried."

"What's that?" she asked.

"You know, at the end of the ceremony when the groom gets to kiss the bride, I'm not certain I know how to do that well enough. And I think we need a lot of practice."

His lips closed over hers, sealing off her protest, and after the first second, Ronnie knew that she would never argue against practicing their kisses.

Harlequin American Romance

Romances that go one step farther...
American Romance

Realistic stories involving people you can relate to and care about.

Compelling relationships between the mature men and women of today's world.

Romances that capture the core of genuine emotions between a man and a woman.

Join us each month for four new titles wherever paperback books are sold.
Enter the world of American Romance.

Amro-1